The Illyrian Voyages, Book 1:

DROPPING INTO DARKNESS

PETER STAADECKER

The verse from the song "John O' Dreams" is included in this book by kind permission of the songwriter, Bill Caddick.

First published January, 2018

This edition:
February 2019.
ISBN 978-1-9990426-3-9
Paperback edition 2.0

PRAISE FOR "DROPPING INTO DARKNESS"

"... fantastic ..."

"... I didn't want it to end ..."

"... gave me the same pleasure that I experienced as a very young reader with an utterly absorbing story. Thank you for that wonderful nostalgia ..."

"... the writing is assured and fluent ..."

"... I love all the various elements that Staadecker weaves together ... ecology, adventure ... humour, love story, folk tale, ingenious inventions, science fiction and ... characters who are so likeable ..."

"... I'm blown away ..."

"... a fabulous book ..."

"... I LOVED this book! ..."

"... I want more ..."

"... A must read ... it is a book I will read many times and get more details and insight with each one ..."

"... If you are looking for a fun action packed story this is it. It is fast paced with charming characters. The only drawback was it was over way too soon. ..."

CONTENTS

Map of Illyria, Tarsis and Kiliman

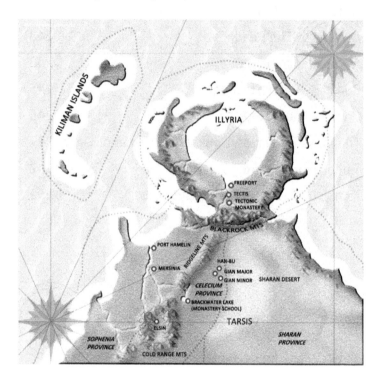

1. Sal

Beginnings are complicated. You could start most stories anywhere and go from there forwards or backwards. Like a circle. Or maybe a helix. If you start on a different loop of the helix, you have a different view back and a different view forward. It's the same helix, but the view is different and the story would have to be told differently.

For now, all I'll say is that there is a boy called Sal, and a girl called Nyx. Don't assume, don't get ahead of the story. They haven't met and likely won't. The world is full of boys and girls that never meet. Sal is on Grand Kiliman, the largest island in the Kiliman Archipelago. Nyx is an ocean and a world away in Mersinia, capital of Tarsis and home of the Duke of Tarsis.

In any case, Sal has more immediate things on his mind than girls he's never met. Like how to survive his stepmother's plans to assassinate him.

He's an unusual boy. A teenager, flip-flopping back and forth like Schrödinger's cat between the man he may become and the boy he was. Next in line for the Kiliman throne, unless his stepmother's plans succeed.

It's how he reacts to the threat that makes him unusual. Outwardly, he's deadpan. Shows no hint of knowing that he's a target. He seems especially amiable, bumbling, clueless. Inwardly, it's different. Inwardly, the boyishness vanishes. His brain speeds up. Time slows down, he's moving so fast. Putting his plans and defences into place. He's playing chess at lightning speed. Figuring out how his stepmother's next move will come, what form it will take, when it will happen. Preparing himself.

She has to make it look like an accident. Nothing obviously planned or tied to her. Her new husband is, after all, Sal's father. So when she asks to see him in her chambers, he thinks he knows how the endgame will play out.

Her earlier attempt was also in her chambers. On the balcony overlooking the harbour from high up. She served him a tea. Sal noticed *she* was drinking water, not tea. A faintly jarring note.

The day was hot. Sal carried the teacup to the balcony table, added two spoons of sugar and stirred. Then he placed the spoon on the saucer and waited. He could still see a few crystals of undissolved sugar stuck to the spoon. His stepmother chatted amiably about this and that, waiting for him to drink, not noticing the oddity. Sal doesn't take sugar in his tea.

A fly landed on the spoon, sipped at the sugary liquid, fell over on its back, struggled once and then froze, immobile. Sal's stepmother, the new queen, didn't notice the dead fly. Sal did. It's why he had put the sugar in his tea in the first place. The stable below was being cleaned out. He'd counted on the flies being there. Cupbearers. Food tasters for the prince. Sal shifted clumsily and knocked over his tea. He apologized, asked for more.

He had a good idea which poison she'd used. The faintest hint of purple colouring on the spoon, just on the border between wet spoon and dry spoon was a subtle indicator. Right where the wet portion became microscopically thin before ending in dryness. You had to know to look for it. Even then, only an expert eye would pick it up. Aphrinnia, whose effects would be ascribed to a heart sickness, not to poison. The onset would have come an hour after Sal had drunk the tea. By that time, he'd have been long out of the queen's chamber. No suspicion would attach to her. Aphrinnia, hard to come by. Very rare. She would not have a second dose. When you're a prince on the Kiliman Archipelago, and have a mind like Sal's for what makes things tick, knowing about poisons is second nature. Curiosity, talent and survival skills in one.

The queen ordered another pot. He poured for them both from the same pot. This time she drank too. He left, nodding amiably. Smiling. Outwardly.

Now another invitation from the queen. It's already night. Which is how he would have played it in her shoes. What he expected. He goes up to her chambers, knocks and enters, smiling. She's writing at her desk. Quill pen in hand. Starts to chat. She's wearing a very low-cut blouse. She leans forward. She smiles. He assumes his most amiable, clumsy air.

She walks him out to the balcony, high above the harbour. The ships below them look tiny from this height.

He's considered whether he should wear chain mail under his shirt to protect his back. But a knife or arrow in the back won't be seen as an accidental death. So he's not wearing chain mail. The current Kiliman fashion allows him to wear a high collar of thick inner fur and stiff outer leather. That protects the back of his neck from a blow from behind. He'd considered the risk of a blow to his head from behind, but he's too tall and she's too short.

He's on the extreme right of the balcony now. The light is dim there. She's dead centre on the balcony, looking out into the night.

"Stand with me, Sal," she says. He walks to where she is, running one hand along the railing as he walks.

She waves her hand at the harbour, using the quill pen to point with.

"One day, Sal, all this will be yours."

He can't resist, even with his life at stake.

"What," he says, "your quill pen?"

For a more astute woman this obvious doltishness would raise suspicion. But she's more greedy than astute. Greedy for the kingdom she wants for her own future children. Her mask slips briefly, showing anger.

"Not the quill!"

Then she smiles to make it sound like friendly teasing. "I meant these islands, Sal, the rich fishing, the seas between the islands, the whole kingdom of Kiliman. Does it mean nothing to you? Come look closer."

She guides him forward up against the railing. The railing is an interlinked heavy black iron chain. Sal has already noticed that the centre links have been repainted, to hide something. A clumsy, rushed touch-up job. A small detail. He notices, because he was looking for it.

Sal obligingly steps as far forward as the chain will allow, the chain that separates him from a drop to his death.

The hard push on his back, and the way the centre chain links part easily under his weight comes as no surprise. He falls.

***

2. The Six Orders

There are six orders of monks in the known world. Two minor orders claim they keep the world spinning.

When they're not fighting each other, they take tribute from the ignorant, so that the world will continue turning. That is, of course, sheer superstition - rampant after the world descended into its new Dark Ages.

The Monks of St. Bacchan claim to have invented the finest distilled wines on the globe. If you can find one of these monks sober, you may even be able to obtain some of the famous products. In exchange for a donation to the monastery. Depending on how sober the monks were when distilling it, it might be very good, or it might make you violently sick for several weeks. That, the monks say, is the will of the gods and a just judgement for past sins visited on those who become sick.

The Monks of St. Ephebius like to smack random strangers and then give them rich gifts, candy, gemstones and trinkets. This, they say, enlightens the recipients to the opposing forces of darkness and light. Their path to enlightenment sometimes succeeds, but has also led to several cycles of escalating mass violence in which the gifts, candy, gemstones and trinkets stage was never reached. Their monastery was rebuilt nineteen times, often on top of the still smoking ruins of the previous rebuild. The twentieth was built in a hidden location. It is believed to be still standing. So far.

The Monks of Han-Bu believe that our world is an obstacle to the universal plan for cosmic harmony, harmony that can only be achieved by the removal of our world. They spend their days rearranging nine towers of over 1200 stones of different sizes, one stone at a time, according to complex rules. Chief among the rules are these: move only one stone at a time, and, a larger stone must never rest on a smaller stone. The Han-Bu Monks believe that when they complete the rearrangement of the nine stone towers, our world will drop out of existence. Cosmic harmony will be restored.

The rules are complex, and the stones are almost the same size, which is why the Han-Bu Monks are now in the 23rd attempt since the monastery was founded. It is said that they got within 22 stones of success after 700 years in the 17th attempt. That was when a novice monk, Ju-Sin (may his name be ever-cursed) sneezed knocking over five stones at once.

The monastery split into two competing factions after this. The traditionalists continue the work of the previous 17 cycles. The reformists say a stone was lost when Ju-Sin (a plague on his memory) sneezed. They spend their days searching the world for the missing stone.

The Tectonic Monks are the oldest of the six orders. They date back to shortly after the third EC, the third eco-catastrophe.

What the Tectonic Monks claim is complicated. They say they protect the breeding grounds of the earth-dragons. The earth-dragons, they say, burrow tunnels under continental shelves, relieving the enormous pressures where these shelves push against each other, relieving the gigantic pressures left from the underground H-bomb explosions used in the third EC. The earth-dragons, they say, are mankind's only defence against mega-earthquakes that can split the globe like a rotten melon, trigger more volcanic ash clouds, trigger five-year-long ash winters, and doom the remnants of human life.

When they're not protecting the earth-dragons, the Tectonic Monks trade, run schools, send doctors into the world and make exquisite pottery from rare earths thrown up from deep in the earth's core by the burrowing earth-dragons. The monks make beautiful shining, delicate cups, saucers, pots, dishes. Tectonic pottery is famed even in the smallest, furthest villages of the globe. The one thing the Tectonic Monks don't make is plates.

***

3. Mushrooms or No Mushrooms?

The Duke of Tarsis is an angel-faced young man with the heart of a rabid ferret coupled with the temper of a bear woken in mid-winter hibernation. The Duke has recently replaced his father as Duke of Tarsis. The young Duke has ambition and dislikes competition.

This has led to a shakeup in the Tarsis nobility. Just recently, four of the young Duke's cousins, and next in line for the dukedom, have mysteriously died. One after another, all within the same month.

Now the commander of the Tarsis police force, Commander Zlod, is standing in front of the Duke.

"Sit Zlod."

Zlod sits. After years of police work, Zlod no longer enjoys people. Or her job. There are good people, she supposes. Somewhere. In her line of work, Zlod doesn't get to meet them.

She especially does not like angel-faced dukes with the heart of a rabid ferret and the disposition of a recently roused bear. The chair though, the chair she likes. Furniture can teach you things. Quiet endurance, silent competence, and how to blend into the background.

She knows that at many levels she's smarter than the Duke. She also knows it pays not to show it. Follow the chair's lead she thinks to herself, say as little as possible. The chair will be her example in this interview.

"Your Highness sent for me?"

"Zlod, you know of this new invention thing, this printing press and newspaper in Mersinia?"

"Yes, Sire."

"Do you read it?"

Zlod wonders briefly how the chair might answer such a question, if it could. The thought is brief enough that the Duke sees no hesitation. Zlod knows what answer is needed. The Duke does not like intellectuals. "No, sire. Only the sports section. I'm a great supporter of the Mersinia and Region Handball Team."

"Very good, Zlod."

The Duke is pleased by this. He continues, "You know my four cousins all died tragically over the last month?"

"Yes, sire. My condolences sire. A great tragedy for your family to lose four such promising young men all in the same month."

Zlod waits. Follows the lead of the chair, silence and patience.

The Duke shoves a newspaper at her. "This, Zlod, is what the newspaper printed after the second death. Read it."

Zlod takes the paper, shuffles to the back page and reads, "Mersinia and Region challenges Celecium handball teams."

The Duke reddens. He has a vein throbbing over his right temple. "Not that. Read the front-page headline."

Zlod slows down her normally fluent reading speed. She reads aloud, slowly, deliberately halting between syllables.

> *"Mush-rooms A-gain??*
> *Joseph-Kalil, a-nother cou-sin and third in line to our Duke, has died of mush-room soup poi-so-ning. This after a death only a week ago of the Duke's cousin, Franz-Kalil, second in line, also of poi-son mushroom soup.*
>
> *How is this poss-ssible? There is only one poi-son mush-room in all of Sophenia Province. It has bright red polka dots that even a two-year-old would avoid."*

The Duke is looking angry still. "That, Zlod, is dangerous slander. That damn press implies that there was something unnatural about two of my dear cousins both dying of mushroom soup within a week of one another. And it gets worse. You know my cousin Isidore?"

"Yes Sire, he died of a broken skull a week after Joseph-Kalil."

"Zlod, read what the newspaper said about my dear Isi's death. Read the headline."

Zlod reads aloud.

"The Dangers of Refusing the Soup"

She bows in the direction of the Duke. "More slander, Sire. Very dangerous slander. May I ask Sire, what did they print after your cousin Oris died?"

"Zlod, you know how Oris died?"

Zlod knows precisely how Oris died. She has a large network of informers, so she doesn't hesitate to say: "No, Sire."

"The court doctor, Zlod, the court doctor himself, certified the death was from a genetically acquired excess of iron in his blood."

Zlod looks down at the chair she's sitting in. The chair wisely says nothing. Zlod knows the court doctor well. A cautious man treading a fine line between professional accuracy and political expediency.

Zlod decides she'd better speak for both the chair and herself.

"Yes, Sire. My condolences again. Oris had great promise. Many of us thought he would have made a great rear-guard for the handball team. If only he had come to our regular practices more often. I hope you are not at risk from the same genetic condition."

There is silence as the Duke glares at Zlod. Zlod wonders if she has gone too far with his country bumpkin act. The Duke may be dumb, but he's dangerous. Zlod holds onto her concerned face. Imitates the chair's expression – I'm here to serve, a piece of background furniture unless I'm needed.

After Zlod's expression of submissive concern, the Duke appears to relax. "This, Zlod, is what the damn newspaper printed after dear Oris died. Read."

Zlod takes the paper and reads the headline.

> *"Genetically acquired – from a cousin?*
> *Was Excess of Iron a Knife or an Arrowhead?"*

"What do you think of that, Zlod?"

Some imp of rebellion pricks her. Against all her judgement she says "Very shoddy, Sire. Half the headline uses capital letters, half doesn't."

"Damn the grammar, Zlod. Look at the content. More slander, Zlod. Treasonous slander."

"Yes, sire. Very upsetting. Do they even mention his handball skills in the obituary?"

The Duke waves this aside. "Focus, Zlod. What's important is to stop this treason. Who is the owner and editor of this scandalous paper?"

"That is Master Sri."

"Does he have family?"

"One teenage daughter, Sire. Name of Nyx. The mother died when the girl was young. Master Sri has not remarried."

"Arrest them both, Zlod. Today. Charge them with high treason against the state."

"Yes, Sire."

Zlod salutes like a damn military puppet, although she's police, and exits.

The chair remains silent. A lesson to us all thinks Zlod as she leaves. Say nothing and you may yet survive this Duke.

***

4. Not Always Calm

Have I already said beginnings are complicated? Everything needs to be explained. Like Nyx. She was about the same age as Sal, that in-between age where you weren't sure whether to call her a young woman or a girl. Once you spoke to her, listened to her, watched her eyes, watched her calm way of managing the world, you realized she was far older in wisdom than Sal was. Usually calm that is. Usually taking control of the world around her. Usually ready to bring order to the world around her. Usually. There are exceptions, of course.

5. Trail Up or Trail Down?

Nyx looks at the map her father has given her, then at the split in the path ahead. She wishes she'd paid more attention to what her father had said about the route ahead, or about reading maps. She'd been too overcome by sadness and trying not to cry when he put the map into her hand. And left her. Even now, the tears threaten. She holds them back, knowing that if they start it will be hard to stop them.

Nyx's mother died when Nyx was three. The only parent she can remember is her father, Sri. He has only two passions in life. Bringing up his daughter is one. Printing his newspaper is the other. Father and daughter are closer than most. Sri was the mother Nyx couldn't remember, and the father that was always there for her. From about the age of ten though, who looked after whom was more complicated. Sometimes he was the parent, at other times she ran their home and his life more than he ran hers. There were times when he was desperately impractical, idealistic without thinking of consequences or whether he'd bought enough food for their breakfast. Then she would become the one running the house and reminding him of what needed doing. Now he was no longer there. Not to look after her, not to be looked after.

The newspaper is the problem. Sri uses it to criticize the young Duke of Tarsis and his mentor, Ham, the Patriarch of the New Church of Sacrifice. This is a recent movement founded by Ham, and rapidly gathering power.

Sri's newspaper commented caustically on the recent deaths of the Duke's cousins. When cousin Oris died Sri insinuated that the death was assassination.

It was then that Sri told Nyx she needed to go into the country. For safety. Far away from him, where no one would find her. To guide her on the first part of her journey he dressed her in boys' clothing and cut her hair. He dressed her in a shapeless poncho that hid the curves of her upper body. Leather chaps on her legs hid the curve of her legs. She was to play the part of a local guide to Sri, as he rode through the country, supposedly searching for Nyx, the teenage daughter who'd run away from home. They re-dyed her hair every three days to make it look like Sri was hiring different local lads to guide him every few days. Every week they stopped and set up camp out of sight. Then he backtracked and did hire a local groom for a day or two before releasing him and coming back to her. This way, he said, if questioned on who the local boys were, he could point to actual local boys.

"Nyx, dearest," he said after two weeks riding, "I've tried to make it look that I've come this far just with local guides, and otherwise alone. But I cannot take you all the way. That would leave a trail I cannot be seen to leave. Here, I turn around, again using local guides. You must go on by yourself. I have marked the trail on the map. A friend from very long ago has agreed to take you in. The map will take you to her. No one else will remember my long-ago connections to her. You will be safe with her. Her name is Elsin. She is a herbalist in the Great Cold Range Mountains. Live with her until I can call you back. If you wish, she will teach you about healing with herbs. It is a great skill for your life. You will like that.

"One more thing," he said, "I don't think anyone is watching, but I can't be certain. You're playing the part of a local guide for me. In a moment I will turn away from you. No hugs. No tears. That doesn't fit the role you're playing. Just a casual wave."

The parting had broken her heart, and his. But there was nothing for it.

The path for the next three days had been clear enough. Now she stares at the split in the trail and the map wishing she'd listened better. The path to the left drops down into a deep ravine. There are trees and a river down below. The path to the right leads up a horrendously steep, almost sheer cliff, in a series of narrow zig-zags and hairpin turns. She remembers that contour lines on the map bunch close together for steep slopes. That doesn't help. Both the slope down to the left and the cliff up to the right will have steep contour lines on the map. She looks at the dotted trail her father marked in pencil and tries to guess which way to turn the map. If the contours don't help her what will? The map shows a blue line for a river underneath contour lines. That must be in the ravine. She lines up her map so that it shows the river on her left. Her father's dotted trail marks go right.

Her heart sinks. Up the cliff is steeper and more dangerous looking than down-slope to the river. But it's the way she has to go. There are a few stunted trees part-way up. They're whipping back and forth under what must be a ferocious wind up there.

She delays the moment by running through a mental checklist. She is riding her own horse from Mersinia. Socks. A four-year-old gelding. They'd disguised him to look like a new horse every few days. Painted over his tell-tale white sock markings. Some days he was spotted, some days not, some days blond mane, some days black. She'd checked his shoes at dawn before setting out. She'd checked his coat for burrs before putting on the sweat-blanket, protector and saddle. She'd checked each of those to make sure there was no dirt on them that would rub his back raw. Now she checks that her packs are still sitting well. He's loaded with front saddle bags, rear saddlebags, a bedroll and two waterproof tarps behind the saddle, cantle bag on top of the bedroll and tarps, breastplate to avoid the saddle sliding backwards and crupper strap to avoid the saddle sliding forwards. All the cinches are correct, the ropes are well tied, and the folds of the tarps and bedroll all face backwards so that they won't catch any branches as they ride. Everything is orderly the way she likes it. There's no excuse to delay further. She nudges Socks forward. The heavy load won't make his climb easy.

As Socks climbs, he walks on the outside of the trail, on the edge of the drop. She tries several times to guide him closer to the cliff, but each time he veers back to the extreme outside. The veering back and forth is making him walk half-sideways to the trail in protest and she gives up.

Now they're entering bands of low clouds that hug the higher cliff. It's like riding into a thick mist. She can no longer see clearly ahead. She wonders whether she'd be safer dismounting, but Socks has a bad habit of skittishness when she dismounts. She can't afford to have him prancing sidewise while she still has a foot in the stirrup. She's committed now to ride until they reach flat land. She hopes the horse can see or feel the path. She cannot. "Dragons guard and guide us," she whispers, touching the dragon talisman hanging from her neck.

Brief breaks in the mist give glimpses of dizzying drops to the side, drops that then disappear in whiteness. The breaks are accompanied by fierce up- and downdraughts of wind, chilling her to the marrow.

There are glimpses of snow far below her now, pierced by sharp rocks that point upwards. On a tight hairpin her horse kicks loose a boulder. The mist hides its fall, but, after seconds of delay, she can hear the crashes and rebounds far below her. She shuts her eyes, swaying in the saddle. With her eyes shut come visions of her father worrying about her. She thinks, "What will become of him? If I die here, it will kill him too. If I disappear over the cliff and am never found, what will happen to him?" Nevertheless, she keeps her eyes closed; swaying in the saddle each time her horse scrapes around another hairpin, or lunges up a steep uneven section of trail. He's panting now with effort. She leans forward to pat his neck and say soothing words, but keeps her eyes closed. Doesn't want to see those unsettling glimpses of the void below. Even with her eyes closed, she can feel the light fading. Along with the thickening mist, the daylight is fading fast now. They lunge and turn and clatter on up interminably.

Then Socks balks. She realizes she's fallen asleep. She hasn't slept well since her father turned back. Worrying about him at night. Now the tiredness has caught up with her. It's the lack of movement, the change of rhythm from lunge and clatter and turn and scrape that has half woken her. Her head has nodded forwards her eyes are still closed. She doesn't bother to open them, just nudges her horse with her heels and hands. He refuses to budge.

What wakes her completely is a voice. A woman's voice. It says "Wake up."

The remnants of her dream disappear. She sits up and looks around. It's night. They're on a flat, rocky plateau. Socks must have been following a trail across the plateau for quite some time. In front of them is a

small cottage. Blocking their path. Vine covered.
Flowering vines, unusual at this height. Flowerbeds, a
vegetable garden with herbs and root vegetables.
Someone has put a lot of work into digging out enough
rocks and putting down enough soil for this. Which
makes Nyx look at the woman. She is slim, fit looking,
dressed in a home-dyed shirt and long pants. As tall as
Nyx. Older though. Maybe the age of her father. Her
hair is greying, but her face is unlined. She's looking at
Nyx curiously.

"I fell asleep," Nyx says.

"You came up the cliff path?"

"Yes," says Nyx, "it was ..."

"A dangerous climb. Especially with the cloud on
the mountain and the light gone."

"It scared me," says Nyx.

"It scares everyone," says the woman. She comes
closer, peering carefully, then relaxes. "I thought you
were a boy at first." She holds out her hand. "I'm Elsin.
You must be Nyx. I've been expecting you for the last
several nights. I wasn't sure when you'd arrive. There's
a stew on the stove. I haven't eaten yet. Rub down your
horse and stable him over there. There are brushes,
towels, blankets, hay, oats and a water trough in the
stable."

She points to a stable around the side of the
cottage, next to a sheep pen and a bird coop. "Join me
once your horse is comfortable."

Nyx smiles at the woman in relief. "Thank you," she
says and climbs stiffly off Socks. She rubs his head and
whispers in his ear, "Come, Socks, there are oats for
you, and I'll rub you down. You did well. Very well."

***

6. The Monastery at Tectis

The Tectonic Monks run schools across the globe. The main school, the mother school, is however in the town of Tectis itself, on the Illyrian Peninsula. Only handpicked students, filtered from the daughter schools by stiff competition, are offered a chance to study at the monastery in Tectis.

There is one other way to gain a seat at the monastery school in Tectis. Arrive on the Illyrian Peninsula by ship in the harbour of Freeport. Climb the zig-zag road out of Freeport up to the town of Tectis, inside the slopes of an ancient caldera. Climb higher to the monastery overlooking Tectis and the harbour. Instead of going to the main monastery entrance, you turn left. Towards the clock tower. The path to the clock tower is difficult. There is a pedestrian bridge across a moat. A thing of rope and planks. Almost never used. The bridge swings violently underfoot. There are no handrails. Near the centre, the drop off the bridge is high. You wouldn't want to fall. If you can calculate a precise walking rhythm that dampens the swings of the bridge - and the rhythm changes as you progress - you arrive at a locked door at the base of the tower. From the door protrudes two large spoked wheels. These are the keys to unlock the door. Move either wheel and the other moves also, in seemingly unpredictable sequences. It is said that the movements offer clues to the correct unlock sequence. Others say the timing of the movements is more important.

If you do succeed in opening the lock, the next puzzle is the door handle itself. It doesn't sit on the door. It sits on the stone wall next to the door. You need to pull the handle outwards - away from the wall -

to open the door. The puzzle is how to reach the handle. It's *inside* the stone wall, inside a twisted hollow pipe carved into the wall. The hollow pipe enters the wall, twists and curves, and then exits the wall a little lower down, like a distorted letter 'U'. The pipe is narrow – too narrow for your hand, and too twisted for a stick. If, in spite of this obstacle, you somehow do pull the door handle outwards and get the door open, a huge bell-rope hangs in front of you, leading up the tower to the massive brass bell.

Ringing the bell is difficult. The bell tower is narrow. It needs huge effort and timing to get the bell swinging. The swinging of the bell amplifies the up and down movement of the rope. If you don't find the right rhythms, the rope will be torn out of your hand before the bell can be rung.

If you ring the bell, five monks will administer a final oral, entrance examination to ascertain whether you have the right to become a student at the monastery.

It's been two hundred years since anyone gained a seat at the monastery school in this way. Until now. A boy named Sal. He arrived by ship from Grand Kiliman. Alone. Rumours say he tested the bridge with one foot on one foot off. Took 15 minutes, pushing at the bridge with one foot, pushing at different speeds, watching it. And then he didn't walk across. He ran in a queer hopscotching fashion. And the bridge never moved. He spent 5 minutes moving the wheels of the lock in various random directions. Then he stood still and did nothing for two minutes. Just stared at the door. After staring, he made two adjustments to the wheels and the lock was heard to click open. A loud click, audible even across the bridge. He took a balled up piece of bread from his pocket, shoved it into the U-shaped channel that hides the door handle, took a mouse – yes a mouse of all things, with a string leash tied around its neck – from his pocket and let the mouse crawl down the channel to the bread ball. A minute later, the mouse reappeared on the lower side of the U having pulled the string leash through the U and behind the door handle. Rumours do not explain how Sal rang the bell. For the last months he's been a student at the Tectis Monastery School.

***

7. The Monastery at Tectis II

Sal soaks up what the monastery offers. For all that it is called 'monastery', there are women 'monks' as well as men. Always called 'monks', never 'nuns'. Doma Anik is the abbess. She runs the monastery. Sal has yet to meet her. Dom Smuel teaches oral history and ecology. Much of what he has to say, Sal already knows, but Smuel has an interesting way of telling things. Dom Bal teaches mathematics. Sal has corrected Bal twice in front of the class. There is now a simmering dislike between them. Dom Bal has taken to heavy-handed sarcasm when he speaks to Sal, pretending to forget his name and calling him fisher-boy instead.

Dom Taane is what Sal came for. The artificer. The man is a genius. He makes and shapes glass and iron in ways that Sal had never known possible. His knowledge and supply of chemicals are endless. His collection of tools and measuring devices is the most sophisticated that Sal has ever seen. Taane is also generous in his appreciation of others.

Sal has created some simple mechanical devices in class that Taane has pored over at great length, chuckling and shaking his head in pleasure at the mechanisms. One is a wind-driven churn for butter. Sal added a speed governor that amazed Taane. Two simple mechanical arms, each with an elbow and a weighted hand. The faster the churn goes, the straighter the arms stretch, increasing the moment of inertia and slowing down the churn. As the churn slows, a spring bends the arms again, bringing the weights back to the centre and allowing the churn to spin faster. Like a figure skater stretching or contracting her arms to control how fast she spins.

Taane and Sal are now collaborating on an advanced horse-wagon design. Among other innovations, Sal has proposed replacing the traditional straight wheel spokes with curved – almost spiral - spokes. That way when the wheel hits a bump the spokes flex and absorb the shock. This, Sal says, will allow the wagon to travel faster with less danger of wheel or axle damage. Sal and Taane are also debating where to source more iron. Sal has ideas.

***

8. Pythons and the Three ECs

"Beginnings are complicated. You could start most stories anywhere and go from there forwards or backwards. Like a circle. Or maybe a helix. If you start on a different loop of the helix, you have a different view back and forward. It's the same helix, but the view is different and the story would have to be told differently."

Dom Smuel looks at the class and asks, "So, who first made that saying famous?"

He pauses. The class is quiet. They've all heard the saying but no one knows where it came from.

"No?" says Dom Smuel, "No one wants to answer? Nu, it was our own Dom Uss. Spelled U-s-s but the 'u' is pronounced as in 'push'. He wrote that now famous saying in his 'Diaries of a Voyage'."

Smuel shakes his head admiringly. "Now there's a monk who's been everywhere. Uss talks about the coils of a helix. Why?"

Again, the class is silent.

Smuel continues, "Because a large python coiled itself around him, somewhere on the border between Sharan and Celecium, in the dense rainforest. Dragon knows what took him there. He has his own reasons, or the Abbess' reasons for what he does and where he goes. Some of us monks would envy him his journeys except for the trouble he gets into."

Dom Smuel repeats, "If you start on a different loop of the helix you have a different view down on the previous coils and a different view forward. It's the same helix, but the view is different and the story would have to be told differently. That's what Uss wrote. What it means is it's a different story if the python's head is latching onto your boots or about to swallow your head."

Smuel pauses and watches the students, then continues. "Dom Uss also wrote, 'Beginnings are complicated. Everything needs to be explained.' When the python first dropped its coils on Uss, he had no idea what was happening to him. He needed an explanation. He says until you've experienced a large constrictor attack five or six times, the attack is always disorientating. Of course, by the time the python had latched its fangs onto his arm, by the time its coils were squeezing the breath from his lungs, by the time the pressure was shutting down his blood flow, no more explanation was needed. Just a solution.

"Incidentally, Uss spent time afterwards studying pythons and their kin. He wrote that constrictor snakes do eventually crush bones and can constrict breathing, but death usually comes because they shut down the prey's blood flow. The constrictor senses the victim's pulse. It applies pressure until the pulse stops. The prey's heart cannot cope with the enormous pressure on its arteries. Dom Uss' observations were groundbreaking. He's a little different, our Dom Uss.

"So, now. Back to our lesson. Let's start at the complicated beginning of today's topic and talk about the history of the three ECs, the three eco-catastrophes. A big picture first. Jao, tell us in 30 seconds or less what you know about the first EC."

Jao stands. He's a lean beanpole of a student from Sharan province. They're all lean and beanpoles in Sharan Province. Something to do with adaptation to desert heat. They don't like talking much either. Another adaptation to desert life. You lose moisture when you open your mouth.

Smuel has been careful to encourage Jao to talk more. He says with only minor hesitations, "The first EC was the great drought and great famine caused by overpopulation and overheating of the earth. The human and animal population shrunk drastically, with only pockets of the globe remaining marginally habitable. That cured the issue of overpopulation and stopped further temperature rises, but the earth's climate didn't re-cool and the issues of drought and crop shortages weren't cured."

He still looks embarrassed though, at having said so much.

"Very good," says Dom Smuel. "Now, Alyx. 30 seconds. Tell us what you know about the second EC."

Alyx stands. She's from somewhere north of Mersinia in Sophenia Province. Alyx has green eyes, and blond hair, typical of the northern Ridgeline Mountains. No hesitation in her voice. "The first EC led to the second EC, which was the famine wars. The remaining pockets of humanity launched wars to compete for scarce water and crops. They used N-bombs, H-bombs, P-bombs, and gene altering viruses. The H-bombs were detonated both at high altitude and deep below continental shelves. The combination of elevated radiation levels and gene altering viruses backfired and led to significant mutations, including the genetic split between carbon-based and silicon-based life forms. The wars did not cool the earth's climate. That remained hot until the third EC."

Smuel nods. "Good. Now Sal. 30 seconds on the third EC."

Sal is almost caught off-guard. He was still thinking about Dom Uss.

> Dom Uss was one of five monks that put him through his entrance exam. At the bell-tower, after crossing the snaky footbridge. The five were Doma Chi, Dom Bal, Dom Taane, Dom Uss and Master Bach.
>
> Doma Chi had shown Sal a selection of musical instruments. Asked him to play one. Sal is no musician. He had shrugged and said 'Maybe I can sing instead?'

He sang a work song he'd learned from the Kiliman deep-sea fishers. He'd picked at a 5-string ud to give himself a rough accompaniment. His ud playing wasn't anything special, but his voice can do a surprising bass. Doma Chi listened with concentration and seemed satisfied.

Dom Bal had asked him some trivial question about the distance flown by a bird going back and forth between two approaching ships, each travelling at velocities blah, blah, blah. Sal had given the answer without waiting for the complete question. The fundamentals had already been given; the rest of the question was a red herring. Dom Bal had been annoyed by having his question cut short, but agreed with the answer. His second question was about an equation for a smooth, continuous curve that approximates the shape of a square. Sal's answer was rapid and added variations that Dom Bal appeared not to have considered.

Dom Taane's questions had been more interesting. More of a discussion really. What other rapid methods might Sal have used to cross the bridge to the clock tower, without radical redesign of the bridge? Sal had rattled off three ideas:

- Dampen the bridge's wild movements by hanging weights at intervals underneath the bridge. Also, hang buckets into the moat from underneath the bridge to act as dampers in the water.

- Carry two poles joined in the shape of inverted 'V'. The bottom ends of the V are weighted, and jut out beyond and below the sides of the bridge. The weights lower the walker's center of gravity and increase his resistance to both bouncing and twisting on the bridge. Works on a similar principle to the tight-rope walker's balance pole.

- Assemble a moving rectangular wood frame. The frame consists of four wooden planks. The bottom plank hangs below the bridge and has a weight on either end. The top plank rolls along the bridge on small wheels. The bottom plank hangs from the top plank via the side planks. The person crossing the bridge rolls the frame across the bridge in front of himself/herself. The weights on the bottom plank again lower the walker's centre of gravity and increase his/her resistance to sudden bounces, swings and twists.

They continued this discussion for several minutes, covering construction times, materials needed, advantages and disadvantages of each method, until the other monks became visibly impatient.

Judging by his title, Master Bach was not a regular monk. He was a short, bald man with a barrel chest and broad shoulders. He had intricate scars on his face and hands and a dragon tattoo on his face. Sal couldn't tell whether the scars were ceremonial, or accidental, or both.

His voice was hoarse. "Put these on, Chickpea," he said to Sal, handing him a padded suit, helmet and gloves. Sal put them on. "Now then, Cabbage Patch," said Bach, "take this here quarterstaff, one for you and one for me and we both climb onto this little plank. First one to fall or step off loses."

The quarterstaves were about the height of Sal plus the length of one of his arms, and thick enough that you could just get your fingers to close around them. They were practice quarterstaves, with the tips covered in padding rather than iron. The plank they stood on was a mere two feet off the ground, and about ten feet long. It was narrow enough that you had to put one foot in front of the other. Too narrow to stand with one foot next to the other.

The quarterstaff is a common weapon across most of the known globe. Easy to make and extremely effective if you have room to manoeuvre. Very effective against swords, daggers, dogs, wolves and bears. Not so much against bowmen. It's most frequently used by cowherds and shepherds to guard flocks, or by travellers in wild places. In the hands of a master, it's a deadly instrument. Sal saw the ease with which Bach was holding his staff. He might be bluffing or might really be good.

They stood facing each other at opposite ends of the plank. Master Bach spoke again. "So what you have to do now, Master Cauliflower, is to knock me off the plank."

"You don't have padding or a helmet," said Sal.

"I won't need them," said Bach, "as long as you're talking instead of trying to knock me off the plank."

"I don't want to hurt you, Master Bach."

"You? Hurt me? I laugh," said Bach, and before Sal knew it, he'd received a warning blow to his left arm. It was very quick. Sal hardly saw Bach move.

"Right," said Sal. He moved down the plank and stabbed his staff at Bach's stomach. Before his lunge was even half complete, his staff was knocked aside. He barely kept his footing on the plank, and, even with the gloves, his hand stung from the impact. He feinted a lunge at Bach's head and then turned the lunge into a sideways swing at Bach's ankles. Again, the stinging of his hands and his frantic dance to keep his balance told him that his staff had been knocked aside.

Bach was still standing in a relaxed pose on the plank, looking bored. Sal moved closer and bounced his weight up and down the plank hoping to distract Bach by the underfoot movements. This time Sal felt Bach's staff smack against his shin padding.

"Stop messing about, Little Carrot," said Bach.

"Right," said Sal again. Bach was holding his staff with the forward hand halfway along the staff, and the back hand on the last quarter. A good position for swinging the staff but not good for spearing your opponent. Not good for dealing with an opponent who's gotten inside the arc of your swing. Which gave Sal the opening he wanted. He flipped his staff horizontally in front of himself and charged at Bach.

And found himself lying on the ground. Bach was still on the plank. Looking bored.

Sal stood up. He was angry at the unfairness of the test. He wasn't a soldier. He wasn't applying to be a soldier. He put down the quarterstaff and took off his helmet. "Did I just fail my entrance exam?" he said.

Bach looked at Dom Uss, the only monk who'd said nothing so far.

Uss looked at the other monks. Doma Chi gave a nod. Dom Bal gave a sour shrug. Dom Taane gave a thumbs up. Bach nodded.

Uss looked back at Sal. "Did you fail? Not yet. You lasted 7 seconds against Bach, which is longer than most. And you didn't make it personal or lose your temper, or pull out that fish knife that you're wearing. So, quite good. But you haven't passed yet either. You still have my questions to answer."

"Ask," said Sal. Still angry and feeling bruised.

"My questions will wait a few weeks," said Dom Uss. You're admitted provisionally to the monastery school until then. Welcome. Be happy and make the monastery an even better place by being here. Bach will show you to your dorm and get you settled."

Uss turned to Bach, "Do you think you could shake hands with Sal, Bach. The civilized way? No twisting his hand and kicking his ankles out from under him? Just shake hands with Sal to welcome him?"

Sal looked at Bach. The little man spat onto his open palm and then held it out for Sal to shake. An old foredeck ritual from the southern oceans. "Dom Uss thinks I have no manners. After all this time. That's hurtful, that is," Bach said.

Sal spat on his own palm, conscious that Bach was watching him carefully, nodding slightly in approval. To not accept the ritual, or not reply in kind, would be ignorance at best or an insult at worst. Sal shook Bach's hand. Cautiously.

"Better wash your hands well, Sal," said Dom Uss, "Otherwise you'll get rabies, or grow short, bald and evil."

"Glad to see you've got manners at least," said Bach to Sal. "Unlike some I might mention." He glanced meaningfully at Uss before leading Sal away.

Now Dom Smuel was asking Sal for 30 seconds on the third eco-catastrophe. Sal stood up and snapped his mind back to the class. Being caught off-guard, his answer was less concise than usually:

"The third eco-catastrophe was the global winter caused by the explosion of the Illyrian volcano. Remnant pressures from underground H-bomb explosions had stressed the earth's crust and contributed to the giant Illyrian volcano. The ash cloud blanketed the earth for five years, causing further crop failures, the regrowth of polar ice caps, extensive glaciation across high-lying areas, and further animal and human deaths. Much of human technology was lost and the surviving humans (both carbon and silicon-based) were set back to a largely agrarian, and often feudal society. In some cases the knowledge for more advanced technologies was still available, but the complex manufacturing interdependencies for a high-tech society were no longer possible."

Dom Smuel nodded at Sal. "Good. What does it mean, Sal, that complex manufacturing interdependencies made highly technical societies impossible? Five seconds only please."

Sal thought a moment how to simplify this. "Dom Smuel," he said, "The problem is how to dig an iron mine when you no longer have the iron to make shovels and pickaxes for digging the mine."

Smuel nods, "And the volcano that caused the catastrophe is where?"

"Right under us," responds Sal. "The monastery today sits on what is left of the caldera, the cone, after the big explosion."

Dom Smuel smiled. "Hokay, Sal. Don Uss wants to see you. Says it's time for you to answer your final admission questions. You are excused. Good luck. The rest of us will continue to explore the impacts of the three ECs on how we live.

9. Elsin

Nyx has brought her saddlebags, cantle bag and bedroll into the cottage. She arranges them in a careful rectangular pile just inside the doorway. "Where do I put these?"

"This way," says Elsin.

She shows Nyx to a small storage room that will be her bedroom. There is a cot by the wall and a window looking out through more vines to the rear of the cottage. She watches as Nyx brings her gear from the front door to her bedroom. Once again, the girl builds her little rectangular pile, this time inside her bedroom door.

"Dragons help us," thinks Elsin. "A neatness fanatic. In my house. For dragons know how long." Aloud she says, "Would you like to eat?"

"Would it be possible for me to wash first?"

"Of course." Elsin shows her the outside shower. There's a tank on a short tower above the shower, painted black to trap the sun's heat during the day. "There's hot water in there. The tank will refill automatically. There's a pipe coming from the river higher up. All gravity fed. The outhouse is down that way away from the river."

The girl doesn't take long; she's obviously efficient as well as a neatness fanatic. Or just hungry.

Nyx steps into the main room of the cottage. It's at once kitchen, living room and herbalist's workbenches.

Elsin is sitting in shadow in a corner watching Nyx come back in. Nyx has discarded the shapeless riding gear and is now very clearly a shapely young woman. Very shapely. The transformation is eye-catching.

Nyx doesn't see Elsin at first. She looks around.

There are racks of books, some in Common Script, most in Han symbols, running across the top half of almost every wall. The bottom half of the walls are covered by cupboards and shelving with bottled seeds, bowls with dried powders, jars with leaves soaked in liquids, distilling equipment, sieves, muslin clothes, scales and weights, pill presses, guillotines, eyedroppers, pestles and mortars, miniature braziers, blank labels, labels with Han symbols, and equipment that Nyx doesn't recognize.

Nyx stares. There is no order to anything. Half-filled jars stand on a workbench in between a half-full pill press, a handful of broken pills are scattered under the workbench, and a broken alembic is stuffed into a basket next to a brand new glass alembic. Some of the powders are mixed in with shelves of tinctures, and boxes of drying leaves are mixed in with jars of liniment. There is a mess of something black and tarry on the corner of the table. There are half-open books scattered amongst weighing scales and one of the scales is filled with quills, inkpots, and scraps of notepaper. Next to the inkpot is something that looks like last week's dinner, congealed on a plate.

Elsin sees Nyx's lips curl. The girl is muttering as she stares at the chaos. Then she sees Elsin in the corner and her face adopts a polite neutral expression as she steps towards Elsin. "The first hot water I've had in weeks. It was wonderful. Thank you."

A large dog on the floor growls at her.

"That's Magnus," says Elsin. "He's very old and doesn't see well. He growls at things he doesn't recognize. Maybe walk a ways around him."

"Would it be OK if I gave him a chunk of something to eat and spoke to him?"

"Try giving him his supper bowl. It's over on the counter. Say the word 'supper' as you approach and go slowly. If the growling gets louder back off."

Nyx takes the supper bowl and bends down to floor level, supper bowl stretched in front of her. She moves forward slowly, saying very gently "Magnus, here comes supper".

Magnus raises his nose. He growls once, then sniffs and lowers his head. His tail twitches. Nyx edges forward, still talking quietly, in calm, soothing tones. Musical tones. Almost a lullaby. Bit by bit, Magnus' growls become softer and the tail twitches become larger, eventually becoming wags as he receives his bowl.

Nyx sits on the floor, far enough away from Magnus that he doesn't feel threatened while he eats, close enough that her smell is with him while he eats.

She waits patiently. He licks the plate clean, then shuffles over to sniff at her. He thumps down next to her and lets her rub his head. She leans against him talking softly.

"Well," says Elsin to Nyx, "I wasn't sure he'd accept that."

They eat at the kitchen table. Nyx is hungry, but she's also starved for conversation. She's had no one to talk to for days. She eats and talks and eats and talks breathlessly, barely waiting for responses, describing the Duke, the assassinations, her disguise as a boy, her trip, the parting from her father, the trip up the cliff. She's full of questions for Elsin too.

"How have you known my father?"

"Long before he met your mother, we went to the monastery school together in Brackwater. I already knew I wanted to help people here in the remote mountains. They have few doctors, few midwives, and I already had some skills with herbal cures. Your father was already obsessed with recreating a newspaper. No one had created one since before the ECs. He said I would cure people's ills and his newspaper would cure society's ills."

"Were you sweethearts?"

Elsin smiles at the bluntness, and the memories. "It was a long time ago."

Nyx pounces on the smile. "I'll take that as a 'yes'. Why didn't you stay together?"

Elsin is still smiling. "We each had strong ambitions that took us in opposite directions."

"Do you regret it?"

"I've been happy. I was also happy to get the request from your father to house you for a while. And, now I'm happy to get to know my old friend's daughter."

Gradually Nyx's hunger for food and talk ebbs. Nyx pauses. She sits over the now empty bowl of stew. Her second very large helping. For all the disorder in this house – not the way she keeps her kitchen in Mersinia – she recognizes that the stew is a miniature masterwork, beyond just hunger making it tasty. There were bits of wild mushrooms, lemongrass, and herbs she doesn't recognize. She feels warm and well-fed for the first time in weeks. She looks around the cottage.

Elsin has listened to the onslaught of chatter with only the occasional interjection. She recognizes Nyx's need to talk. "More stew?"

"Thank you, no," says Nyx. "It was very good. I haven't eaten this well in weeks. Here, let me wash up."

She gets up with dishes in her hand. Elsin watches. "I wonder how this will work out," Elsin thinks to herself. "The girl's got grit. Not many would have made it up the path in that weather. But being way up here in isolation with just Magnus and me week after week won't be easy for her. I told Sri I'd do it, but it won't be easy for me either. I've grown used to a quiet home."

The girl is now wiping down the counter. The dishes are already, washed and stacked in an obsessively neat pile on the draining board. Nyx has ordered them from large to small. The knives are in the drying rack with the knives, the forks are with the forks, the spoons with the spoons. She's still talking.

"Elsin. You're a herbalist?"

"Yes."

"My father said you might teach me something of what you do."

"Perhaps. If you have the aptitude and the desire."

"I don't sleep well these days. Do you have a herb for that?"

"Nyx, if ever you become a herbalist, the first thing to learn is when *not* to give herbs and potions."

"I thought a herbalist would have something to help me sleep."

"Nyx, why don't you sleep well?"

"I worry, mostly about my father."

"And why do you worry about your father?"

"He's my father."

"That's not a reason."

"He's a good man, a very good man, he's in trouble, and I love my father, he's the only parent I have."

"Ah."

Nyx looks at her. "Why 'Ah'"?

"I'm wondering whether you'd like a herb to make you forget that your father is in trouble, or would you prefer a herb to forget that you love your father?"

Nyx looks embarrassed. For the first time that evening her gush of words stops. "No." She says. Just the one word.

Elsin leans forward, "Being worried for your father is natural. Don't fight nature, girl. Accept it. It's part of having a father or a child or a sweetheart or husband or friends. Those are good things. Tomorrow think about how your worry can lead you to do something for your father. Worry without constructive action is destructive and must be deferred. In any case, I don't think sleep will be a problem tonight for you."

The girl wipes the sink clean and then reaches for a broom to sweep the kitchen floor.

Elsin again sees how tired she is, and interrupts, "No, no, put the broom down. Sleep time for you."

"But I want to hear more about you and my father. I have many questions, Elsin."

"Sleep first Nyx. We'll have days and weeks to discuss all that. There is no rush and it's late. Tomorrow I start early. If you wake after I've left, help yourself to whatever food you want. Use the day to relax. I'll be back by evening. The vegetable garden is the one in front. Any herbs in there you can use for food too. The garden in the back is medicinal herbs that should never be used for food. Leave those alone."

The girl leans over to rub Magnus' head then hesitates. She walks up to Elsin and gives her a long hug. "Thank you," she says, "I can see why Father liked you," gives her another long hug, and then goes to her room.

Elsin sits back. "I didn't expect that," she says to herself. She looks at Magnus and says, "And what got into you? Letting a stranger rub your head? Are you getting senile as well as losing your sight?"

The dog has one more surprise for her. He grunts at her, gets up and goes off to lie in Nyx's room.

***

10. Democracy meets Feudalism

Tarsis under the old Duke was a reasonable place to live, at peace with the world and its own citizenry. The new Duke and Ham, Patriarch of the New Church of Sacrifice, and advisor to the Duke, are changing that. They've expanded both the military, the police, and created a new institution, the Militant Police of the New Church of Sacrifice, commonly called the MPs. Taxes on the citizens have increased. Every town must erect a bronze statue of the new Duke, and increase donations to the New Church of Sacrifice. Every town has a contingent of MPs to supervise the morals of the citizenry and their willingness to sacrifice some of their wealth and income for the good of the church and state.

The farming villages of Upper Sophenia Province make the mistake of thinking they can air their grievances at these changes. They send a delegation asking for an audience with the new Duke.

The Duke meets them in a giant hall, Ham next to him.

"We were thinking that we might help Your Honour know your people by sending a representative member from each of Your Honour's provinces. We would elect one member from each province and send that member to sit with Your Honour as an advisory council. Electing members by voting is something useful we read about from before the first EC. It was called universal suffrage."

The Duke looks blank. "What?" he says. Ham leans forward and whispers in his ear. The Duke grunts in agreement. Ham addresses the room. "The Duke thanks you for your excellent and patriotic willingness to share in the burden of rule. Both he and the New Church of Sacrifice welcome your willingness to endure and espouse universal suffering. This is a worthy idea you have brought to us from before the first EC. The Church of Sacrifice will examine the principles and aims of universal suffering more closely and incorporate them in our doctrine.

The Duke also welcomes the willingness of one of you to give up a member. He is curious to know whether the member will be an arm, leg, foot, hand, head or some more private member. Please return to Upper Sophenia, think about it and let His Honour know when you reach a decision. In his great generosity, His Honour says there is no urgency. We are ready to continue the discussion whenever you wish.

The Sophenian delegation leaves. Hastily.

The Duke has further business with Patriarch Ham. Illyria and the Monastery at Tectis. Under the old Duke, the Tectonic Monks and their satellite schools were valued. There is even a satellite school in Tarsis, at Brackwater Lake, in Celecium Province. But Illyria is a thorn in the young Duke's side.

"Ham," he says, "Illyria. They are so closed to the outside world. No one knows what they could be plotting. To their south, the Blackrock Mountains are a barrier between us and them. To their north, entry to Illyria by sea to Freeport is blocked by reefs everywhere. Only the damn Illyrians know how to navigate past those. So. They know what's happening in Tarsis. We don't know what's happening in Illyria. Is that just?"

"No, Sire." Ham watches the Duke. He thinks he knows where this is heading.

The Duke continues. "I sent a small hunting party into Illyria across the Blackrock Mountains. Very hard going. They say they were lucky to get out. They were lucky with the weather. Even so, two of them fell off a cliff and died, one lost toes and fingers, frozen in a snowstorm. Separately, we bought a map from one of your contacts inside Illyria for navigating the reefs. We sent a ship with the map to guide it. The idiot captain still ran his ship onto a rock. The Illyrians impounded the ship and set the crew adrift. It seems the only way to get inside Illyria is on an Illyrian ship."

"Sire, the Illyrian ships do carry passengers from all nations. I could arrange for a few of our more dedicated Militant Police to pose as common passengers. Traders come to barter goods at the annual Illyrian trade fairs. They could easily stay for a month and ferret out gossip and contacts. Perhaps bribe a few permanent contacts."

The Duke considers. "Very well," he says. "I have been reading some pre-EC texts. The texts point out the danger of having one's spies captured. They might reveal *my* plans to the Illyrians if captured. I don't want Illyria to know the extent to which I'm expanding my military and your MPs."

"I will pick only the best, the most loyal MPs, Sire."

"Ham, my late father's pre-EC texts suggest an additional solution."

"Yes, Sire?"

"Hand-pick a half dozen of your MPs for this role, Ham. Have them each fitted with one hollowed out tooth."

"Painful, Sire, but I'll ensure that their love of country and duty will overcome any reluctance. What should be placed in the hollow tooth?"

"Enough poison to kill them in seconds. If captured they must bite hard enough on the weakened tooth to crumple it and release the poison. See to it, Ham."

"Sire."

"And, Ham?"

"The men you pick, make sure they're trained not just as spies, but also as assassins."

"Of course, sire. Full training. Poisoning, stealth, dagger throwing, crossbows, garrotting, venomous spiders in the pyjamas, scorpions in the shoes, infected needles in the ends of a glove, adders and poison powders in the target's bedsheets."

"Exactly Ham. There are more ways of taking over Illyria than just invasion."

"Indeed, Sire."

Ham leaves. He smiles. It seems he has just been promoted to head of the Tarsis Secret Service. Who knew? He hums a happy tune.

***

11. Who Goes First?

Sal finds Dom Uss in the stables getting two horses ready. "Dom Smuel said you wanted to see me, Dom Uss?"

"Yes. Ride with me and we'll talk."

They saddle up the horses. Sal is casting sidelong glances at Uss. The man is medium height, lean but muscular, no fat on him. His hair is grey, yet his face looks young. Sal judges he might be forty years old. There's a curious imbalance to his frame. His shirt is short-sleeved, showing a right forearm that is visibly thicker than his left. His right shoulder appears larger than the left too, although that's partially obscured by his shirt, and harder to judge. Sal wonders whether this imbalance is the result of some childhood injury. Dom Uss steps into a stirrup and swings himself up onto the horse with complete ease. Whatever has caused this imbalance, he's obviously totally fit.

Dom Uss lets the horses walk. They ride abreast and talk.

"Dom Taane says you think you've found signs of iron deposits up on the ridge ahead, maybe enough to be worth mining, is that right, Sal?"

"Yes, Dom Uss."

"Show me, please."

Dom Uss moves his horse into a trot and encourages Sal to go ahead.

After an hour, Sal halts the ride by a stream high above the monastery. "Here, Dom Uss. See these shiny black pyramidal crystals. That's iron-bearing hematite. See the red soil where the stream has cut into the rock. That red is iron oxide. See how the streaks come up vertically from below the surface? The surface deposits aren't rich enough to be worth much, but this caldera, this is the inside of an old volcano. These iron traces came up from deep in the earth. What I've been discussing with Dom Taane is whether the iron deposits become rich enough at depths we can dig to, or whether the rich deposits are too deep for us to reach. Also, there are similar iron-rich tells in different places upstream from here. We don't know which place is best to do a trial dig. The iron would be really useful to the monastery and to Dom Taane if we could find a good, reachable deposit."

They dismount and tie the horses to some trees. Below them lies the monastery, the town of Tectis, and below that the harbour of Freeport. All of these lie on the southern half of the old caldera. The northern half of the caldera was ripped away by a mega-eruption during the third EC. The space where the northern wall once was is now open to the sea. The approach is littered by reefs left by the eruption.

If you're an Illyrian skipper who knows his way past the reefs, you can find a sheltered and very deep mooring nudging against the shore where the southern half of the caldera meets the ocean. Too deep for any anchor, but you moor against trees on the shore. Two hundred fathoms below your keel is the floor of the ancient volcano. It's one of the most impressive moorings in the known world. Ahead of you, the southern half of the caldera rises up to Tectis, then further to the Tectis Monastery and then far higher to the snow-covered Black Rock Mountains. Further south yet, if you can get across the Black Rock Mountains, lies Tarsis.

Dom Uss surveys the scene slowly then looks upstream. He rinses his hands in the stream, and drinks. Then he looks around.

"Sal," he says, "Dom Taane speaks highly of you. Says you have uncommon skill at analyzing rocks and soil back in his lab, says you know how to do chemical tests for all kinds of minerals. Have you looked at the wild fig trees growing all the way up the stream?"

"No, Dom Uss."

"In Tarsis, in Celecium Province, miners pick where to mine with the help of trees like these. The trees put down their roots to variable depths. Where the rock below them is hard, the roots stay near the surface and the trees stay small. Where the rock below them is fissured, the trees put down roots up to 300 feet deep. And the trees grow larger there. Of course, the roots bring up minerals according to the depth of the root system, and deposit the minerals in the leaf structure. Might be worth taking leaf samples back to Taane's lab and doing some analysis on the leaves. Find out in which locations on the stream the leaves have most iron content."

Sal looks embarrassed. "I did not know. I did not even think of that." Then he starts to smile. "That's brilliant. Thank you Dom Uss."

He looks at Dom Uss' arms, points and says, "Dom Smuel was telling us about your fight with a giant python in the Celecium rainforest. Are those bite marks on your arm from the python's fangs?"

Dom Uss looks surprised. He looks at his arm. "I'm not sure. It was all a long time ago. And Dom Smuel is a great storyteller, he probably exaggerated the story."

Sal watches Uss. He's beginning to like this quiet monk. Where others would boast this man does not. And he has great ideas about mining. Sal grows serious again. "Dom Smuel said today you would give me my final entrance questions."

"You'd like to stay at the monastery?"

"Yes, Dom Uss. I still have much to learn here."

"Good. I have two questions for you. The first is how you left Kiliman and why. I wanted to hear from my own sources before questioning you. Now I need to know your version. I will say that my sources reveal your father is King on Kiliman. I need to make sure there are no political ramifications for the monastery. We keep good relations with Kiliman."

Sal hesitates. "Dom Uss, I would like to answer, but the information could damage relations deeply between important families in the Kiliman Archipelago."

Dom Uss nods. "I will swear to keep what you tell me to myself unless there is wrongdoing involved on your part or danger to the monastery. I will swear it by the oath we Tectonic Monks keep, and by the oath of your own islands, by our dragons and by your mother sea. If you cannot answer openly my question, I will not press you, but you must leave the monastery."

Sal watches him. He guesses that Uss has already gathered some of the facts. "Very well. My father is, as your sources say, king on Grand Kiliman. He cemented an important alliance with a major island family by marrying one of their daughters after my mother died. The marriage is important for the peace between the islands. The new queen plotted to push me off her balcony. She hopes her future children will be first in line for the throne. I left the island."

Dom watches the boy carefully. "My sources say the queen *did* push you off her high balcony. Yet you survived. How?"

Sal sighs. "I had hints ahead of time about her plan. She invited me at night. It was dark out on her balcony. Before I went to her, I hung a rope from a higher balcony down past the right-hand edge of her balcony. I had blackened the rope. She didn't see it in the dark. We went out onto her balcony. I walked over to the right-hand edge, as though looking at the scenery. I wore a harness under my cape. I attached the rope end to my harness then pulled some slack into the rope, so that the slack loop hung below her balcony out of sight. I walked back to her at the middle of the balcony. She didn't see the rope coming up from below, nor the rest of the rope to the right of her balcony. Then she pushed me off the balcony."

Dom is still watching the boy intently. "That must have been a hard tug on the harness when you hit the end of the rope?"

"I ran the rope from the coil on the ground up to a high pulley above the queen's balcony and then back down to me. As I fell, the rope rose from the coil on the ground. I had placed a 15-pound weight every five feet on the coiled rope. The further I fell the greater the counterweight on the rising rope, and the slower I fell. By the time I touched ground below the castle I was barely moving. I had swung to the right of the queen's balcony on my descent. She could not see me in the dark. She believes I fell into the tidal rocks below the castle and was washed away by the waves. I stood up, untied the rope from my harness. The rope ran off the pulley and fell to the ground near me. I tossed the rope and the weights into the sea. I boarded an Illyrian vessel to come here. We left that same night. The little pulley that remained several balconies higher will not be noticed. It is outside an unused room. By the time anyone sees the pulley this event will be long forgotten."

Dom Uss is following the explanation carefully. "And Sal, your father, does he believe you disappeared?"

"I left a note for my father, where only he would see it. He knows where I am. But for the peace of the island, he will pretend that the marriage is happy and stable for a few years. He will see to it that there are no children by his new wife. Without children, his council will eventually annul. At that time, the ex-queen will retire to seclusion in a religious hermitage. No one will question it. Perhaps then, I will reappear. I leave that to my father's judgement."

"Could your father not have prevented this?"

"Dom, that would not have ended the threat to me, just made it harder to foresee. Besides, my father needs this marriage to appear to work, at least for a few years."

Dom Uss looks at the boy carefully. Thinking. Then he says, "Your second question now."

"Yes, Dom?" Once again, Sal's mind is moving at lightning speed. He's playing another chess game, trying to put himself in Dom Uss' shoes. What would he do? He would ask about something trivial but embarrassing to gauge whether he was getting truthful answers from Sal. Still, when Dom Uss' question comes, it surprises him.

"Sal, Dom Bal handed out a math exam to your class last week. The exam was handed out face down. When he said 'you may now look at the questions' the side with the questions was so faded it was almost blank. Unreadable. Tell me your part in that."

Sal is shocked. He says, "Dom Uss will I be expelled for this? I really do want to study at the monastery."

Uss' face is unreadable. "Answer the question."

Sal breathes deeply and straightens his back. "Yes, it was me."

"Tell me how you did it."

"Dom Uss, there are chemicals that I use in Dom Taane's laboratory that make ink fade after a day. Dom Bal had printed his exam a week before he gave it to us. I added the chemicals to his printing ink before he printed the exam. The questions looked fine for a day, and then faded."

Uss' probes further. "And how did you get into the printing room? It is locked, and the only window is three stories up."

Sal finds he is sweating in spite of the nearness of the cool stream. His stomach is knotted.

"Dom Uss, there is a ledge between the windows on that floor. If one has a head for heights one can move into the print room from a neighbouring room."

Uss looks at him. "I hear that Dom Bal is riding you, tells you Sal is a girl's name, calls you fisher boy. I know plenty of Kiliman fisher-people. It's a tough and honourable profession. And I know good men called Sal. Short for Salvatore in an old language."

Sal says, "It's not that, Dom. I don't care about that. I don't like him because he rides some of the students who do feel it and don't know how to defend themselves. He rides Alyx because she's bad at maths, tells her she can't get by on looks in his class. He rides Hanum for his poor handwriting, but Hanum's hand was badly broken when he was young. Hanum does the best he can with a badly mended hand. They're all good students, but he makes it hard for them to be good."

Uss thinks a moment. Then he says, "Leave Dom Bal to me and to the Abbess. She already knows of this. I need your word no more pranks against him, or you're out of the monastery. Give me your word and then you and I will forget this conversation, Master Sal."

Sal breathes a sigh of relief. "Thank you, Dom Uss. I give you my word."

They mount to ride back to the monastery. Dom Uss lets Sal go first.

Sal looks over his shoulder and asks, "Dom Uss, how did you escape the python?"

Uss snorts, "Smart youngster like you, I thought you'd have guessed."

Sal thinks, "Crush-proof armour?"

"Nope. Too heavy and hot in the rainforest."

Sal tries again, "Lightweight armour, lined with outward-facing blades, so that when the snake coils itself on you, it cuts itself on the blades?"

"Nope, never even thought of that. And outward facing knives? Sounds like you'd cut off your nose the first time you sneeze."

Sal thinks again, "You got an arm free and strangled it?"

"Nope, I couldn't move a finger, never mind an arm. You're missing the obvious solution."

"I give up, Dom Uss, what did you do?"

"Me? Nothing. The fellow walking behind me, *he* cut its head off. Damn near cut my arm off too. Thanked me for going first. Otherwise, I might have been the one nearly cutting his arm off. You see, young Sal, sometimes having the right companions is more important than having the right technology. Worth remembering."

Uss pauses, then resumes, "Also, Sal, always make deliberate decisions on whether you want to go first, second or third when walking or riding in the wild."

"Dom?"

"Yes?"

"What happens if you go third?"

"For pythons, nothing. A rock-viper now, a rock-viper will sleep on your path. The first one to walk by wakes it up. The second one annoys it. The third one gets bitten. The teeth are like nails, they'll go through leather boots. Easily. And they hang on like bulldogs till all their venom is emptied into you."

"Good thing there are only two of us today, Dom Uss."

"True."

"Dom Uss, are there pythons in Illyria."

"Not according to most books."

"Then, out of politeness, shouldn't I let you ride ahead of me."

"Not until we find out if the books are right."

They ride back to the monastery in silence.

***

12. Elsin II

The morning after Nyx's arrival, Elsin leaves before sunrise. There's a farmer a half day's ride away that Elsin has been treating for a foot infection. The foot is slowly mending but it's time to check on him and renew his liniments. Elsin saddles up her horse. Nyx is asleep still. Obviously exhausted. She hasn't even woken after Magnus took over half the bed next to her.

By the time Elsin has treated the farmer, inspected the rest of his family, discussed silage making with the farmer, and helped him treat a calf for scours, it's time for the return journey. She mounts up and sets her horse to a steady walk, wondering what Nyx has been up to. She sings to herself as she rides, an old habit of solitude. As she approaches her cottage, the singing stops. A frown creases her face. There's something odd about the cottage, something different but she can't put her finger on it yet.

Nyx hears her stabling her horse. She runs out to the stable looking excited. There is a smile across her face.

"Elsin, I have a surprise for you."

She grabs Elsin's hand and pulls her to the cottage entrance.

"Close your eyes," says Nyx. "I'll guide you into the cottage. Promise not to look until I tell you to look."

Elsin feels a growing sense of foreboding but says, "OK."

She shuts her eyes and is guided into the cottage.

"You can look now Elsin," says Nyx.

Elsin opens her eyes and staggers. The blood drains from her face. She comes close to falling.

She's aware of Nyx guiding her to a chair. "Sit," says Nyx. "Breathe deeply."

Nyx feels Elsin's forehead. "Don't get up," she says. "Breathe. Breathe. Elsin, are you sick? What's wrong? Was the ride today too much for you? What happened to you today? Wait don't talk, I'm going to get you water."

Nyx scurries away. Elsin looks at her cottage again.

The wood floor of the cottage is a shiny yellow instead of the normal brown. It gleams in reflected light from the kitchen window. Like new wood. Elsin looks at the window. The vines that were crawling across the kitchen window are cut back to the edge of the window. The glass is so clean you can barely tell it's there. She's looking out of the window with the mountains in clearer view than they've been for years. Her heart stops again when she looks at her workbench. She can barely breathe. That idiot girl has not only cleaned and polished the floor, she's polished the wood workbenches and tidied her herbs, her measuring equipment, her notes. The tar deposit on the edge of the table is gone. Her shelves are completely rearranged. The measuring equipment is all on one shelf. The mortars, pestles, alembics, guillotines, pill presses, braziers are all on the shelf underneath. The next shelf contains strainers, pots, funnels and neatly folded muslin cloth. The muslin looks whiter than it's looked in years. The girl has washed it. There's a shelf for just her notes, quills and inks. The shelves ... the shelves have labels and numbers. The broken pills have disappeared, the broken alembic is gone, Dragon only knows where. The once open jars are now neatly corked on the workbench with a stack of blank labels waiting next to them.

"I'll kill her," thinks Elsin, "Dragons damn me if I don't." She now knows what seemed odd when she approached the cottage. The damned girl has also weeded her flower garden. Elsin's head is spinning. She feels faint. "Nyx!" she shouts in fury.

The girl arrives with a large glass of water and Magnus, the traitor dog, following, looking adoringly at the girl. Elsin attempts to stand up and let the girl have a piece of her mind.

"Elsin!" says Nyx, "sit, you're not looking well at all. You're pale as fury." She holds Elsin down with one hand while holding out the glass for her. The girl is surprisingly strong. Or maybe Elsin is weak from shock. She tries to stand again and the impasse is broken by a knock on the door.

It's Jurl, from two farms over. "Mistress Elsin, please come. Hannah's water has broken."

Elsin finds her strength again. "Out of the way, Nyx. This is important."

"You're not well," says Nyx, you've already had too long a day. I'm coming with you."

"Whatever," says Elsin, "I've no time to argue."

They mount up and leave.

By the time Elsin and Nyx get back to the cottage the stars are fading in the east. It was a long complicated birthing. Took all night. But. A new day is coming. Hannah has a new child; all is well. And Nyx was a big help. Nyx's extra pair of hands was invaluable. The girl followed instructions quickly and well. She had good instincts too, knew how to manage Jurl and keep him from interfering. Elsin knows she's still going to have to scold Nyx severely for rearranging her workbenches, but now doesn't seem like the right time. They're both too tired and hungry.

"Nyx, did you have any supper last night?"

"No. I cooked for us both but we didn't have time to eat. First, you fell ill, then Jurl arrived. So no supper. We could have it for breakfast if you feel well enough."

"What did you make?"

"I caught a beautiful trout upstream from your cottage and smoked it all day while I was cleaning your cottage for you. I pulled some asparagus and sautéed some potatoes from your vegetable garden to go with it. I'll get the fire going, heat up the potatoes and breakfast will be ready in no time."

They eat. The trout is amazing. The sautéed potatoes are manna. Nyx is babbling about which wood she uses to smoke fish. And how beautiful Hannah's baby is. The first that Nyx has ever delivered. So lovely. The magic of being allowed to tie off the umbilical cord. And Hannah is thinking of naming the baby Elsin. What a joy for Elsin this work must be. And how the stars at dawn are lovely.

Elsin puts aside her fork, barely listening to the girl. "I'd better get the scolding done with now," she thinks to herself.

"Nyx," she says, "What I do up here in the mountains is very important for the health of all who depend on me. There are few doctors. I am often all there is to keep people and livestock healthy. It's a heavy responsibility. Just one person supporting so many. And herbalism requires a process, one that I know and have studied and made my own. It's a difficult field and it has to be done just right. There are ways of preparing herbs that I've perfected over several years. You do understand that, don't you?"

Nyx's face is glowing. "I understand Elsin," she says. "It's too much for one person. You've decided to teach me. I'm so glad." She capers around the room, comes back to Elsin and gives her a huge hug and a kiss on the cheek.

"Thank you, Elsin."

Elsin shakes herself. How did that go so wrong? She must be tired. "I'm going to bed," she says.

"Do you need help?" says Nyx. "I'm worried about you. You really didn't look well, last night."

"I'm fine," says Elsin, gritting her teeth.

The last thought she recalls as she falls asleep is that her newly clean bedroom window shows a lovely view of the mountain.

***

13. Vegetables that Start with 'P'

There are no classes on Friday afternoon. Some of the students are in "The King's Hand" down at the dock, drinking spice-wine and playing Tarot or Klaverjas, some are sprawled on the monastery lawns reading, some are playing handball, some are practicing archery at the butts. Sal, Hanum and Alyx are strolling idly at the docks, in Freeport, below the monastery. Hanum is big for his age; he towers above the other two. He and Alyx are usually together. Alyx is one of the most attractive girls at the monastery. Sal would be jealous of Hanum, except he likes both Hanum and Alyx; they go well together. He's musing on his mixed feelings quietly when Alyx points. There's a 60-foot ketch at the dock. 'Dragon Wings'. A beautiful ketch. Not sleek and shiny like a rich man's toy, but solid, powerful, meticulously maintained, designed for all weather. Two crewmen are scrubbing the deck and rinsing it down with buckets of seawater. Astern of the wheel, Master Bach is sitting at ease mending some netting. Alyx strides forward to lead the way up the gangplank from the dock. Sal places a restraining hand on her shoulder. "Bad manners," he cautions her. "Always ask first. Like walking into someone's home."

He raises his voice, "Master Bach? Permission to come aboard?"

Bach glances up. He grunts and waves his hand towards the cockpit. He grunts again at one of the crew, "Cookie, some coffee for the pumpkins please."

Cookie is a giant, even taller than Hanum. He smiles at the newcomers and reappears from below a moment later with three steaming mugs.

Bach shakes Hanum's hand with genuine warmth. "Sit, Hanum," he says, "and your friends also."

Hanum points, "Alyx and Sal."

"Know them both," says Bach, handing each one a mug. "G'day Potato-heads."

"My name is Sal, Master Bach," says Sal, trying to make a point.

"Must be confusing for your parents, you having all those names," says Bach. "Still they bring it on themselves. If they'd stuck with just pumpkin or potato, there'd be no problem."

Alyx apparently knows Master Bach's naming conventions. "It's a 'p' day," she says.

"Really?" says Bach. "I was having a good one myself."

Sal is grinning in spite of himself.

"Master Bach," he says, "I never found out what you do at the monastery."

"I'm a Ranger, Little Peanut."

"Ranger?"

"Yeh – haven't they taught you about us Rangers, up there in the seat of all learnin'?"

Sal shakes his head.

Bach spits over the side. "If that don't beat everything. We do all the work, and the hoity-toity teachers never bother to mention us. Hanum knows though. Hanum's going to do a tour of duty with us starting next month. You want to tell them, Hanum?"

Hanum looks embarrassed. He tries to make himself look smaller, curving his back down. "Alyx knows too, it's just Sal being new. Sal, you know about the second EC. How gene altering viruses ran out of control, the mutations from carbon-based into silicon-based life forms, how the H-bombs stressed the earth's crust, and the mega-volcanoes during the third EC."

Sal nods.

"Well," says Hanum, "the earth's crust is still overstressed. We'd be having more catastrophic volcanic eruptions, more mega ash clouds blocking the sun, more five-year winters, darkness, freeze-ups, crop failures and starvation. Except for the earth-dragons. They mutated during the second EC. Silicon-based life forms. They burrow into the continental bed rocks deep below the surface. Their burrows lubricate the points where continental shelves would otherwise collide, compress, break and build up new mega-volcanoes. Because of the burrows and lubrication, pressure is released early, before it builds to catastrophe."

"I know that," says Sal. "What's that got to do with us, with the monastery?"

"What they didn't teach you in Grand Kiliman, Little Peach Pip," says Bach, "is that here, in Illyria, all along the shore, in the soft sand shelves, is where the earth-dragons lay their eggs to hatch. The only place in the world. It's that special. No other place like it. Needs protection. Poachers try to get in across the Blackrock Mountains to steal eggs. We patrol up there. Mostly the snowstorms, the crevasses, the ice on the cliffs kills those or turns them back. Then there's poachers that try to get in by sea to steal eggs. Most get wrecked on the reefs. We guard our maps and our knowledge of the approaches well. Still, some get close. It's us rangers that take care of those that get too close. And don't make dumb puns about poached eggs. We've heard it all. What we do is no joke."

Sal looks at the netting that Bach is mending. "That's no fishing net. That's a net to stop boarders."

Bach looks at Sal sharply, as though seeing him for the first time, "What else have you noticed, Little Parsley-Leaf? Walk up to the bow and back and tell me."

Sal was born in the Kiliman islands. Practically born and raised on boats.

He shakes his head at Bach. "Don't need to walk up to the bow. I'll tell you from here. Ketch rig, that's nice for reducing sail in sudden storms, nice for manoeuvrability among reefs, and nice for sailing short-handed – if the crew is busy with something else. Overly large crow's nests. That's bad for sailing. They force you to use shorter sails or taller masts with deeper keels. Either way that's not good boat design. Unless there's a reason, something important. I'm guessing if I climb up there I'll find the reason. Maybe a neat rack of crossbow bolts and crossbows. Enough space for three marksmen. Over there on the rack by the main mast, those aren't fishing gaffs, those are boarding pikes. I see cutlasses too. And that's not fish blood your crew is washing off the deck."

Bach nods approvingly and leans back. "Not quite as green as you're cabbage looking, are you?"

Alyx is looking alarmed, she leans against Hanum and clutches his arm.

Bach says to her, "Hanum will be fine, Young Mistress. He's a smart lad. He won't run towards trouble over-early, and I'll see to it that he can walk away from it afterwards too. Or at least limp away."

Hanum frees his arm from her clasp and wraps it around her shoulders. "It's important work, Alyx. And I want to do it."

She nods miserably and leans her face into his side.

Sal feels a twinge of jealousy again. He'd like to reach out and comfort Alyx, give her a hug, but he can't. She has all the comfort she needs right next to her.

He addresses Bach instead, "what do you do with poachers?"

"A few are happy to see us. When they've run onto a reef and the waves are about to shred their miserable bodies against the reef. There are a lot of very inaccurate charts of our waters. Rocks charted incorrectly. Markers and lights shown incorrectly. Other poachers are less happy to see us. In either case, we subdue them, disarm them, confiscate their equipment and sink their boats."

"And what happens to them?"

"We mark them with a tattoo, put them on a raft with some fishhooks, a tarp and water, a small solar still, and let the raft go with the Harran current. The Harran current has many swirls before it touches land. If they're careful, they'll reach land in about six months. Far away from here. More humane than a life behind bars. The tattoo is so we recognize second offenders."

"Do you have second offenders?"

"Once every few years. We add a second tattoo, put them back on a raft in the Harran current. A smaller raft, smaller tarp, less water, only two or three hooks, a smaller solar still. We've never seen a third offender. It takes them much longer to get back to land on the smaller rafts. And they have to be really careful how they go. Don't want to come back here after that. Your hoity-toity monks call that 'aversion therapy'."

"You've got tattoos, Master Bach. One I recognize. On your right hand."

Bach says, "Oh?"

His tone is challenging.

Sal returns the steady gaze. "That's a Harran pirate tattoo. From the Harran Islands. North of Kiliman. On Kiliman if you're caught with that tattoo you'd likely be hanged for piracy."

Bach gives a minute nod of his head. "I was one, once. Pirate. Not anymore. Water under the barge. And I avoid Kiliman. They're antisocial when it comes to ex-pirates. No sense of humour about piracy. Hard to get a laugh out of any of them. Did try to hang me once. And their beer tastes like sewer water. So I'm a Ranger now. Work for a monastery. That makes me almost religious. Almost a saint. My dear old parents would be proud to know. Especially my father. Very big on religion he was, especially Lettuce Gods. He'd be proud to know I was almost Saint Bach. Patron Saint of Dragon Eggs. Almost as good as being Patron Saint of Lettuces."

He stares at Sal. Challenging Sal to disagree with or laugh at his almost-sainthood.

When Sal remains serious, Bach says, "You've sharp eyes on you, young Sal. And you know boats. We could use you as a Ranger. You'd be good. If you were a Ranger, you might even find a young woman looking at you the way this one looks at Hanum. Think you might like that?"

It's the first time Bach has called him 'Sal'. It deserves a politeness in return, so Sal appears to weigh the question before responding.

"I've got a lot to learn at the monastery first, Master Bach. Maybe another year."

Bach gazes at Alyx, as though inviting her to volunteer. When she doesn't, he returns his gaze to Sal.

Bach grunts, sips his coffee and says to Alyx and Sal, "You come see me when you're ready, young Parsnips. Might even teach one of you how to use a quarterstaff properly."

Sal notices that he's back to being a vegetable.

It's a dismissal. Hanum and the two parsnips say their farewells and leave.

***

14. Marching Orders for Nyx

The months since Nyx came to Elsin have shot by. Elsin has never known a girl to learn so fast. Nyx has mastered Elsin's standard Han texts, 'The Herb-Root Codex', 'The Annotated Materia Medica', 'The Wild Herb Canon', and several more. She is completely reliable in identifying common herbs and compounding the most important disinfectants, anti-inflammatories, tonics, laxatives, purgatives and anaesthetics. They have stitched up cuts together, delivered calves, lambs, foals and babies. Nyx has helped Elsin prepare poultices, tinctures, tonics, eye drops and ointments for everything from croup in people to ringworm in sheepdogs to hoof cracks in horses. Elsin even finds she enjoys cooking with Nyx. She'd never thought she'd enjoy sharing her stove, but they work well together. They've worked out a truce on tidiness too. The girl can tidy whatever she wishes, provided Elsin's main workbench is left untouched. Nyx is fast becoming the daughter Elsin never had. A joy to have with her.

Today, though, Elsin's heart is leaden. It's early morning. Elsin has barely slept. She had a visitor from Mersinia during the night who brought messages. She didn't wake Nyx. Better Nyx didn't see the messenger. The fewer in the resistance to the Tarsin Duke that know each other's faces the better.

Now Elsin will have to tell Nyx to move on.

A cruel blow to both of them. Elsin reflects how hard the girl's life has been over the past months. First a separation from home and father, now a separation from what might have, with time, become her second home, here with Elsin.

Elsin, sighs, then thinks to herself, "Keep it brisk and no-nonsense to focus the girl on what lies ahead. Any display of emotion from me, will sink Nyx into needless self-pity."

Over breakfast, Elsin tells the girl.

"Nyx," she says, "I had a messenger from your father during the night. Didn't want to wake you. The messenger came and went while you slept. Your father sends his love."

"To you too?" asks Nyx.

In a different mood, Elsin might blush. Not today. "He was being polite. "

"How is he? Where is he?"

"He's still in hiding. The warrant for his arrest is still there. The Duke's men, the MPs, have destroyed his printing press. Your father has helped build small, secret printing presses scattered throughout Mersinia. There are people still printing the truth about the Duke and distributing leaflets secretly, mostly at night. They call themselves the Underground Press, but they're much more than that. They've found out that the Duke has been sending hunting parties into Illyria, across the Blackrock Mountains. The Duke is looking for an Illyrian Lynx pelt to wear at his coronation as Emperor."

"He's killing Illyrian Lynx?"

"Yes. It's very bad. Your father needs you to go to Illyria."

"Why?"

"In a moment I'll show you why. First the how. He says you should go to the monastery school at Brackwater Lake, here in Celecium province. You'll need to ride. It's autumn. Crossing the Cold Range Mountains will already be difficult. Worse if you delay. Late fall snowstorms will block the passes."

"When do you think I should leave?"

"Today. I packed for you last night."

"Today!"

Nyx looks at her hand. The spoon in her hand is trembling, dripping porridge. She can't believe how casually Elsin is giving her this news. Elsin, the woman she has adored being with, her teacher, her companion, who took her in, who taught her, who talked with her about love, life, birth, death, joy, sadness and everything in between, is throwing her out.

Elsin is still talking," Once you're down on the plains again the going will be easier. Your father has sent ahead a letter of introduction and a payment. That has guaranteed you entrance at the Brackwater School as a student for some weeks if needed. Also to live in the school hostel. Go to the school. You can't disguise as a boy this time. You'll go as a girl under your own name. You needn't give a last name. The school is expecting a girl called simply Nyx. In fall there are monks from the Tectis monastery that come to Brackwater Lake. They run competitions for the Brackwater students, choosing some to come to Illyria. Wait for the monks. You shouldn't have to wait more than a week. Join them and go with them when they travel back to Illyria. Here. This is a letter from your father. I haven't opened it. For you. And this is what the messenger also brought last night. This is why you need to go to Illyria."

She carefully opens a small cloth bundle and shows it to Nyx.

Nyx peers in. Her face becomes paler still. "Oh, oh no."

***

15. Marching Orders for Nyx II

Nyx is riding. The precious cloth bundle is slung across her chest, snug and hidden under her poncho. Her saddlebags, bedroll and cantle bag are carefully strapped to her saddle. Elsin has also given her a basic herbalist's kit in a slim teak box. The box is a marvel. Little brass catches to keep it closed. Inside, satin lining over padding to protect the contents: a selection of key herbs, a small assortment of equipment, glass containers, and a slim reference book on key botanicals. A truly precious thing in a world where books and glassware are so rare.

Nyx doesn't know how to reconcile the magnificence of the gift, with the casual matter-of-factness of Elsin's parting. She half wishes she *had* hugged Elsin when they said good-bye. But Elsin's manner during their parting made that impossible. Nyx feels a surge of anger at the woman. Fury. Elsin stood by as calm as a Wednesday morning while Nyx mounted. All Elsin said was, "Good luck." That was all. No expression on her face. Didn't even watch her ride away or wave. Turned and went back into her cabin and shut the door. After all they'd been through together. The calves delivered, the late night urgent rides, the good companionship, the long conversations, the laughs. Nyx can't figure it. Then when Nyx is ready to curse the woman aloud, she thinks of all the nights Elsin sat up late to explain how to grind up this or that root, how to boil off the toxins and dry a this or that herb, how to calculate correct dosages. An endless treasure of knowledge, given freely and lovingly. Nights when Elsin was already tired by a hard day's work and travel.

It's the casualness of "good luck" before turning away that hurts.

Now as she rides, Nyx tries for the hundredth time to put that aside. Instead, she mentally reviews her father's letter to her. She can recite it by heart.

> *My Dearest,*
> *E. will have already explained to you where to go. And why. By the time you get there it will be late fall or early winter. Too late for you to return to E. through the Cold Range passes with their storms, snow and avalanches. Join the monks that return to*

Tectis. Carry the burden E. will have entrusted to you. It must go back to Illyria. In Illyria, go to the Tectis monastery. Show your amulet to the Abbess. I have no time to write all I wish to say, the messenger is already mounted on his horse and will leave with or without my note to you.

Know there is no day I will not think of you with all love.

In great haste,
Your father.

An odd letter, Nyx muses. Odd for what he does not say. He does not name the burden she carries, does not name the school at Brackwater, does not name Elsin or talk about himself. He usually signs himself 'Sri', not 'Your father'. Yet the brushstrokes are unmistakably his. Clearly, he is being cautious in case the letter is intercepted by the Duke's men. His reference to her amulet is also curious.

She touches it. The action is unconscious. An unthinking habit. A last link to her mother. Who in turn got it from her mother, Nyx's grandmother. Nyx cannot remember either one. All she has left of them is the amulet. It's made of some hard stone, almost black, that flashes rainbow colours when the light catches it sideways at just the right angle. It is shaped like a dragon claw holding an arrow. The arrow point pierces a heart. The rear of the amulet carries the inscription 'The Hand of God'. An enigmatic object. Nyx has no idea what the inscription means. Some days she holds the amulet in the light wondering if, when held just right, it might not bring back a clearer memory of her mother. It never has. She sighs, put away thoughts of the amulet and her father's letter and concentrates on the trail ahead.

16. Marching Orders for Uss

"Uss, old friend," says the Abbess. "Welcome. Sit. Have some coffee."

"Do you have tea?"

"Come Uss, you know I won't give you tea and you shouldn't ask."

Uss shrugs.

"If you are in pain," says the Abbess, "talk to me. Don't drown it in tea."

"An old reflex," says Uss. "Coffee is fine. Let's not talk about it. I'm not in pain"

The abbess stares at him closely.

"Very well. Let's talk of other things. The monastery has need for you to travel."

"Oh?"

"I'm going into seclusion for some weeks to meditate," says the Abbess. "My usual autumn meditation. This year Dom Bal will be in charge while I'm in meditation."

It's Uss' turn to stare. "An odd choice. You have a reason, I suppose, Abbess?"

She grimaces. "I do. I'm also well aware of his character. And his petty dislikes. I want you and the other petty dislikes out of harm's way. So, I have a mission that will take you to Tarsis while I'm in seclusion. Several missions."

Uss cocks his head sideways. "Oh? Several?"

The abbess counts off on her fingers for him.

"Number one, go to Mersinia. Deliver a coronation gift to the Duke of Tarsis, soon to be crowned Emperor of Tarsis. We have a set of our finest earthenware cups, saucers and dishes for him. Quite priceless.

"Number two, the Duke has succeeded in killing an Illyrian lynx. He sent a poaching party into our territory through the Blackrock Mountains. He doesn't know that we know. He intends to wear the pelt for his coronation as Emperor of Tarsis. We cannot allow the pelt to be shown in that way. The lynx numbers are too low as it is, and they are vital for the dragon eggs. If the pelt is seen on an emperor, every minor earl, baron and lord will send hunting parties to shoot one for themselves. You know how it is. If the emperor has one, everyone else dreams of having one.

"The pelt is being cured by a furrier outside Mersinia. We have information where to find the furrier. The workshop is probably guarded. You need to remove the pelt. Bring it back or destroy it but don't let the Duke wear it at his coronation. Don't let him know our involvement in removing it. He must remain convinced that we knew nothing about it. Going to Mersinia to present him with the pottery is your excuse for being in Mersinia.

"Number three, it is time to select some bright students from the Brackwater Lake School and award them scholarships here in Tectis. Another good reason for you to be travelling in Tarsis.

"Number four, I have had in the monastery for some time a stone that may be very important to the monks of Han-Bu. I want you to take it to them."

Uss sits up. "Not the missing stone? The one that was lost when Ju-Sin sneezed?"

The Abbess looks serious. "Quite possibly. The history of how it got here is cloudy. We've had it at Tectis for over two centuries now. We found it again recently during a clean-up of our storage rooms. I've been studying it closely since then. It may be the genuine article. The markings are correct, the weight and size are right, the composition of the stone, everything matches. I've written to the Abbot of Han-Bu and let him know we'll be sending it with you. They can ultimately decide better than I if it's real or not. Here. I've put it on a temporary chain. Wear it around your neck. Keep it close."

Uss slips it over his neck and frowns. "And if it's real? Will you be destroying the universe by giving them the missing stone?"

The abbess shrugs. "If it's real, then I must return it to its rightful owners. Keeping what is not ours would be equally harmful to the universe. Also, I think the universe is more resistant to annihilation and to having the stone towers completed than the Han-Bu know. It was likely no accident that Ju-Sin sneezed before the stone towers could be completed. The universe had a hand in that sneeze. Ju-Sin was merely its tool. I predict that if ever the Han-Bu stone towers again near completion, something else will interfere with success for the Han-Bu."

Uss bows silently. "Very well," he says, "are there more tasks for me?"

"One last one. As I said, I want you to take two of Dom Bal's petty dislikes out of harm's way."

"Who?" says Uss.

"The boy, Sal. He knows more mathematics than Dom Bal, and it's causing a problem between them."

"Might be easier if I just took Dom Bal with me and left the boy? Perhaps lost Dom Bal while I was travelling. Lost him overboard? No? Ah, I can but dream. So, the boy, Sal?"

The Abbess nods. "Do you know the boy? Will you take him?"

"Yes, I know him. Normally I wouldn't take a student on a trip like this. It might put him in harm's way, or he might put me in harm's way. But I set him a hard question recently. He didn't evade, didn't lie when most would have. I trust him. Very well, I will take him. Who else?"

"Your black-hearted pirate, Bach."

"He's a Ranger, and a very good one, Abbess. We're lucky to have him."

She smiles. "Yes, a good Ranger, with a heart as black as a farmyard cesspit on a moonless night. I like him, mind. But he's fallen out with Dom Bal."

"Dragon's-breath," says Uss. "What has he done to Bal? I've sworn Bach to non-violence outside of his Ranger work. He's always kept his bargain."

"Not exactly violence," says the Abbess. "You were travelling when we had our annual Rangers' dinner in the summer. You know the one. The summer equinox, the end of spring.

. Midsummer. The night when the Rangers cook dinner for the monks and students. The Rangers lay on steaming hot spice wine, freshly caught fish, diced raw vegetables called 'crudités', and various dipping sauces. All cooked and eaten down at the shore on the third sand shelf."

"Yes," says Uss. "It's fun. A good night. What on earth could go wrong?"

"Ha! Nothing unless you have an ex-pirate like Bach, heart as black as sin, who doesn't like Dom Bal at the best of times. Dom Bal, curse his airs, ordered Bach around like the basest scullery-hand, and demanded a bottomless cup of spice wine and more crudités, on the double. So Bach pretended to misunderstand. Dragons know where he got it, but he held an actual bottomless mug over Dom Bal and poured the scalding spice wine in a never ending stream through the cup and onto Bal's lap. He accompanied all this with a string of the worst crudities and accusations against Bal's ancestry that I've heard in many a year. Bal wasn't actually scalded, thank the Dragons, but he ran around like a monkey with a burnt bum, and of course, he's never forgiven Bach."

Uss winces. He looks at the Abbess. "Did you keep a straight face, Abbess?"

"Uss!" she says in mock shock, then grins, "don't ask. Just take that piratic piece of evil with you when you go to Tarsis."

***

17. Cold

Nyx is cursing. Unusual for her normal calm. It's an icy morning. The cold woke her an hour before dawn. Snow has piled up deep near the rock that is shielding her and Socks from wind. Her fingers are numb. She had to spend the night above the treeline in the Coldwater Range. She hopes to cross the pass that will lead down off the mountains today. There was no way to cross the pass before dark yesterday so she camped below the pass. She brought some hard camelthorn wood from the lower slopes of the mountain. Cutting the wood was difficult and took forever; it's such a hard wood. Maybe without stopping to cut the wood she might have made it over the pass before dark. Then again, she might not.

So many decisions and events over which to doubt herself. Why had Elsin been unmoved by Nyx's leaving? Nyx had tried so hard to be helpful to Elsin. There had been clear and deep affection on either side, Nyx was sure. What had Nyx said or done to change that? Had she offended Elsin? Would Nyx have been better off trying the pass in the dark? But the trail would have been dangerous for Socks at night. She shudders to think of what a broken leg for him would mean. And the wood was vital. A safety net. She tied it in a bundle and dragged it on a rope behind Socks. She cooked supper over it, a hot stew to give strength. She melted water for Socks. Best of all, the silicon mutation in the wood ensured that the big pieces burned all night and provided some added warmth against the biting cold.

She stomps her feet and jumps to get some blood flowing. She's wearing several layers of clothes under her shapeless poncho. The precious bundle that needs to go back to Illyria is snug against her chest covered by a sweater and the poncho.

She had picked a camp spot where there was wind shelter for Socks too. He's a mountain breed that can withstand cold, but in spite of a horse blanket, even he was restless towards dawn. Another decision to raise self-doubt. Horse blankets. They help if they're well-made, waterproof and windproof. They may do more harm than good if the weight compresses the horse's coat and reduces its natural insulation. She thinks the blanket helped. She hopes so. She's never camped with him in such cold weather.

She stands next to him. He bends his head back to look at her reproachfully. He's telling her how cold it is. "Soon, old friend," she says. "Soon you will be in a warmer place. Patience." His mute suffering distresses her more than her own cold. She can't bear to put a cold iron bit in his mouth at these temperatures. She rigs a bridle for him with just a noseband. "No bit for you today," she says.

Next, she removes the horse blanket, starts to saddle and load him.

Normally she can talk to him, pat him and soothe him while getting him loaded. Now her cold fingers and divided attentions betray her. One of the saddlebags falls before it's closed, contents bouncing, spilling and leaping off the pebbles underfoot, some items spraying and leaping into the deep snow next to her. She curses again and painstakingly gathers up the scattered objects. A notion that something is still missing nags at her, but she can't think what it would be. Everything that ought to be there seems to be there. She checks the ground again and even runs her fingers through the deep snow where some of the objects came to rest. She shakes her head. Too cold to stay here and dig. She needs to get over the pass. She kicks a mound of snow over the camelthorn coals to extinguish them. That will leave some unburnt coals and wood for some future needy traveller. She cinches the errant saddlebag into place and mounts. The saddle and stirrup leathers are so cold they squeak and creak as Socks moves forward. They move slowly up towards the pass, their breath making icy plumes in the air.

***

18. Mersinia – The Furrier I

Dom Uss, Bach, Sal, the horses and wagon disembarked from their sea voyage at Port Hamelin. They've made good time on the road to Mersinia since then. They've already reached the unpopulated backcountry not far from Mersinia. Dom Uss, Bach and Sal are camped out there with their wagon and horses. It's unlikely that they'll be seen. The land is a series of hills that hide the valleys. The valleys are lined with trees that provide further shelter from view. They've bought a small flock of sheep as cover. If they are spotted, they will look like drovers fattening a flock in the valleys before driving them to market in Mersinia. They've given the wagon a temporary coat of grey paint, and put on a green mottled canvas cover to make it harder to spot. The camp spot they've found is idyllic. There are fish to be caught in the river, rabbits to be snared, a wild apple tree upstream. During the day they slip into Mersinia, leaving at least one of their group behind to fish, hunt and guard the wagon and sheep.

In Mersinia they observe the furrier. He is on the outskirts of Mersinia, where the town gives way to farmland. This is the furrier who is preparing the Illyrian lynx pelt for the Duke's coronation. The pelt they have to remove. Silently. Before the coronation.

At night, back at their wagon, Dom Uss polls the others.

"So," he says, "we've seen two armed guards on each shift, day and night in the furrier's house. The furrier's there too, of course. The house contains both his living quarters and his workshop. And the pelt. Probably being pickled in brine or being stretched out to dry by now. We've not approached the house itself too closely. Don't know the inside layout. But viewed from the nearby market, it's a one-storey building on top of a small hill. There's a garden gone wild out back, and the main approach from the front. The approach crosses a small pond and then climbs up the hill to the house. Any suggestions how to get in and remove the pelt?"

Bach clears his throat. He looks at Uss. "Release me from my vow of non-violence. Or call this valid Ranger work. In which case my vow doesn't apply. I'll knock on the door and, once they open, I'll have all of them laid out cold before you can say 'gut the fish'."

Uss shakes his head. "No. Your vow stands. Unless we or you are in danger. I'm a physician. I don't plot bloodshed and bone-break. How about you, Sal. Ideas?"

"Can we set the building alight?"

Uss again shakes his head. "Not easily. It's standard Mersinian construction. Brick walls, clay tile roof."

Sal tries again, "Can we lure them outside with some pretext of an emergency outside."

Uss considers. "I don't see it yet. See if you can come up with details that make a solid case. Bach, any more thoughts?"

Bach shrugs. "Wait for shift change, capture the incoming shift, put on their uniforms, relieve the outgoing shift."

Uss furrows his brow. "Maybe. See if you can come up with details that cover all the weak points. Meanwhile, let's all sleep on it and see what additional ideas come in the night."

The solution does not emerge in the morning. Sal and Bach's suggestions from the previous night all have obvious flaws. The solution comes only a day later, at breakfast. They're sitting at their campsite. Sal has caught some tiny finger-length fish from the river. They're cooking whole on a grid on the campfire. When crispy they make delicious mouthfuls.

They're also eating bread from the Mersinia market. Bach, a man of surprises, has not only found a wild bees' nest in a tree downriver, but also knows how to get honey from it. So bread with honey for breakfast.

Sal asks, "How do you know about getting honey from bees, Master Bach?"

Bach looks up from his bread. "I was raised on a farm. We grew lettuces mainly, but there were hives out back. I was good with them. Got so I didn't need the jacket and veil most time to protect me. A bit of smoke, and moving slowly and the bees were fine with me taking a bit of honeycomb for our breakfast today."

Uss was reaching for another crispy fish from the grid. He freezes, withdraws his hand, drops the fork he was holding and sits up. His breakfast is forgotten. He has questions for Bach. Many questions.

***

19. Mersinia – The Furrier II

Sal is on the roof of the furrier's house. He's climbed up unseen through the tangled trees of the back garden. He's bent low over the chimney, two ropes sliding slowly through his hands into the chimney. The roof is broad. As long as he stays crouched down, he's invisible from anyone to the front of the house, but still visible to the back garden, where Uss is hidden amongst bushes and trees, watching Sal.

Sal pays out more rope slowly, down the chimney. A foot more, then another foot. Soon. A knot in one of the ropes bumps against his hand, trying to slide through his hand and down the chimney. Sal halts the ropes there. No further. The knot indicates that the load on the end of the rope should almost have reached the fireplace below. There is no fire in the fireplace today.

That's key. He gives a sharp pull on the second rope. That releases the load from both ropes and undoes the sacking around the load. Sal whips the ropes and empty sacking back up and out of the chimney, then rapidly seals the top of the chimney with a wooden block. The block has a long string tied to it. Sal waves thumbs-up in the direction of the trees where Uss is waiting. Then he climbs back down to join Uss, the long string to the block trailing behind him.

They don't need to wait long. There is a shout from inside the furrier's house, then more voices shouting, then screaming. The front door is flung open violently and a man runs out – one of the guards. He runs down the path and dives straight into the pond at the bottom of the hill. Sal and Uss hold their breath. There. Barely three seconds afterwards, the remaining two occupants charge out of the house, down the path and also dive into the pond. A curious grey cloud follows behind them and hangs over the pond. The cloud shimmers, sometimes losing shape and becoming transparent, then coalescing again into a dark grey mass. Uss rushes to the back window of the house, lifts the window and climbs in. He's dressed in a curious loose canvas outfit covering his entire body, including his hands. His head is covered by an even stranger hat with a veil down to his shoulders. He's carrying a canvas bag. He emerges barely a minute later still with the bag. He quietly closes the window behind him, runs back to Sal, strips off his strange garment, and folds it into his canvas bag. He taps Sal on the shoulder and says, "Got it, let's go."

Sal pulls on the long string. The wooden block drops off the chimney into the garden. Sal hastily retrieves it. He and Uss disappear quietly through the tangled garden.

Back at the wagon, Bach is waiting for them. He's bad-tempered from being left out of the action. Uss claps him on the back. "Don't fret, Bach. We did it. You were key to this. You were the one who got the bees and their nest off the branch and tied into the sacking. You were the one who stitched up my protective clothes and veil. Without you none of this would be possible."

"Never mind the fake thank-you. How did it go?"

"Like clockwork. Sal lowered the sack into the house, released the bees nest and blocked off the chimney. Once the bees were out of the sack, they must have been furious. It didn't take long for the guards and the furrier to run out of the front door and me to run into the back. I've got the pelt."

"What do we do with it?"

"That's evidence that will hang us if it's not destroyed now. We cut it into pieces and burn it. Now. Afterwards we dig a hole and bury the ashes."

They each start cutting. Bach has the fire going in no time and the little strips are rapidly consumed.

Bach has another question. "How long before every guard in the country, every policeman, every soldier is turned out to look for the missing pelt?"

Uss smiles. "I've bought us a few days' grace. The real pelt was being pickled in a brine bath. It was probably meant to stay there for another week. I substituted a fake pelt for the real one. Superficially, the two look alike. A few days after the fake comes out of the brine bath, the furrier will see the difference. With luck, they won't connect that to the bee attack."

"No?"

"They may assume the bees built a nest in the chimney during the summer, which came unstuck now."

"And where are we going next?"

"To Mersinia, to give presents to the Duke."

Bach makes a face. "They tried to hang me on Grand Kiliman Island. I have a feeling they're going to try again in Mersinia."

***

20. Drawn, Hung and Quartered

Commander Zlod is once again sitting in front of the Duke of Tarsis. Soon to be crowned as self-announced Emperor of Tarsis. The future emperor is angry. The vein is throbbing over his right temple again.

"I sent a hunting expedition into Illyria, across the Blackrock Mountains, Zlod. They were meant to bring me back the hide of an Illyrian Lynx. The rarest of all furs. Almost pure white. For me to wear at my coronation. The fur went to our best Mersinian furrier for curing. Now it appears it's a fake."

Zlod knows exactly what the substitute fur is. Her connections across the city have informed her accurately. She thinks it politic to pretend ignorance. "What was the fake fur, Sir?"

The Duke jumps up. He bangs his fist on the table. "Zlod," he says, "This is for your ears only. If you tell anyone else, I'll have those ears nailed to the palace gates."

"Yes, Sire."

"Instead of a lynx fur, someone had taken several skunk furs – can you believe the insult – SKUNK –

bleached and dyed them almost white – cut them to shape and stitched them very carefully, almost invisibly, into the shape of a larger lynx fur. If it ever gets out that I was going to wear skunk fur for my coronation, I'll be a laughing stock. Not a word to anyone, Zlod, on your life, understand?"

"Yes, Sire."

Zlod sits even more upright to show her full understanding. She hears and feels a microscopic squeaking and shifting of the chair under her. Could a chair be laughing? It's a fleeting thought only. She gives the armrest a warning squeeze. The Duke may be slow, but he's dangerous. She gives her attention back to the Duke.

"Do you suspect the hunters or the furrier, Sire?"

"I don't know Zlod. I'm tempted to deal with all of them the same way."

"Which way, Sire?"

"I've been reading some of the pre-EC texts in my father's old library. Ancient punishments that appeal to my philosophy."

Zlod feels a question is called for. "Which philosophy is that, Sire?"

The Duke puffs out his chest. "My philosophy, Zlod, of finding a just punishment to fit an outrageous crime against the state."

"Yes, Sire?"

"Unfortunately the details are missing from the old texts. How do you have someone hung, drawn and quartered, Zlod?"

The imp of rebellion is once again whispering in Zlod's ear. She appears to consider the Duke's question carefully before replying.

"I had a famous grand-uncle, Sire."

"Yes?"

"General Karpov. He put down the Sharan Province rebellion many years ago. He became famous throughout Tarsis. The great portrait artist of the time, Klim, did a very good pen and ink drawing of the general. The drawing was hung in the Mersinia National Portrait Gallery, Sire. It's still there."

The Duke considers this. "I see. Drawn and hung. That doesn't seem like a fit punishment for the Lynx fur fakers, Zlod."

"No, Sire."

"How about the quartering?"

"When General Karpov was putting down the Sharan rebellion he was based in the town of Nali. He and his officers were quartered in the mayor's own house, in Nali. The General's diaries from the time say the quarters were small but comfortable."

The Duke is clearly disappointed with this very civil form of pre-EC punishment. "Damn," he says, "We're missing something vital in the details. Forget hung, drawn and quartered. Maybe I'll have their heads cut off instead. However, that is not why I've called you here."

"Sire?"

"There are three Illyrians in town. What do you know of them, Zlod?"

"Dom Uss is the head of the group, Sire. From the Tectis Monastery. He is a physician who comes to Tarsis yearly. He is much loved in Tarsis, Sire, for his healing skills. Many families owe him the life of a son, daughter, father or mother that he has saved from illness or injury over the many years he has come to Tarsis. This time he is accompanied by a young student, named Sal, and a servant named Bach. They have detoured to Mersinia to present gifts for your coronation. Afterwards they leave to go to the Tectonic school at Brackwater Lake to select students who want to study at the monastery school in Illyria."

"They go to Brackwater Lake every year, Zlod?"

"Yes, Sire. Dom Uss does. It's the first time for the student and the servant."

"The gifts they brought me are an insult, Zlod."

"How so, Sire?"

"They brought Illyrian pottery, from the Tectis Monastery. Rare-earth cups and bowls and saucers and the like. Settings for up to 16 people."

"Yes, Sire. The pottery from the monastery in Illyria is a rare, priceless gift. Things of wonder and beauty."

"Zlod, there are no plates. The gift is glaringly incomplete. What message are they trying to send? Is that a commentary about me? About my rule? About our nation?"

"Sire, I understand that is the tradition of the Tectonic Monks and the pottery they make. They never make plates."

"I don't like it, Zlod. I don't like them. I don't trust them. They could be spies for Illyria, looking at our military capabilities. They could be stirring up insurrection. I want you to follow them on their journey to Brackwater Lake. You personally, Zlod. Follow them until they're out of Tarsis."

"Very well, Sire."

"My local eyes, my Militant Police of the New Church of Sacrifice, the MPs, will observe any foreign travellers closely in each town they pass through. But you, Zlod, have the training and the experience that the MPs don't. Follow Physician Uss and his party Zlod. Report to me by carrier pigeon if you need any instruction from me."

"Very well, Sire."

"If you need to take action against them, do so without hesitation. Do so on the slightest suspicion that they are acting against our state. If you need extra men, call on the local constabularies, military commands or MPs for whatever you need. Here is my letter of authorization, with my seal."

Zlod shifts her position on the chair to take the letter, then leans back again. Some air is squeezed out of the upholstered seat back. It sounds like a sigh. Zlod pats the armrest. A motion small enough that the Duke won't notice.

It occurs to her that the chair has been in this office during the reign of several dukes before this one. The little sighs and squeaks may be signs of age, wear and neglect. A reminder from the chair perhaps that Zlod too is no longer as young and eager to serve as she once was. Is the chair telling her they both need a change? That they've served too many dukes in the past to want to serve this one now? When she retires, she will miss the chair. It is in many ways a trusted colleague. Sympathetic and discrete. Maybe she could ask for the chair as a parting gift. She could give it the maintenance it needs. Clean, it re-varnish it, wax it, renew the upholstery, tighten any loose joints. An interesting, restful project perhaps.

Zlod stands, salutes and leaves.

***

21. The Brackwater Thief

Uss, Bach and Sal are camped out on the town commons in Brackwater Lake. Today they're in town to buy food and supplies. It's market day and the streets are busy with a steady stream of people.

Sal has the purse. He's in the butcher's shop buying meat. Bach is ambling through the craft market far ahead looking at jewellery stalls. Uss is leaning against the wall opposite the butcher's sipping a cup of hot tea, a distant look on his face.

The events that follow are so quick it's hard to put them all together in sequence. There's Uss sipping tea. Here's Sal ambling out of the butcher's shop carrying a brown-paper wrapped, square rectangular parcel of meat. It's tied off neatly with butcher's string. The string curves around four sides of the package and emerges on top in a big knot. The package is big. Sal is using both hands to carry it, walking slowly carefully. As he comes out of the shop, a slim figure collides with him. He's off balance for a moment, arms and package stretched in front of him for counterbalance. The figure grabs the meat from his hands and runs up the street. Sal is completely unbalanced now. All he can do is shout, "Thief!"

The noise from the people in the street drowns out his shout. Uss is lost in his tea dreams. The figure with the meat package is darting up the centre of the street.

And then.

Out of the throng of people.

A uniformed woman on horse steps her horse out of the shadows, reaches down, and effortlessly lifts the darting figure. Lifts her off the street, with the meat, and lays her over the saddle in front of her. She guides her horse down to where Uss is standing. Her knees alone steer the horse. Her hands are on the figure lying across her saddle in front of her. The figure isn't even struggling, exhausted from shock and the adrenalin rush, just panting so heavily you can hear each breath wheezing in desperate pulls of air.

The uniformed woman stops in front of Dom Uss.

"Welcome to Brackwater Lake, Dom Uss," she says. "You of all people should know better than to be drinking that. She nudges her horse into a small sideways step and the mug of tea is knocked from Uss' hand."

He looks up at her. Refocusing his thoughts seems to be an effort. Then he snaps into the present from wherever his mind was. "Commander Zlod," he says, "Dragons be with you. It's good to see you. You're well I hope?"

She nods. "Thank you, yes, Dom Uss. Do you wish to lay charges against this thief?"

They look at her. It is a young woman, almost a girl still. She's face-down with a hood up, so not much face visible. She clutches the meat, her lungs heaving so hard she can barely get enough breath to speak. For all that she's been snatched off her feet and landed across a saddle, head almost lower than her feet, she refuses to drop the meat. Would rather fall than let go the meat. Refuses to free a hand to grab a bridle or stirrup if that means dropping the meat. Between gasps she manages to say, "...NOT a thief, I gave more than fair value ... wheeze ... to the idiot boy who was carrying the ...gasp ... meat... Let me DOWN."

"Not yet," says Zlod. She applies pressure to the now squirming girl until she lies still again.

Uss calls Sal over. "Sal, is the purse still in your pocket?"

Sal puts a hand in his pocket. He pulls out the purse. It is still tightly closed. And obviously still full. There is also a slip of paper crumpled on top of the purse.

"This is not mine," says Sal, picking at the scrap of paper.

"No," says Zlod, "she put her hand into your pocket when she collided with you. I thought she had taken something from your pocket. I was wrong. She left something."

"Let me see it, please," says Uss.

He un-crumples the paper. A hasty scrawl in Han symbols says, "Exchange for the meat. Your horse has a loose shoe, nearside front. Fix it or you'll lame him. Idiot."

They glance over to the rail in front of the butcher's where the horse is tethered. Hard to see from across the street, but he does seem to favour that leg, even while standing.

Uss looks up from the paper, "Please Commander, let the young woman go. She appears to need meat badly. I give it to her. A more than fair exchange. She may have done us a great service."

Zlod carefully lowers the girl to the ground. Zlod has to do double work because the girl still won't use her hands, is still clutching the meat with both hands as though her life depended on it. Her feet touch the ground and she's off running again, without a word to them. For a moment they glimpse her face, white as death with shock, lungs still gasping and then she's gone, hood still hiding her face, lost in the throng of passers-by.

"Well," says Uss, "Two mysteries in one day."

"Two?" says Zlod.

"Two," says Uss. "Why does the girl need the meat so badly that she's willing to steal? She's no trained thief, for sure."

"And?" says Zlod.

"And what are you doing here, Commander?"

Zlod looks at Uss steadily.

"You're camped out on the green are you, Dom Uss?"

"Yes."

"I may drop by this evening for a more private conversation. Too many people here."

"You know you're always welcome, Commander. Would you care to eat your evening meal with us?"

"It's business tonight, Dom Uss. So, thank you, no. No tea either, please."

Uss nods. "Very well," is all he says.

They watch the Commander ride off. "And that," says Uss to Sal, "is the bigger mystery, by far."

***

22. The Butterfly of Chaos and The Wine of Wrath

The principal of the Brackwater Lake School looks forward to the yearly visit from the Tectonic Monks. This year again, Dom Uss has brought him a jug of Bacchan wine. Dragons know where and how he gets those jugs. Then again, Dom Uss seems to know everyone.

Dom Uss' visit is an occasion for him to gather his staff to discuss students with Dom Uss. Tradition has it the discussion should be accompanied by a mug of this wonderful wine for all. The gift this year is exceptionally precious. Instead of the usual sealed clay jug, Uss has presented them the wine in a large corked glass bottle. Made by Dom Taane at the Tectis Monastery. When held up to the light, the wine gleams golden yellow in the light from the oil lamps.

They're gathered now at a big oak table. Twelve of them sipping from small portions that the principal has carefully poured for them from the bottle. Has been forced to pour, because of tradition. When he'd much rather keep it all for himself. There are mutters of appreciation around the table at the taste of the wine.

The principal has set the bottle in a small clay pot packed with cold water to cool the wine. The bucket obscures the bottom quarter of the bottle.

The languages teacher whispers in the ear of the history teacher next to him, "Just wait. Now that the level of wine has dropped below the rim of the bucket, he'll say it's empty. Wants to keep the rest for himself. Penny-pinching sod. Same trick every year."

Some of the staff are already holding up empty mugs, indicating they wouldn't mind another measure. The principal looks regretfully at the bottle. "All gone," he says, and puts the supposedly empty bottle in the clay pot under the table at his feet. In the dark under the table, no one will be able to confirm or deny this.

The history teacher winks slyly at languages, and stretches his body, arms, legs and all, in an exaggerated yawn. There is a clinking noise as his feet catch the bottle next to the principal, a clank as the bottle and bucket tip over, then a faint gurgling sound of liquid spilling.

"Oops. Good thing the bottle was empty," says the history teacher to no one in particular.

The principal pales. He attempts to say something, then realizes he cannot. He sits back sourly, eyes down, lips moving silently, and lets the table chatter continue.

When the social pleasantries are taken care of, the principal turns to Dom Uss to report.

"We have some exceptional students this year. However, none of those have ambitions to go to the Monastery School in Tectis. We have one other student who does wish to go to Tectis. We're not sure if she merits it. Opinions are divided amongst my staff."

Uss nods in a way that indicates he'd like to hear the opinions.

The Earth Sciences teacher speaks first. "She's the best, brightest student I've ever seen. Brilliant. She knows far more than I do about flora. Take her to the monastery. She'll make her mark on the world one day in a big way."

The mathematics teacher is next, "An absolute dolt of a girl. Shows no interest, doesn't do her assignments. Doesn't show up for half the classes."

The languages teacher chimes in. "I don't know what to think. Half her assignments are brilliant. Absolutely brilliant. The other half are never done. I can't make her out. She won't speak about why she's intermittently good or bad."

The music teacher is next. "She's never shown up for my classes. Says she's too busy, but won't say with what. I'd expel her if it was my call."

The history teacher says, "She has an outstanding grasp of history. Her opinions though, conflict with the ideas of our new Duke. She is a danger to herself, unless she learns to control her tongue better. My attempts to teach her have failed so far."

The activities master smiles. "Dom Uss, you'll hear every shade of opinion. I find her extraordinary. More than that. Her archery and riding are better than any student I've ever taught. She could teach as well as I could, or better. I don't say that easily."

The provost shrugs. "An odd girl. Very intense, as though she has more important things on her mind than school. Odd in other ways too. Her board and lodging here are paid for, included with her schooling fees. Yet, when she first arrived, she wouldn't sleep in the general dorm with the other girls. We don't know where she lodged when she first came. Rumour has it that she camped somewhere in the forest behind the school. We eventually gave her a private room. Which incidentally she keeps locked when she's not there. The standard school lock plus a padlock of her own."

The history teacher jumps in again, breaking the sequence around the table. "Odd in other ways. The other students like her well enough, but she doesn't socialize with them. At meals, she'll often enough gather her food and take it up to her room, instead of eating with the other students."

The provost says, "Interesting about the food. Early on there were suggestions that she had stolen a jug of milk from the school kitchen. It was never proved conclusively though. We still have a problem that small quantities of milk seem to disappear from the kitchen at night. We don't know how."

Uss interrupts, "How about meat theft?"

The provost is surprised at the question. "Curious that you should ask. We had suspicions that we were missing small amounts. We put a lock on the cold room just a day before you got here. Everything seems fine now."

Uss is rubbing his chin thoughtfully. "What is the girl's name?"

"Nyx," says the provost. "No last name. You know how it is with the children from remote farms. First names only."

Uss shrugs. "Don't know anyone by that name." He looks at the principal, "Would you like me to interview her for admission to Tectis?"

The principal, still visibly soured by the knocked-over bottle at his feet, says, "Having heard all this again, I've made up my mind. She doesn't merit a chance of studying in Tectis. I will meet with her tonight and let her know."

Uss nods briefly. "Very well. Your decision, of course."

And so, in a blink of an eye, the threads of many lives can be changed. All by a knocked-over quarter bottle of Bacchan wine. And a history teacher who should have known better. After all, if history teaches us anything, it's that an event as small as a bottle knocked over, may irrevocably alter the future.

***

23. Interpretations of Disease in an Agrarian, Feudal Society

It is interesting to note that the history teacher was wretchedly sick all night after the meeting with Dom Uss.

The cause of disease has, of course, been a subject of long debate in agrarian, feudal societies. Dom Uss, the physician, blames disease on little organisms that are too small to see with the naked eye.

Master Bach, the ex-pirate, is of a more scientific bent. He likes to argue cause and effect based on purely observable phenomena. For instance, he cites the sudden feelings of nausea and weakness that overcame the notorious Harran pirate, Half-Hand Glim. Bach relates it to the observable axe head that he had just buried in Glim's back.

Glim himself believed that the four bodily humours and their imbalance explained all of the body's ills. For instance, when Glim stabbed Bach's friend, Otin, at a game of cards, he blamed an imbalance of ill-humour in his own body for Otin's demise. That was seconds before the axe in his own back.

The Abbess at the Tectis Monastery relates many illnesses to what she calls Newton's law of history. Namely, that anyone who changes future events will feel an equal and opposite backlash from the forces of fate and karma. This backlash causes feelings of grave foreboding that the body often manifests as physical illness.

The history teacher, in turn, blamed it on a bad glass of Bacchan wine. The others who had sampled the same wine slept like babes and woke to a new day refreshed and energized. They smiled at the history teacher and talked about the judgement of the gods as the cause of his illness. After which he ran outside to throw up again.

***

24. A Warning from Commander Zlod

After meeting with the Brackwater School teachers and principal, Uss walks back to the camp on the green. The night is dark. Bach and Sal have a small campfire burning. Uss joins them and is telling them about the school meeting when Commander Zlod rides into the circle of light. They look up at her in surprise. None of them heard her approach. Out of the shadows and darkness.

"A word in private with you Dom Uss, if you please."

Uss rises. "You can speak freely in front of my companions. I trust them."

Zlod shakes her head. "No. In private."

"Very well," says Uss. "Lead on."

She walks her horse out beyond the campfire light. Uss follows. She looks around to make sure they're unobserved, then speaks in a low voice.

"Dom Uss, I owe you a favour. In return for the healing skills you've brought my family over the years. I'm trying to repay the favour now."

"Yes?" says Uss.

"We have a new Duke in Tarsis. The old Duke is gone. The new Duke does not like Illyria. He may have military designs on Illyria. To expand his empire. He doesn't like Illyrians here in his domain at this time. He fears Illyrian spies and insurrection."

She pauses to make sure Uss is taking in every word. He grunts to show his full comprehension. She continues. "It would not take even a small excuse for him to have you and your group locked up as spies. He has his MPs, his church police, in every town watching strangers closely. It would be wise for you to leave Tarsis quickly and quietly."

Uss nods. "Thank you, Commander. I am grateful for the warning," he says. "I have one more piece of business in Tarsis and then we leave."

"What business, Dom Uss?"

"We ride a few days north to Gian Major. A courtesy visit to the monks of Han-Bu."

"And then?"

"Then we ride back to Port Hamelin and take a ship back to Illyria."

"Very well, Dom. Tell your people to keep a low profile. Offend no one. Do not discuss the new Duke, his coronation as Emperor, his army, the new high taxes, Ham, the New Church of Sacrifice or the Militant Police."

"Thank you, Commander."

"And, Dom ..."

"Yes, Commander?"

"This discussion tonight. Remember: it was a routine police check. That's all. Otherwise, my neck hangs with yours."

"Understood, Commander. You visited my camp to check on some strangers in town. A diligent police officer. You questioned us on who we were and where we plan to go. That's all. And thank you."

Zlod nods at him once. She wheels her horse around and disappears into the darkness. Her visit so brief and silent, it almost didn't happen.

Uss walks back to the firelight.

***

25. The Empty Room

Directly after the meeting with his staff and Dom Uss, the principal walks up to the student rooms. He knocks on Nyx's door. She calls out "One moment." There is shuffling within. She quarter opens her door, squeezes out and shuts the door tightly behind her. "Yes, principal?"

He stares at the door, then shrugs. He has better things to do tonight then ask what she's trying to conceal. He has more important news for her. "I've just met with my staff and the Tectis monastery monks. I am not proposing you as a student candidate for Tectis. My staff could not unanimously support that."

She pales.

"That is all," he says. He turns his back on her and goes down the stairs. Her look of shock is some compensation for his rage over the spilled wine.

The next morning the principal is in a sour mood again. The loss of the Bacchan wine still rankles. His mood sinks anew as he thinks of the sheer waste. Even seeing that wretched history teacher looking ill is no recompense. If anything, it rekindles his anger. He needs an outlet for the anger. He decides to go again to Nyx's room. It's time to tell her that if she doesn't get better reports from ALL her teachers, he will expel her. It's still early and students are in their dormitories and rooms.

He knocks on Nyx's door. There is no answer. To his surprise, the door is not properly closed. It swings open under the pressure of his knocking. The extra padlock is gone. The room is unnaturally neat. Bed made, sheets squared, floor swept. But empty. No belongings, no clothes, not suitcases, no books. No Nyx.

The principal walks out of the dormitory and across to the school stables. The stall for Nyx's horse and tack is empty. Swept clean and neat, but empty.

"Well," he says to himself, "good riddance. She was more trouble than she was worth. Obviously, she's gone back to whatever remote farm she came from. She can go back to being a farmer's wife, bear a dozen squalling children, milk the cows, muck out the barn, and cook for the farmhands."

***

26. Chon

Uss, Bach and Sal are riding to Gian Major. The wagon trail is overgrown from lack of frequent use. The three of them are in the covered wagon. Two heavy draft horses pull the wagon. The saddle horses follow behind the wagon on long tethers. Trees crowd in over the disused trail, spinning dense, dark shadows over their path. The day was warm but with dusk falling, there is already a chill in the air.

Sal is driving the wagon team. Bach has been teaching him. Sal is enjoying the new skill. He's never worked with draft horses until this trip. These two, named 'Duke' and 'Farmer Joe', or 'Joe' for short, amaze him. Their grandeur and dignity startle him every time he looks at them. There are no horses like this on Kiliman. They're black Clydesdales, a very old bloodline, pre-EC. He's spent every early morning grooming them for the past weeks, and their coats gleam silver in stray rays of light. He concentrates on holding the reins the way Bach has told him. Gather the reins between the little finger and ring finger of each hand, up through the fist, and feed the ends out between index finger and thumb of each hand. The near-side horse, Duke, has a habit of swishing his tail over the reins and then bucking in annoyance at the trapped reins. Sal has to keep his left arm wide to avoid this. The strain is beginning to tell on his arm. He's thinking about asking Bach to take over for a while, but Bach seems preoccupied. Uss has noticed it too.

"Something?" Uss says.

Bach says to Sal, "Stop the wagon a moment, will you, Peach Pip?"

Sal says, "Sal." It's an almost mechanical response to a losing battle about his name. He brings the horses to a stop.

Bach listens. "Yes, something," he says to Uss. "Bird noises behind us. Flying up from their roosts. Alarmed. Shouldn't be hearing that at this time of day."

Uss listens and nods. "Someone on the trail behind us?"

Bach listens again. "Maybe. I noticed the same thing yesterday." He waits for Uss to comment.

Uss says, "Let's ride on. We'll camp at the next water we come to. If there's someone behind us, they'll come to the water too to camp, or overtake us."

Bach says, "Maybe" in a tone that indicates a million other possibilities.

They ride on.

The next stream to be crossed is not far. There's flat ground just off the trail on the edge of the stream to place the wagon, hitch the horses and build a cooking fire. There's grass for the horses. Sal has the billy simmering with a stew, while Bach is stowing the harness gear.

Uss is pacing restlessly. "I'm going back up the trail a ways; I want to see who is behind us on the trail."

Bach pauses in straightening the harness leathers. "You want I should come along?"

"Come if I'm not back in an hour. I should be fine. I'll hear the horseman or horsemen long before they see me. I'll get the first look at who and what they are without them even knowing I'm there. A man standing in trees next to the trail in the dark is almost invisible."

He takes a longbow out of oilskins in the wagon, strings it, gives it a few test pulls, slings it and a quiver on his back and walks into the darkness.

Bach goes back to examining the harness for twists and frays.

"Bach," says Sal, "Aren't you worried for him?"

"No need to worry," says Bach, "Uss can more than take care of himself. He wasn't always a physician you know. He's been in more rough and tumble hot stramashes than you've had warm breakfasts. It's the horsemen out there you should be concerned for. Pity them, if they mean us any harm."

"Oh."

"You just take care of the stew, little Cabbage Patch."

Sal turns his back on both Bach and the road to show how unconcerned he is. And how he dislikes being called 'Cabbage Patch'.

Well before the hour is up the horses raise their heads and look up the road.

Then Bach and Sal hear voices approaching them.

Sal turns his back to the stew to watch the road. Bach is already watching.

Uss' voice and a second voice, in leisurely conversation, interspersed with equally leisurely thud-thud of hooves of a walking horse. Then Uss and the horseman come into view, deep in conversation. Uss is walking level with the stirrups of the rider. The rider, in turn, has slowed his horse to Uss' pace, and has his head bent down the better to talk to Uss.

They step into the circle of firelight. The rider is dressed in a shapeless poncho, hood over head, features hard to make out. Uss motions to where the other horses are tethered. "Tie your horse up there if you wish," he says to the rider. "Then join us for Sal's stew."

Uss waits with the rider while he ties up his horse. They walk back to Sal and Bach together. The rider is stripping off the shapeless poncho.

Uss says, "Bach, Sal, this is Mistress Nyx. We're taking her to Illyria."

Sal stares. "It's the meat thief," he blurts out.

The girl glares at him. "How's your horse, idiot boy? You're welcome. Or hadn't you said thank-you yet? And, your stew's burning."

Sal curses, hurries to the fire and lifts the burnt smelling stew off flames.

Bach is unmoved by this exchange. His eyes are on Uss. "Why do we take her to Illyria, Dom Uss?"

"Let's eat, Bach, and Mistress Nyx will explain. Sal, can you dish up for us all? We'll share the burnt bits equally."

Sal blushes. It's unusual for Uss to criticize. It's also rare for Sal to make mistakes, and he doesn't like being called on it. Especially in front of an outsider. And if it weren't for her, he wouldn't have burnt the stew.

The girl is ravenous, absorbed by her plate of stew, so it takes a while for her story to come out. She is cautious in the telling, leaving out some names and places that might incriminate others, sticking to the barest essentials.

"My father and some of his friends," she says, "are resisting the rule of the new Duke. They call themselves 'the underground resistance'. Their underground newspaper accuses the Duke of murdering his cousins to eliminate competition for the throne. What the underground also found out is that the Duke sent a secret hunting party into Illyria. Sneaked in over the Blackrock Range. The Duke had an Illyrian lynx killed and its pelt brought back. He'll wear the pelt at his coronation."

Uss stays quiet at this, giving no hint that he, Bach and Sal already know about the pelt. Both sides are being cautious with what they share.

"That information has leaked out," says the girl. "What is less known is that lynx was a mother with cub. The hunters brought the cub back too. The underground knows how vital the lynx is to the Illyrian ecology and the earth-dragons. They stole the cub back and sent it to me to bring back to Illyria."

Uss is nodding. He has already learned this part from the girl when they first met on the road. "Show Bach and Sal, please Nyx," he says.

The girl has a sling over one shoulder, running diagonally behind her back, round to her opposite side hip, up across her chest and back to the shoulder. There is a cloth bundle where the sling crosses her chest. She carefully peels back the edges of the bundle to show the contents.

Two luminous green eyes stare out of the semi-dark at them. Tiny, but bright as gemstones. It's hard to look away from them, they're so commanding. When Sal and Bach do look further, they see black lines on the golden-white fur, running back from the outside corners of the eyes. The lines give the eyes an almond-shaped slanted appearance. They can make out outsized tufted ears. The little animal yawns, showing off a brown nose, a row of black dots on either side of the nose where the whiskers stick out, a very pink tongue and tiny, needle-like teeth. It stretches out an oversized paw, spreads the toes, showing off little claws, and pink pads under the paws. Then the eyes and mouth close and the little animal snuggles itself against Nyx's chest. Nyx runs a finger very gently across the little animal's head. She bends so that her mouth is touching its ears and murmurs something very quiet to it. The little creature snuggles deeper against her and sighs, once, twice, and then is soundly asleep.

Bach's expression is hard to read. Sal is entranced. He'd like to touch the little animal, run a finger up against the tiny paw pads, but equally, he has a fierce wish to guard its sleep against any disturbance. He just wishes the little animal was being carried by someone with a softer nature. He thinks of Alyx back in Illyria. She would be a perfect guardian for the cub. Not only does she have a kind, gentle soul, but her green eyes, blond hair and the animal's green eyes and almost white fur are a perfect match. They'd be stunning together.

"This is Chon," says the girl, snapping Sal out of his thoughts of Alyx.

"He'll need to eat soon, and have some space to romp. He's still at the age where he sleeps more than he wakes. But if he could have some space marked off in your wagon where he can both sleep and run around during the journey, it would be better than what I've given him so far."

Uss nods. Bach says, "I'll put up some canvas and netting in a corner where he can sleep or run around without falling out of the wagon. We can put a litter box in there for him too. I'll also make him a small collar and leash so that he can go for walks with you when he's ready. Maybe our young Potato-Head can put up a curtain rod over that section of the wagon so that Mistress Nyx can have a private area for changing."

"Potato-Head?" says the girl. There seems to be a snigger as she says it.

Sal ignores her with a mature calm that he doesn't quite feel, and looks at Bach. "Easily done," says Sal. "So the girl will come with us to Illyria? She's not just handing over the cub?"

Uss says, "I offered to take the cub further for Mistress Nyx. She says she has instructions from her father for further business at the monastery. And nowhere else to go. And the cub is used to her. So, *Sal, Nyx* will travel with us."

It seems to Sal that Uss put deliberate emphasis on their names, Sal and Nyx, not *Potato-Head* and not '*the girl*'. Trying to set some direction for civil travel together. Sal wants to say, "I can be civil if Bach calls me 'Sal', and thief girl gives up on 'idiot boy'", but he decides to swallow it.

"Dom Uss," he asks, "Why are the lynxes so important for earth-dragons?"

Uss smiles. "We have a complex ecology in Illyria. It's the only place where earth-dragons lay their eggs. They lay their eggs on sand shelves just above the high-water mark. The sand is held in place by spinifex, a grass that grows on sand. Without the spinifex, the sand washes away and the earth-dragons have nowhere to lay their eggs. Illyria also has deer herds and geese that love to eat the spinifex. The lynx keep the deer and geese numbers low. That way the spinifex survives and the sand stays in place for the dragon eggs. In recent years, the lynx population has declined. We can't let that decline continue. That's why every lynx, including

Chon, is important. To the world. Without the lynxes, no sand. Without the sand, no earth-dragons. Without the earth-dragons, another mega-volcano, another five years of winter and mass starvation."

Sal nods. Still, he is not ecstatic about the girl travelling with them. He's happy to do something for the cub though, give it something to make up for the thief girl it too has to put up with. He looks at her, "What does Chon need to eat?" he says. "I can prepare something."

"I've got some raw meat. If you could mince that as fine as ever you can, just one teaspoon for now. Please make sure your hands, the knife and your cutting board are absolutely clean. And please heat some water in a big pot. I have milk for him that I'll warm for him inside the pot of hot water. I don't like putting the milk directly on the fire in case it scalds."

Sal puts a pot of water on the flames, takes out the cutting board and knife, then adds, "You're welcome. Or hadn't you said thank-you yet? Sorry, I wasn't paying attention to you."

And afterwards as he chops up the meat, he can't stop himself asking her "Why didn't you just buy the meat you needed?"

She's clearly not pleased to have this brought up again. She pauses, then decides she should answer. "I came to Brackwater Lake over the Cold Range Mountains. One of my saddlebags broke open and spilled its contents into deep snow. I lost my purse and my money in that snow. My own lodgings and food at Brackwater School, and stabling for my horse were already paid for. Ahead of time. But Chon needed meat and milk. I had no money for that."

She glares at Sal. He grunts "ah" in what he intends to be a conciliatory grunt, but realizes that it may sound like a sceptical grunt. Well, so be it. Her comments about not burning the milk on the fire, and ensuring his hands were clean were probably jabs at him. Too bad Dom Uss has decided to take her to Illyria, rather than to just accept the cub and let the girl go back where she belongs.

***

27. Newton's Theory of History Revisited

It is interesting to note that at about the same time that Nyx joined Uss' group, the history teacher at Brackwater Lake said, "I feel better now."

He stopped throwing up and ate his first meal in days.

Those who adhere to Newton's Theory of History say this is quite typical. They say a person who caused the future to deviate from its intended path will feel sick only until the future gets back to its intended track.

Opponents of Newton's Theory say this is hogwash. They say many sick people just get better if you wait long enough. With time they say, the body can eliminate that truly terrible wine you were foolish enough to drink, or eliminate the microscopic disease-causing organisms, or a Good Samaritan may pull the axe that's making you nauseous out of your back. This is known as the theory of "Just wait, it will go away."

Yet another group of theoreticians believe that waiting won't cure anything. They point out that when

Glim's friends removed the axe from his back, he did not get better. He simply stayed dead. This is known as the theory of "Just wait, it will go away, and so will you."

In the absence of any agreement between these theoreticians, experiments with bad wine, disease-causing micro-organisms, and sharpened axes are likely to continue.

***

28. Solomon's Kidneys

The next morning Nyx is making breakfast. Sal is grooming the two Clydesdales, Duke and Farmer Joe. The two heavy horses are always happy to see him in the morning. They rub their muzzles against Sal's chest, neck and shoulders and blow noisy raspberries in his face. They're completely trusting of Sal, letting him walk behind them and letting him brush their bellies.

Sal can feel Nyx watching him with a critical eye while she cooks breakfast. "At least this time," he thinks, "she can't complain about how I'm looking after the horses."

By the time breakfast is ready, he's done with Duke and Farmer Joe and given each of them their customary carrot as reward. He tastes her porridge carefully, hoping to spot traces of burnt food, but it's just standard porridge. No burnt traces.

After breakfast, the girl who, Sal sees, is clearly a neatness nut, announces she is going to tidy the inside of the wagon. Meanwhile, a debate breaks out between

Bach and Sal. Bach has made a collar for Chon. Sal has made the matching leash. They argue about who should walk Chon on his new collar and leash. Bach argues that since he made the collar he should be able to give Chon his first walk with the collar. Sal argues that since he made the leash, he should be able to give Chon his first walk with the leash.

Dom Uss puts on his most magisterial expression and says, "I see the judgement of a Solomon is needed. Sal, Bach, hand me the leash and collar."

He puts both on Chon who is frisking in the grass. "Now," says Uss, "Bach, stand 10 paces east of me. Sal, stand 10 paces west of me." He waits for the two to take up position. "Sal and Bach, count aloud together to twenty-five, slowly. Then call Chon without changing your position. Whichever one of you Chon goes to will be allowed to give him his first walk on the collar and leash."

And while Sal and Uss are counting out aloud, Uss walks due north, straight between Bach and Sal and on beyond them into the trees. Chon happily follows Uss on the leash, batting at butterflies and grasshoppers. Uss looks back briefly as he disappears into the trees and shouts "Remember, no moving before you reach twenty-five."

"I think we've just been had," says Sal.

"The wicked, scheming little bugger," says Bach, "and I don't mean Chon, neither. If I hadn't given him my word about no violence we'd have his kidneys for a second breakfast."

Uss returns with Chon a half hour later. He hands Chon up to Nyx for stowing behind the safety netting and announces it's time to move out.

***

29. Great Green Lettuce Gods

Uss and Nyx choose to ride the saddle horses that day, while Bach and Sal drive the wagon. Sal senses there's a new comradeship between them after Uss' trickery.

"Master Bach," says Sal, "how is it that Uss swore you to non-violence."

Bach glares at him. "You'd prefer kidneys for breakfast then?"

"I'm curious," says Sal.

"You already know," says Bach, "that I was a pirate when I was young. Your age."

"Right," says Sal, waiting for more.

Bach reflects. "I was caught. The whole shipload of us. On Grand Kiliman. Before your time. Your grandfather would have been king, I think. First, they sentenced us to hang. Then they had a trial to find us guilty."

"Seems like a backward way of arranging things," says Sal.

"Gave 'em time to build the gallows, while the trial was going on. On account of us already being found guilty. Very efficient, your granddad was. Wasted no time. That was more or less the story."

"But you survived?"

"Well, Dom Uss was visiting Grand Kiliman at the time. He knew your granddad, knows your father too. Didn't like to see a green young cabbage like me hung with the rest of them black-hearted pirates. Thought there might be some good in me yet. Thought maybe I'd been led astray. Made me an offer. Said if I foreswore violence, he'd bargain for my life with the Kiliman folk. Also offered me a job as a Ranger if I wanted it. Said my vow of non-violence wouldn't apply if I was defending the earth-dragons against naughty poachers. I liked that. Was kind of like being a pirate all over again, this time on the side of saints and angels, with the blessing of the monks and all those holy types. Still makes me feel very righteous to sink boats and slit throats in a good cause."

"What did he have to give to my grandfather in exchange for you?"

"He never would tell me. I do know your grandfather liked to bargain almost as much as Dom Uss does. The two of them tried to out-bargain each other. Lots of theatrics on both sides. Each one saying the other one's offer was ridiculous, was an insult. Your grandfather got so angry, he twice shouted he was through with bargaining and his people should just hang me. Dom Uss acted the reluctant buyer, walked out twice on your granddad and shouted what did he care if they did hang me. A lot of theatrics, of course. They were having a fine time getting each other's measure. But a couple of times I thought they meant it. See the rope was around my neck while those two old so-and-so's enjoyed their little games. Got tighter too, each time one of them walked out on the bargaining session."

Sal is thinking hard. "How come Dom Uss knew my granddad. Uss he's not old enough, no?"

Bach spits. "You don't know tiddly, little Cabbage Leaf. Don't you know Dom Uss is an SI?"

"An SI?"

"He's silicon-based, a post-EC mutation if you want to call it that. They have far longer life spans than us regular carbon-based life forms. The Abbess back at the monastery too. She's about seven hundred years old. Looks as spry as any fifty-year-old."

"I didn't know," says Sal.

"Well you wouldn't, would you?" says Bach. "It's subtle. They can withstand higher temperatures, like your earth-dragons. They're not so good in cold, although that's harder to tell. Don't have as many children as regular carbon-based folk. Some foods they're funny with. Tea is not good for an SI. Don't know why Dom Uss insists. Sneaks a cup every now and then. Then there are other things they can eat that carbon people can't. A bit of sand in their stew is fine for them. The big tell is how long they live. Of course, if you're not around as long as them, that's hard to pinpoint. In other ways, they're just regular folk. Some good, some bad, some boring, some not. Known a fair number. Liked some, not so much others. Just like most people. Uss now, I've always taken a shine to him. Course, he did save my neck, so maybe that's why. Also, he does like to cure people. There's plenty of folk that owe him their health and lives. Used to be a rough diamond, might have made a good pirate himself, but then gave up all the fighting and other careers he's had. Now he seems to really like being a physician."

Bach pauses to click his tongue at Duke. The big horse has his tail caught on the reins again. Bach gently flicks the whip tip on Duke's shoulder to angle him briefly to the side until the rein is freed. Then Bach continues. "He's more than just a physician. The country folk know that he's got a good head on his shoulder. They bring him all kinds of problems to sit in judgement on. He wasn't kidding this morning when he talked about giving the judgement of Solomon. He's done that many a time. I've seen it."

They ride a mile in silence. Then Sal says, "How did you know who my father and grandfather were?"

Bach smiles. "My Ranger, Cookie, recognized you. You remember Cookie on my ketch, Dragon Wings? He's originally from Kiliman. Used to work in the palace. Used to see you around when you were a little one."

Sal looks worried. He tries to say something, but can't get the right words together. Bach interrupts him, "No worries, Cauliflower. My Rangers won't blab. A fair number of my Rangers have to hide their real names and their former lives. We've grown the habit of being blind to each other's pasts. Don't know what you did on Kiliman, don't know why you had to leave in a hurry, don't want to know, and we won't repeat what we do know."

Sal nods gratefully. They ride further in silence. Finally, Sal said, "Master Bach, how did you become a pirate?"

Bach stares at him. "You thinking of applying, young Parsley-Leaf?"

"No."

"Wouldn't suit you anyways."

"No."

"The interview process is tough."

"I guess."

They ride a while further in silence. Sal waits. Bach looks at him.

"So no one believes this story. I'm telling you only once. And if you don't believe it, I don't want to hear it. Understand? If you don't believe it, you shut your trap and say nothing."

"Yes, Master Bach."

Bach eyes him again to make sure he's serious.

"I grew up on a farm. We grew lettuce, of all things. My father was a religious nutcase. Believed in the Lettuce Gods. Had a temple on the farm devoted to the

Great Green Lettuce Gods. Of course, I didn't know better. Thought it was true. Didn't know he was a loony. That's how kids get the strangest religions. Because their idiot parents teach it to them. Mind you, no one knows for sure. There might well be Great Green Lettuce Gods after all. Then my loony father would have the last laugh on me.

"The farm lay on top of a mountain pass. The trail up the pass crossed part of the farm. Travellers were allowed to cross that part of the farm provided we could spray them when they arrived to get rid of any pests dangerous to lettuces. Mainly we worried about a fungus called clubroot. Devastating to lettuce farmers that is. Used to spray the lettuce regularly. Same spray for the travellers. Didn't want any of them coming up the pass to have picked up the fungus on their arms, legs, shoes while walking through the scrub up the path. You with me?"

"Yes, Master Bach."

"So my job was to stand at the top of the pass with an anti-fungal spray. Was what you call an alkaline spray. Killed the fungus. Dead. Had to spray it mainly under the soles of their shoes, sometimes arms, legs and hands if they looked like they'd been shortcutting through the bushes. So these groups of people would traipse up the pass. We'd see them coming from a long ways away. Then I'd rush out to meet them with a bottle of spray held up high.

"They'd say, 'What's that?'. And I'd say ..."

Sal looks at him attentively, waiting.

Bach continues, "...and I'd say, 'Lettuce spray for your soles.'"

"Then they'd all stop, bow their heads, and pray for their souls."

"What?" says Sal, bewildered.

Bach is impatient. "Get with it, Cabbage Roll. They misunderstood what I told them. Struck me dumb the first few times it happened. There's me, this kid saying one thing, and they're so messed up about religion they hear another. People are weird. Just because of club root fungus. Anyway, the next part gets even weirder. If I got to spray their arms next, I'd say, 'and now for your arms'. Strike me down with a feather. They'd dig into their pockets and backpacks and give money, silver, jewellery and all. I made a fortune from it."

Sal doesn't get it. "What?"

Bach looks at him, even more impatiently. "Arms – alms. They thought I said 'alms'. Anyhow, my dad eventually found out what I was doing. He went spare. Said I was taking the name of the Great Green Lettuce Gods in vain. Said I was tricking pious travellers into donating to no gods at all. Told me I'd have to make amends or I'd spend an eternity being reincarnated as clubroot mold, leaf-rot or root-worm. Told me I had to make good by spreading the true word of the Lettuce Gods. Gave me a backpack of his finest lettuce heads, packed in ice, and a horse. Told me to ride like the wind until I came to a place where the people didn't know what lettuces were, even if I showed them. Told me that when I found that place I should erect a temple to the glory of the Great Green Lettuce Gods. Made me promise him I would."

Bach falls silent, lost in memories. Sal prompts him, "So ..?"

Bach snaps back into the present, into the telling of the story. "I ended up in a waterfront bar in Port Vieux. This rough-looking feller, name of Glim, tried to rob me of my backpack. Right there in the bar. I smacked him a good one. Then he bought me a beer. Asked real polite to see what was in the backpack. I showed him the lettuces. And he said, 'What in the seven hells of Jupiter is that?'"

"See, he was a seaman. They don't get to eat much green stuff on board. Mostly salt pork and hard tack. The only vegetable he'd seen in years was barley and hops if you get my drift. Hah, seaman. Took me all of two minutes to figure out he was actually one of the worst pirates up and down the coast. Anyway, he listened to my story. I think he'd had one too many rums in the bar. He proposed I turn his ship into a lettuce temple. I'd sign on as a 50:50 partner for a decent upfront investment on my part. My alms from the religious groups crossing our farm land. Well, I was tired of farming. You've no idea how repetitive lettuce farming is. I tried cross-breeding lettuces one year. Couldn't tell the difference no matter what you cross-bred with what. And there's no excitement on a lettuce farm. Not like you can ride out in early winter to bring in the wild ones, rogues and mavericks, off the range. Practised with a lasso as a kid, but it just smashed the lettuces. Made my father mad too. Told me I'd be reincarnated as a desert slug. Well, Glim gave me a chance to do something different while still fulfilling the promise I'd made to my lunatic father. Glim and I renamed his ship, now my ship too, 'Temple of the Lettuce Gods'.

"Great name for a pirate ship. None of the merchant vessels we captured could believe that a ship with such a name was a pirate ship. Couldn't believe it until it was too late for them. We had a good few years, but then Glim developed a sudden back problem, took poorly and died. Funny thing how old age creeps up. One moment you're playing cards with the man, he's smiling and happy. The next moment he's complaining of back pain and dies on you. Shocking. Truly shocking.

A few months later one of your granddad's naval vessels caught us napping and took us all for hanging. The rest I've already told you."

Sal looks sideways at Bach. He's considering a comment.

"Shut your trap," says Bach.

They ride on in silence.

***

30. Probability

Later that day Sal has a quiet moment to speak to Uss. Away from the others. He says "Dom Uss. I've been chatting to Bach. How much of his stories are true?"

Dom Uss ponders, then says, "All of his stories are true ... some of the time. And also ... some of his stories are true all of the time."

And that's all that Sal can get out of Uss on the subject.

***

31. Religious Cults in a Feudal, Agrarian Society

It is often thought that evolution and natural selection applies only to living organisms. That is incorrect. Evolution and natural selection also shape social customs in human society.

For instance, the worship of the Great Green Lettuce Gods began after the third EC, originally as a cult that worshipped the power of nature on mountain tops during lightning storms.

Subsequently, in the hotly disputed First Council of Hallan, the surviving members of the cult decided instead to worship the power of nature in coconut groves during hurricanes.

Two years later, in the Second Council of Hallan, the further reduced membership agreed unilaterally on the worship of lettuces during periods of gentle rain or drizzle.

This marked a renaissance for the cult during which membership and the cultivation of lettuces flourished.

***

32. Small Mysteries

Nyx enjoys the morning riding with Uss. It's a relief to know that Chon now has space to stretch in – or sleep – as he chooses. She and Uss have much to talk about. She confides in him her training with Elsin. Uss knows Elsin. He holds her in high regard. He's pleased to hear that Elsin was training her. Nyx almost says that Elsin *is* training her, but that seems dishonest given the abrupt parting. Nyx doesn't feel she can ever go back to Elsin. But that's a private matter and not one she talks about with Dom Uss. Nyx talks about the various herbal remedies she's using. Uss nods. He knows many of the ones she talks about and uses several more she has not yet learned about.

At lunch, they find a meadow to stop in. There's a brook with a series of pools and cascades. The men go downstream to bathe and wash and let Nyx take one of the upstream pools where the trees screen her from view. Then they take a lunch of bread, dried meat and cheese. The horses are still grazing so Nyx and Dom sit to one side to compare books and notes about herbal remedies. She's excited by the first of the books he shows her. It starts where Elsin's teaching stopped. Uss' book has far more information about how various herbs' potency will vary with season, maturity of the plant, type of plant, type of soil and rainfall. She flips pages with delight.

"I'll come back to this and read it slowly," she says. "Show me the other one please, Dom Uss."

He hauls out the larger set of his notes. This one is about fungi, roots and seeds. She flips it open and stares in embarrassment and dismay. She makes a show of flipping pages, but her mind is a blank. He stops her at an illustration of a shitake mushroom, and asks her to read the text. She mutters an apology.

"Perhaps another time, Dom. I'll go check on Chon now. He needs his milk."

She gets up to warm the milk. Uss watches her thoughtfully.

***

33. The Biggest Problem in Gian Minor

By mid-afternoon they're almost within reach of Gian Major. One more day will see them there. They've stopped one village short, in Gian Minor.

They've asked a farmer if they can camp in his pasture. He's fine with it, once they guarantee that the big draft horses won't destroy his fences.

"Awful on fences, those big 'uns," he says. "Them leans half their weight on the railings, an' the railings fold like wet paper. Them wouldn't even notice it. Too heavy. No more 'n they'd notice a mosquito. Look at the size of them. And the size of them hooves. Them'd walk through brick an' not notice."

Before long news has spread that Dom Uss is there. A message is sent to their pasture from the mayor of Gian Minor. Would the famed Dom Uss please join them at the Gian Minor town hall for a banquet in his honour? Uss doesn't know any of the locals, but apparently, his fame as physician, monk and judge with the wisdom of Solomon has spread. All four of them are tired of campfire cooking so they accept. They get the horses comfortable in the pasture; then they wash and dress in whatever finery they have. Nyx notices that the boy may not know about or care anything for the saddle horses, but he has a genuine bond with the big draft horses, Duke and Farmer Joe. He speaks to them while they graze. They nuzzle his shirt even when there's no prospect of a carrot for them. Too bad the boy is intellectually slow. Can't look after saddle horses, can't cook stew, is servant to the wagon driver, doesn't understand the ecology of his own country. What did

Master Bach call him? Potato-Head? That's sad. Not very nice of Bach to make fun of the boy's limited abilities. Then she sees Bach approaching Dom Uss.

"Dom Uss," he says, almost embarrassed, "I have a favour to ask."

His embarrassed manner makes Nyx keen to hear what his ask will be.

"Yes, Bach?"

"We've travelled together many years, right?"

"Indeed."

"And we've been to many of these village banquets, what with you being somewhat famous, right?"

"Indeed."

"So, I know how the evening goes. The mayor gets up and makes a speech on how honoured their little town of Whatsit-upon-Whatever is to have such a famous monk here, all the way from Illyria. How almost no one in the little town has travelled further than the neighbouring village of Thingme-unter-den-Linden. And they wouldn't go there except for the annual handball match either, because everyone knows, there's nothing worth seeing in Thingme-unter-den-Linden that Whatsit-upon-Whatever doesn't have a better one of. Including they're going to whop the Unter-den-Linden team at handball, again. Right?"

"Right, Bach. That's pretty much the standard pattern."

"Then, you, Dom Uss, get up and make a speech on how beautiful the town of Whatsit-upon-Whatever is, how friendly the people are, how intelligent the children are, how beautiful the women, how strong the men, and how good the bread. You mention that you've travelled the world, but the inhabitants of this little corner of heaven should be justly proud of their community and their world-famous handball team.

Then everyone cheers you and pours you great wines and makes a fuss of you. A little girl gives you roses, and if you're lucky, a pretty young woman gives you a kiss on the cheek and calls three cheers for you. Then we all eat and have a great time. Right?"

"Right, Bach. What's on your mind?"

"Well Dom, just for once I'd like to have the little girl give *me* the roses, the pretty young woman to kiss *me* on the cheek and have the room cheer for me. How about we switch? Let me pretend I'm you. I know how to give your speech of 'I have travelled the world and you can be justly proud...' You pretend to be me, the wagon driver and ex-pirate turned Ranger for the monks. How about it? Just once?"

Uss laughs. "Bach, you madcap, if that's what will make you happy tonight let's do it. Here, wear my monastery signet ring. That goes on this finger; let me put it on for you. Don't lose it."

"No worries, Dom Uss, er, I mean no worries Wagon Driver, Jenkins."

"Jenkins?" says Uss.

"Jenkins," says Bach in a firm voice.

"Jenkins sounds very menial," says Uss, faintly resentful.

"Jenkins, you are my driver. A servant. I can call you whatever I wish. Tonight you are 'Jenkins'. Understood."

"Understood," says Uss, making a face to Sal and Nyx.

"Understood, what?" says Bach.

"What?" says Uss.

Bach repeats wearily, "Understood, what?"

They glare at each other.

"Understood, Sir" says Uss, finally.

"Very well, Jenkins."

And so, Uss is demoted to wagon driver Jenkins for the evening. He throws himself into the role, putting on a full-length black driver's coat, black top hat, black leather gloves, and a white shirt with a high collar. The overall impression is of a manservant so stiff and formal that he could drive a hearse if called upon.

Bach puts on a light grey jacket, a white shirt, grey top hat, grey silk handkerchief in pocket, a boutonniere of small yellow field flowers, and a tasteful yellow tie. He looks like the relaxed physician, a country gentleman of exquisite taste, a spinster's dream, ready for a night of banqueting.

Outside the town hall, the mayor is waiting to greet his guests. Uss, in his role as driver Jenkins tips his hat to the mayor, says "Evenin' Yer Worship," climbs down to offer a hand to help the others descend. For each one he tips his hat and murmurs, "Young Master," "Young Mistress," "Sire" as appropriate.

Bach in his role as physician/Solomon/Uss shakes the mayor's hand, introduces his students Nyx, Sal, and his driver 'Jenkins'. The mayor escorts him into the banquet hall leaving the others to follow.

Gian Minor has outdone itself. The mayor escorts Bach to a magnificently laid head table. Silver cutlery, ceramic vases, earthenware mugs, and even one glass crystal decanter is set out. The town councillors rise to greet Bach and shake his hands.

Sal, Nyx and 'Jenkins' are seated at a lesser table, one of many that crowd the town hall.

As Bach had predicted, the evening starts with a speech from the mayor.

"Gian Minor is honoured to receive such a distinguished guest tonight. Dom Uss." The mayor bows to Bach. "Dom Uss is famous throughout Tarsis as a physician, a healer and a man with the wisdom of the greatest of judges, even the wisdom of Solomon. I flatter our town only a little when I say it is that wisdom that made him choose Gian Minor as a stopover on his journey this year." The councillors and the quality sitting in the front tables and most of the room applaud. The mayor ignores the lone heckler at the back shouting, "it wasn't to hear your speeches" and continues.

"Since this is the first time that you have visited Gian Minor, dear Dom Uss, I'd like to ensure you and your companions are aware of the unusual place that Gian Minor holds in Celecium Province, and indeed in Tarsis as a whole."

Bach nods at the mayor encouragingly. He's enjoying playing the role of honoured guest.

The mayor continues. "We hope you and your entourage will take time tomorrow to visit our justly famous cheese factories. For all that our town is called Gian Minor and our neighbours have mistakenly been called Gian Major, it is our Gian Minor's goat cheeses that are known throughout Tarsis as the best there are. Our own Gian Minor goat cheeses have won the Celecium Province award for washed-rind cheeses three years running. Our own Gian Minor aged sheep cheeses won the Gold Harp award at the Mersinia annual fair four years ago. Our own Gian Minor flavoured mountain goat cheeses are this year winning prizes at agricultural fairs across the province for their unique flavouring with cherry leaves. We will be serving some of these to you and your guests, Dom Uss, tonight. In fact all of the cheeses you will taste tonight are made here in Gian Minor."

"Our neighbouring village, Gian Major, mistakenly claims to have equally good cheeses. This is parochial delusion on their part, as you will see tonight. Before the banquet starts, we wish to present you two special keepsakes for the evening. First, we have our very own Miss Aged Goat Cheese from Gian Minor to present you with a basket of cheeses for your journey. If she could come up to the head table now?"

A smiling woman carries a basket up to the head table. She is definitely not 'aged' in spite of her title. She is young, bursting with vitality and good cheer. She is dressed in a green leather apron over a frilly white blouse and skirt, green stockings and yellow wooden clogs, with alpine flowers stuck in both puffed up sleeves. This is clearly the traditional cheese-making dress for women in Gian Minor. She plants two amiable kisses on Bach's cheeks. Then she holds out the cheese basket for him to take. He surprises her by planting two kisses on her cheeks in reply and only then takes the basket. The room roars. She curtsies and retires.

"Now," says the mayor. "We know that many towns would have a young child come up to present you flowers. That's nice, but it's not memorable. We want you to remember your visit to Gian Minor for many years to come. So we have a little intellectual puzzle of the kind you're so famous for, and so adept at solving. We have a dispute here in our own town that none of our wisest councillors can solve. It is a land dispute between three siblings. It has puzzled our best minds for the last year. Your visit is our opportunity to settle the matter. May we lay it before you?"

Only a few people in the room notice that the wagon driver, Jenkins, has turned pale. Most of the room is gazing at the head table. Bach is relaxedly examining the cheese basket while listening to the mayor. He looks up from the cheeses, smiles amiably and says, "Of course, Your Worship. I'd be happy to settle whatever village land dispute you wish to lay before me."

"Very well," says the mayor. "I will summarize the facts briefly. Afterwards, if you wish, you may examine the land titles involved, the deeds, and the original inheritance papers. I have them all here."

He lays three thick stacks of documents in front of Bach. Each stack is thick enough to keep a team of lawyers busy for a year. Bach pats them affectionately, as though he's just received a longed-for gift. He nods to the mayor to continue, with the confidence of a man who has already solved the case. The mayor is encouraged. He resumes.

"If you wish, we will also call the siblings to give testimony to you afterwards. The case in its bare bones is this. One of our foremost sheep farmers died a year ago and left his farm to be shared equally between his three children. Two sons and a daughter. The will stipulated that the children could sell their share to one another, but that their shares could not be sold outside the family for at least twenty years. The will also stipulated that the children could divide the farm between themselves, however they wished as long as the divisions they marked off were equal size and mutually agreed. And indeed the children did agree which portions of the farm each one wanted, in accordance with the will. One brother took an upland portion, one brother took a portion on the slopes of the hills, and the sister took the flatland at the foot of the hills."

"The dispute arose because the brother on the slope of the hills started to mine the hill for coal. This spilled mine tailings into the river that feeds down to the farm of the sister on the flatlands. She demanded that the mining be stopped."

"The brother on the upland farm, above the mining, demanded that the mining continue. He claimed he should receive a share of the mining profits, because he said, while the farmland had been equally disposed of, the mineral rights had never been divided, and were still held in common by all three siblings. He threatened that if the mining stopped, or if he did not receive a share of the profits, he would divert the river from the uplands away from the two lower farms. This river is vital for the two lower farms."

"The sister in the flatlands said that if the mining continued she would shut off the road access to both the higher-lying farms. They need these roads to get their produce – and any coal – to market. She further reminded the coal mining brother that the farm could not be sold outside the family for twenty years. She claims that selling coal – which is part of the farm hillside – is equivalent to selling off part of the farmland to outsiders and is against the stipulation of the will."

"Neither our councillors nor our best lawyers have been able to agree the matter. Would you please settle it for us?"

Sal glances at 'Jenkins'. Jenkins is sweating even more profusely and glaring at Bach. Sal has never before seen dismay on Uss' face. He's seeing it now. No one else notices. They're all watching Bach.

Bach rises calmly from the head table. He surveys the room, the councillors at the head table and finally turns his gaze to the mayor. "Is that the most difficult question you could find for tonight?" he asks the mayor in disappointed tones.

The mayor shows surprise at the question, then nods.

Bach feels all eyes of the room on him. He savours the moment to again inspect the cheeses in the cheese basket while all eyes are on him. He sniffs the little boutonniere of flowers in his jacket lapel. The room is deathly silent. He has the audience in the palm of his hand. He looks at the mayor and says, "That so-called 'big' problem, that question, is so trivial that even my wagon driver could solve it for you."

He looks down to where the real Dom Uss is sitting. "Jenkins," he says, "Jenkins my man, stand up. Don't be shy. Speak so all can hear you and be so good as to tell the room the correct solution to their little puzzle."

***

34. Logograms

Back at the camp after the banquet, none of the four are ready for bed.

Bach is still too wound up over all the compliments he received. For how well his servant 'Jenkins' solved the farmland problem. Bach listened as 'Jenkins' delivered the proposal, with the air of a master testing his student on a simple problem. Then he blessed the student's solution with his own sage nods. Upon receiving the nods from Bach, the three siblings accepted the solution without hesitation. Peace was restored. And, as is the nature of such events, Bach got all the credit and 'Jenkins' got none.

The mayor said to his own children, "See. Even if you're just the driver for such a great man, some of his methods and wisdom will rub off on you." The children looked at Bach adoringly. The youngest even said shyly, "Sir, could I become your driver when I grow up?" 'Jenkins' stayed in his humble role all the way back to the camp.

Now, changed out of his disguise though, Uss' face reveals that peculiar look that comes from an indecision whether to laugh off a painful incident, or to strangle the person who caused it.

Sal stokes the campfire. Bach feeds Chon, staying well out of Uss' way. Uss puts aside the evening's events and takes Nyx to one side for a private conversation.

"I've been thinking about my notebooks on herbs and root medicines," he says. "You read one avidly; you refused to look at the other."

She shifts uneasily.

"I've also been thinking about what the languages teacher at Brackwater School told me about you," he says. "He said half your assignments were brilliant, half went undone."

She looks down, refusing to look at him.

Uss continues. "One of my notebooks was written in Han symbols. You loved that notebook. The other was written in Common Script. You refused to look at it. Could it be that you cannot read Common Script?"

Nyx blushes. She is still looking down. She says in a very low voice, "My mother died when I was young. My father was preoccupied with the underground press. I had to run our household much of the time. There was never time for learning Common Script."

Uss says quietly, "If you wish to be a healer, and for many other tasks, you *must* learn."

Nyx breathes out deeply. "Very well. You are right. I shall learn. Perhaps when we're at the monastery."

"No," says Uss. "You are putting off the decision."

"When then?" says Nyx.

"Sal can teach you. Starting tomorrow in the wagon."

"Sal?"

"Sal."

Nyx stares at Uss. "But Sal is ..."

She doesn't know how to say that Sal is a simpleton, without sounding condescending or rude.

She tries again. "Is Sal capable to teach me Common Script?"

Uss says, with heavy irony, "If he works very, very hard at it."

Nyx doesn't hear the irony. "Very well," she says doubtfully.

She wonders how this will go. She will try hard not to be condescending to the boy, provided he's not rude again to her. It still annoys her that he called her 'thief girl'.

The following morning Bach is back in his role of wagon driver, still smirking over his handling of the mayor of Gian Minor. Uss sits up front with him, feeling irritated by the smirk, but unable to do much about it.

The saddle horses follow the wagon on a tether. In the back of the wagon, Chon sleeps and Sal is teaching Nyx Common Script.

Nyx is holding on to her patience while the boy teaches her Common Script. To Nyx's surprise, he's very organized. He shows her the twenty-six letters of Common Script. He's using chalk on the back of a shovel blade, cloth and water to erase the blade. Then he goes through the phonetics of a subgroup of letters and makes her repeat them together with a little physical action for each sound. She's reluctant to learn at such a dumbed-down level. He assures her the actions will help her to memorize the sounds and the letters. For instance, for the sound for 'a' he makes her say 'ant' and mime an ant crawling up her arm, 's' is for snake and he makes her wiggle her hand in s-shapes as she says it. Soon she is writing and reading short words three letter words, with letters composed only of the subgroup. She asks Sal to let her see Uss' Common Script notebook. She'd like to see if she can understand it with her new knowledge. He refuses.

"It's too soon," he says. "It's pedagogically unsound. You're not ready. It will undermine your new confidence. We'll break for today and expand on the lesson tomorrow."

She's taken aback. Where on earth did the boy pick up a phrase like "pedagogically unsound"? It also sounds condescending. "You do know I read and write in Han?" she says, to bring some balance back into the situation.

"Of course," he says, "doesn't everyone?"

She looks at him sharply. "Do you?"

He looks surprised, wipes down the shovel blade and writes in very rapid and elegant Han logograms "The student doubts the teacher."

She is not sure what to reply to that. Is he some kind of idiot-savant? Can't cook, can't look after a horse, is assistant to a wagon driver who calls him potato-head, but has language skills?

"I agree," she says, to reassert some control over *her* lesson. "We've done enough for the day. We'll do more tomorrow."

He gazes at her as though *she's* the idiot. "Isn't that what I just said?"

***

35. Me Doctor, You Jane

An early lunch finds them near a ford across a river. Word spreads that the famed doctor, Dom Uss is passing through. The nearby community is small. Nevertheless, before their lunch is done a number of patients present themselves for treatment by the doctor. Uss sees them, one at a time in the back of the covered wagon. He asks Nyx to assist him. Sal and Bach are outside the wagon chatting to those who are waiting to see the doctor. There is a mother with an infant who's running a high fever; an old miner with a chronic cough from his days breathing coal dust; a boy with a splinter of wood buried under a fingernail, and a woman who complains of stomach pains.

Sal listens to the murmurings from inside the covered wagon. He can hear Uss consulting Nyx and discussing options and diagnoses with her. Between patients, he compliments her. Listening to the tone of the compliments it seems to Sal that Uss sees Nyx as bright and very capable. With some of the patients, Uss lets her take the lead role, merely murmuring a suggestion or an agreement. Sal is surprised. He saw what a quick learner she was at Common Script, but didn't know that she was an accomplished healer. She seems particularly good and patient with the infant and its mother. Sal can hear how reassuring she is, and how clearly she gives instructions to the mother. She's very different in tone from when she called Sal an idiot.

They're almost done with the patients when one more arrives. He's an old man who keeps rubbing miserably at a reddened, inflamed left eye. There's a trail of dried tears running down from the eye.

Bach eyes him cheerfully. "What do you need then, Sunshine?"

The man mumbles something in the dialect of the river people.

Neither Bach nor Sal catches what he's saying.

"What's that, Sunshine?"

The old man switches haltingly to Common Tongue.

"Eye doctor," he says.

"You doctor?" says Bach in a puzzled tone.

"NO," says the man. "EYE Doctor."

"Got one already, thank you, Buttercup," says Bach.

The man insists. "Eye doctor."

"Listen, Sunshine," says Bach pointing to the wagon where Dom Uss is, "Him doctor."

"Eye doctor?" says the man.

"NO," says Bach again pointing first to the wagon then to the man. "HIM doctor. YOU patient."

"Patient?" says the man.

"Yes."

"How long?"

"What?"

"How long have to be patient?"

Fortunately, Uss emerges from the wagon. The old man and Uss switch into the dialect of the River People. Before long the old man leaves with a compress, eye patch and a small jar of eye drops. He waves his fingers at Bach. "You very bad man. Dom Uss and young woman, good people. You, stupid bad and evil."

Uss shakes his head at Bach. "Really, Bach, having fun at that poor old fellow's expense with the 'Him Doctor, you patient' routine. He's right. You're evil."

***

36. Trouble at Gian Major

They arrive on the outskirts of Gian Major a day ahead of their planned meeting with the Han-Bu monks. The roads have been dry, no mud. The river crossings were easy, the rivers low. They've made good time. "Better early than late," says Uss. I'll go up to the Han-Bu monastery tomorrow to see the Abbot. It's just the other side of town.

Bach doesn't comment. For the last several miles, Bach has been battling with the near-side draft horse, Duke. Duke has been holding back, letting his partner, Farmer Joe, do more than a fair share. Bach has repeatedly had to swear at Duke and touch his rump with the whip. He's conscious that in a very short time his student wagon driver, Sal, has developed a better understanding with the two horses. This doesn't improve Bach's temper. In addition, Uss has taken to calling him 'Jenkins, my good man' that adds to his irritation.

It's mid-afternoon. They find an agreeable farmer and set up the wagon and a camp in one of his fields. Once the horses are grazing, Bach says to Uss, "I need to relax. I'm going to ride into town and have a quiet beer and lunch somewhere. I'll be back for supper."

Uss nods minutely, "See you at supper."

When darkness falls, Bach has not yet returned. The other three eat without him. Nyx has cooked. Sal is washing pots when they hear a horse turning into their field. It's clearly not Bach though.

"Commander Zlod!" says Uss, looking up as the rider approaches, "Dragons be with you. Welcome."

Zlod looks down at the three of them. "Ah, the Brackwater Lake thief has joined you? Isn't that interesting?"

"It's complicated," says Dom Uss. "She was a student at Brackwater Lake. She's gifted but has a severe case of kleptomania. I'm hoping to cure her back in Tectis."

He senses Nyx is about to launch into an angry outburst. Fortunately, she realises any other explanation will put the stolen lynx cub at risk of discovery. She splutters then subsides.

"No matter," says Commander Zlod, "I have other pressing business with you. Walk a little ways into the field with me."

Uss stands and follows her until they're out of earshot of the wagon.

Zlod remains mounted. Uss stands at her reins to hear her better.

"Your man, Bach," she says, "was taken by the MPs, the church police, tonight. He's charged with sedition and inciting rebellion against the state. He's imprisoned at the MP garrison at the town square."

"What has he done now," says Uss, despairingly.

"He was heard cursing our Duke as you rode up the wagon trail, at Folger's Hill this afternoon."

"Cursing your Duke?" says Uss in bewilderment.

Zlod looks at her notebook. "He was heard to shout repeatedly, 'Duke, you lazy, scupper-sucking, no-good, bilge-crawling rat, stop sponging off Farmer Joe's hard work.'" She looks up from her notebook.

Uss doesn't know whether to be amused or frustrated. "Our draft horses are called 'Duke' and 'Farmer Joe'."

Zlod shakes her head. "I doubt the tribunal will believe that, and even if they did, they would consider your use of 'Duke' as a name for a carriage-horse another act of sedition. However, there's more to his arrest. He spent the afternoon in a public house called 'The Boar's Head'. The publican has an accordion. Bach played songs in exchange for beer from the locals. He gathered quite a crowd."

"Yes," says Uss, "he's quite the musician. He would gather a crowd. Very entertaining."

"Not a good thing," says Zlod. "One of his songs was a clear incitement to rebellion. It was called 'John O' Dreams'. Do you know it?"

"Yes," says Uss, "I've heard him sing it before. It's an ancient pre-EC melody about the pleasures of sleep at the end of a hard day. John O' Dreams is the song's fictitious ruler of sleep and dreams, no?"

"Could be," says Zlod. "The church police noted down a verse that Bach sang."

She consults her notebook, "Here is a verse that he sang:

'Both man and master in the night are one
All men are equal when the day is done
The prince and the ploughman, the slave and the freeman
All find their comfort in old John O'Dreams.'

"The MPs say this kind of verse undermines the authority of the Duke, that it's clear sedition, that it tries to tell the listener they're as good as the Duke. The more radical MPs don't believe that John O'Dreams is a fiction. They think he might be an actual rebel leader."

"Dragon's-breath!" says Uss. "They actually believe that?"

"They either believe it," says Zlod, "or they'll pretend to believe it in order to make an example of

Bach. A warning to others, and to the fools in the pub that stayed to listen to Bach. The smart ones put down their beers, even unfinished beers, and left very quickly."

"What happens now?" says Uss.

"The MP Sergeant sent a pigeon message to Mersinia. He explained the capture, the charges and asked what the Duke wishes done with Bach."

"Yes?"

"The Duke ..." Zlod pauses, and interrupts herself, "You understand, Uss, that our meeting is private. I will deny what I am about to say if you quote me?"

"Yes," says Uss.

"The Duke enjoys violence. When it's directed at others. He is fascinated by long-forgotten pre-EC methods of violence, torture and death. There's a word for people like that."

Uss volunteers "Sadist?"

"No," says Zlod. "I was thinking of 'vicious little dung-heap'. In any case, he sent back a pigeon message. I believe he meant to say 'Death by a thousand cuts'."

Uss waits in shock for Zlod to continue, his head lowered as though expecting more bad news.

"Fortunately the Duke's handwriting is notoriously bad. Either that or there is pigeon crap on the message. The message appears to say 'Death by a thousand cats.' The sergeant is very literal-minded. He may be puzzled, but he won't dare question the Duke's orders. He will gather as many cats as possible over the coming days, until he has a thousand. Perhaps he believes that your man, Bach, is allergic to cats. That will buy your man a few days' time – unless he really is allergic - but eventually the Duke will demand an update. Then the actual message will be clarified."

"What should I do, Commander?"

"You can do nothing for Bach. Go home without him. Until now, I have pretended ignorance of the precious load your thief girl brought you. I know how important lynxes are for the world. I want it safely back in Illyria. I don't want to have to search your wagon. Go home as quickly as ever you can. My family and I owe you some favours, Uss, but that goes only so far. I am a loyal commander of police of the state of Tarsis. If you attempt further sedition, or attempt to free Bach, I will hunt you down and recapture you and your precious lynx cub with all the resources of the state at my command. I can shut down the harbours from which you might sail home as easily as swatting a fly. I may not like it but I will do it. I am good at what I do, Dom Uss. Make no mistake. Have your meeting with the Han-Bu monks tomorrow and then turn around home. Quickly and quietly."

Zlod turns her horse around without waiting for a reply. That in itself is a display of her total command of the situation. It doesn't matter to her whether Uss accepts her advice or not. She can control the outcomes whatever he does.

He watches her riding off, swearing softly to himself, and at Bach. Then he returns to the campfire and gives the news to Sal and Nyx.

"What shall we do?" they ask him.

"I will have my meeting tomorrow with the Monks of Han-Bu. I'd like the two of you to stay with me until after that meeting. There may be a message for the Abbess. After that, I think you two, Chon and the Wagon need to return to Port Hamelin and ship back to Illyria as quickly as you can. I will stay here to see what I can do for Master Bach."

Sal is horrified. "Maybe the girl, Chon and the wagon can go back. I could stay and help you and Master Bach?"

Uss is noncommittal. "Let's sleep on it, and we'll make our final decision after I've seen the Abbot at the Han-Bu monastery."

***

37. A Stone to Destroy the World

In the morning, Uss rides through Gian Major and out on the opposite side. Towards the monastery at Han-Bu.

Nyx had asked what the Han-Bu monks do. He reminded her. The Monks of Han-Bu believe that our world is an obstacle to cosmic harmony. Their duty, they believe, is to remove that obstacle. They spend their days in rearranging nine towers of over 1200 stones of different sizes, one stone at a time, according to complex rules. Chief among the rules is moving only one stone at a time, and a larger stone must never rest on a smaller stone. The Han-Bu Monks believe that when they complete the rearrangement of the nine stone towers our world will drop out of existence. Cosmic harmony will be restored.

Now Uss rides. He carries what may be the missing stone, lost centuries before when Ju-Sin the Accursed sneezed and knocked over a stone tower.

Houses give way to fields; fields give way to steep mountain slopes, strewn with rock. The path up to the monastery is short but steep. The monastery is built like a fortress. There are two moats to cross via drawbridges, and then a portcullis with a small iron grating inset. A large brass disk, curved like a shallow bowl, the diameter of a heavy shield, hangs in front of the door. Uss vaguely remembers the protocol. He picks up the mallet that leans against the portcullis and beats the gong twice, pauses, then beats again twice.

An eye appears at the grating. A number of arrowheads emerge from the slits in the masonry surrounding the portcullis. They point at Uss. With all the charm of a bunch of cobras emerging from the masonry. He has no doubt there is a loaded crossbow and an itchy trigger finger behind each. The monks of Han-Bu have become very careful over the years. Not everyone wants the world to end. Some people would happily run off with all their stones.

The eye behind the portcullis says something of which Uss understands only every second word, "? *Honoured Vermin, what, entrance desires, into, Abode of Eternal Peace, Han-Bu, blessed by all gods? Quick answer, or open heart, accept arrows there, many as porcupine and eternal damnation.*"

Uss curses under his breath. It's been many years since he had to speak the Han-Bu dialect. It's too early for this. He tries in Common Tongue. "Dom Uss, sent by the Abbess of Tectis, to speak to the Abbot at Han-Bu."

He waits. The eye waits. Then he remembers the rest of the protocol. He picks up the mallet and starts to beat out six more strokes on the gong.

The eye behind the grating shouts, this time in Common Tongue, "Enough already. Bad enough I have a headache without this ruckus."

There is a grating of bolts, a squeaking of hinges and a small, ancient monk becomes visible cranking on a winch to open the portcullis. The little man is all skin and bones, hard to believe he can raise the portcullis by himself, even with a winch.

"I'm not raising it any higher. My arthritis won't stand for it. Not for you, and not for no one. You'll have to get off your horse and walk in. And the rest of you put away the crossbows."

He glances back at Uss while cranking and mutters, "Crossbows. Ha. It's all fun and games until some poor soul loses an 'I'."

The creaking stops. The portcullis is just high enough to admit a horse without a rider. Dom dismounts. He and the horse squeeze under the door.

The old man is not mollified. "I was having my breakfast too. Cold now. Look."

Dom looks at the monk's breakfast. An egg, some fries, and a cup of tea. "Are you the friar?" Dom asks. The old monk smiles, folds his hands together in prayer, shuts his eyes. A beatific expression illuminates his wrinkled face. Then he opens his eyes, glares at Uss and shouts angrily, "Nah. I'm the chipmonk. Look at my breakfast which you've ruined."

He laughs evilly. This seems to make him feel better. "Give me a hand lowering this door again, and I'll take you to the Abbot. You better mount up for that though. You're supposed to sit on the horse in style, and me, the lowly monk, will guide you and your horse up the garden path. You just sit on your bum. Excuse me Master Horse, I did not mean you, I meant his bum. What was I saying? You Dom Uss sit on your rear end and look regal. I'll do the work. Like usual. They're making a big fuss about your visit. We're supposed to give you the full ceremony. Just in case you've brought the real stone. You don't know the half of it, mate, the fuss you've created."

Uss looks in the direction he's being led. There's a stone path leading through a small garden, then across a large stone plaza, to granite steps leading up to a colonnaded monastery entrance.

Flowering plants are hung from every tree in the garden, in colours of yellow and red. There is a water canal on each side of the path, with candles floating on the water. The plaza is lined twelve ranks deep on either side by monks. Yellow robes to the left, red robes to the right. Two of the yellow robes to the left have giant alp-horns stretched ahead of them. They're producing low, almost subsonic, booms with a slow regular rhythm, at about the pace of a funeral march. Two of the red robes to the right have giant drums on which they're beating a matching rhythm. On the steps at the entrance to the monastery stands a monk in yellow, a monk in red, the abbot in white, and another figure dressed in black.

The old monk guiding Uss says, "For the first time in centuries we've got both Han-Bu factions together. The ones in the yellow robes is the traditionalists, they deny a stone was ever lost. They've been trying to make their stone towers without any lost stone. Hasn't worked so well, so far. As you can see. Since you, me and the universe is still here. Pardon me, Mr. Horse, you're still here, of course, too. A word to the wise, Master Uss: no telling if the traditionalists will be happy to see you bringing a stone they claim doesn't exist, or will execute you for heresy. Things could go either way. The good news is they won't take it out on your horse. He's safe. Always look on the bright side is what I say. And if you'd rather turn back now, I could lead you back to the portcullis, for a nominal fee. A few measly shillings to save your life."

He pauses and cocks an eye at Dom Uss. Dom Uss is scanning the ranks of traditionalists. No smiling faces in yellow. The old monk watches him, then continues.

"No? Now, the ones in the red robes are the reformists. They've been searching the world for the stone you might be bringing them. Another word to the wise. No telling if they'll be happy with you for finding it, or want to kill you for having kept it from them. "

Dom Uss looks carefully at the monks in red. If anything, they have an even greater sullen, mean look on their faces.

"Then there's a monk in black, up on the steps. That's the 'great-great-great', I don't know how many times over, grandson of Ju-Sin the Accursed. The Accursed is the one who sneezed and knocked over the stone towers all those years ago. This one here today is called Ju-Sin Junior, in our dialect that would Ju-Sin-Kinly, but he don't like the diminutive. Better you stick with Ju-Sin Junior. He seeks to find the lost stone. The Oracle of Om says he alone can find it, in order to clear his ancestor's name. He carries the holy sword of truth to help him on the quest. Hah! Don't know what's holy about it. It's a regular sword, for killing people what gets in the way of his quest. He might be very annoyed with you claiming to have a stone that he's supposed to find. Course, if he cuts your head off and that nice necklace you're wearing with the stone drops into his hands, on account of you no longer having a neck, then I guess he'll be satisfied. It's not too late to turn back to the portcullis, if you're considering a few shillings donation to an old monk. If we keep going forward, I'm also supposed to translate in case you don't speak our Han-Bu dialect. What's it to be Tectis man?"

Uss regards the old man, then says, "I too have consulted the Oracle at Om. Would you like to hear what it foretold about my death?"

The old man glances up at Uss then addresses Uss' horse. "I suppose we're going to hear it, if we wants to or not."

"The Oracle," says Uss, "foretold I might be hanged for strangling a nasty old monk someday soon if he doesn't shut it."

The old monk shakes his head. "That's the trouble with being a monk, these days. Used to be monks had a sense of humour. A laugh a minute when I was a novice monk. Wouldn't believe the pranks we got up to. Humour. Harder and harder to find. Come on then, I'll introduce your horse to the Abbot, and you too."

At the foot of the steps, Uss dismounts and ties his horse to a post. The alphorns and drums fall silent. Uss and the old monk mount to meet the four monks on the steps. The abbot, dressed in white, steps forward to embrace him. "Uss, old friend it has been too long."

"Good to see you, Abbot Yan. My abbess sends greetings."

Yan points to the old monk who opened the portcullis.

"I hope our porter, Svalbaard, greeted you with appropriate joy and respect."

Svalbaard perks up. Even though both the abbot and Uss are talking Common Tongue, he translates for them. "The abbot welcomes you and says you're lucky to have that gem of a monk Svalbaard to lead your horse up the garden path."

Since translation is not needed, it's more like a subtitle.

Uss ponders the Abbot's question briefly. He knows the Han-Bu dialect appreciates overblown poetry. "He was as welcoming as a fountain in the dry season."

Svalbaard offers another subtitle. "Tectis man says fountains are dry in the dry season. Useless for quenching thirst, but should be appreciated nevertheless for their ornamental beauty, age and grace."

Yan looks apologetic. "Svalbaard looks after our stables. Traditionally he has also been the porter. We feel this role may be too much for him as he ages, but he insists on doing it. Dom Uss, I think we know each other long enough that you can overlook any eccentricities in his welcome and translations?"

Svalbaard translates. "The abbot says I prefer horses to people, but I get tuppence extra, and a double helping of fries, for every time I crank open the door and offer to translate, and no one's going to con me out of that."

Uss ignores Svalbaard and smiles at Yan. "We are both afflicted. You have Svalbaard. I have a man called Bach."

Yan coughs. "Let me introduce you to the Prior of the Traditionalist Monks, and the Prior for the Reformist Monks."

The monk in yellow steps forward and says something in dialect. To Uss it sounds vaguely like "*! Humble welcomes, man who tell lies about stone, may your lies grow wings, large teeth with, eat you slowly from the feet to head, special delight in eating liver!*"

Uss wants to reply, but Svalbaard holds up his hand. "First I translate. Then you reply. Translation: The Prior of the Traditionalists welcomes you. Even though you claim to have found something that was never lost. He looks forward to demonstrating the error of your ways to you, starting with your toes. Your horse, however, is guaranteed safety, and will be cared for scrupulously by Svalbaard the Ostler, in the event of your demise, which will be declared a day of mourning for all by our revered Abbot."

Uss says, "Please tell the revered Prior that I thank him for the care he will offer my horse."

Svalbaard smiles, looks at the monk in yellow and gabbles something too fast for Uss to follow.

Then the Reformist Prior steps forward. He bows very low and mumbles something in dialect like *"! Welcome to humble abode. Full well know Tectis abode more humble. Accept apologies we better!"*

Svalbaard translates. "The Prior regrets the magnificence of our monastery. He knows that Tectis is a mere hovel by comparison, and therefore spiritually more worthy. He says your horse will enjoy its new magnificent stables here with Svalbaard after your demise. With yet another horse to look after, poor, ancient, overworked Svalbaard will complain until the revered Abbot cuts him a deal."

Uss notices the Abbot is staring off into space pretending not to hear this. Uss bows low to the Reformist Prior and says, "Thank you for the welcome. Indeed your monastery is known far and wide as more spiritual and far more humble than Tectis. I will remind the world."

Svalbaard rattles off something to the Reformist Prior who nods with grim satisfaction. The only words that Uss understands are *"... Tectis man say if searching for dung to roll in, best choice, Han-Bu monastery, humble hovel fit for swine, highly recommended."*

The abbot's attention focuses back on Svalbaard. "Please take Dom Uss' horse to the stables and water it and guard it until Dom Uss calls for it."

Svalbaard leaves. The abbot sighs. "He becomes more eccentric by the day. We're not sure what to do about it. We owe him something. He's been with us for three centuries. The severance pay, if we retired him, would bankrupt us. An SI, of course. He was ancient before he came to us. He also wants to unionize our monastery. We have to let him translate a bit, but he's happy to get back to looking after the horses. Your horse is safe while we talk. So, let's get down to business. Have you brought the stone?"

"I have, Abbot Yan."

"Do you not fear what the stone means, Dom Uss? That with its help we will complete our stone towers and the world will blink out of existence?"

"My Abbess believes the world will resist extinction. She believes the world used Ju-Sin as an instrument of resistance to extinction all those centuries ago, when he sneezed and lost the stone. She believes that the world will find a way to resist again."

Abbot Yan considers. He shrugs. "Regardless, it is our duty to attempt the completion of the towers, to attempt to extinguish the world and restore cosmic unity. Please show the stone. First to Ju-Sin Junior, then to the two Priors, then hand it to me."

Uss takes the chain off his neck and offers it Ju-Sin Junior. Ju-Sin Junior takes the stone examines it wordlessly for two long minutes. Then he kneels, kisses the stone, holds it above his head and murmurs a prayer. From one end of the plaza to the other, the ranked monks can see tears streaming down his face. He remains kneeling, holds the stone above his head offering it back to Dom Uss.

Dom Uss hands the stone next to the Reformist Prior. He examines it even longer, then he turns to the red monks massed on one side of the plaza and shouts in a deep voice. Uss can make out one phrase repeated three times. "*!It is found. The day is come!*"

The files of red monks take up the chant. "It is found. The day is come." Their huge drums are beating a bass note in time to the chant. The monastery walls vibrate to the sound. The Reformist Prior hands the stone back to Uss with a deep bow.

Dom Uss offers the stone to the Traditionalist Prior. The prior puts his hands behind his back and refuses the stone. He shouts in a harsh voice that rings across the plaza "*! Demand a test, we!*"

His followers take up the chant in time with the booming alphorns. "*! Test, test, test!*"

Uss looks at Abbot Yan. "What is the test?"

The abbot holds up his arms to silence the shouting monks. The plaza falls silent. Expectant. Yan says to Uss "The traditionalists don't believe there is a missing stone. The reformists believe this is the missing stone. The reformists have recreated the stone tower up to the point where the missing stone was removed. They believe that if the missing stone is placed on the tower, the cosmos and the world will offer us a sign that the stone is real. That is the test."

"The two priors, Ju-Sin Junior, you and I will now go into the tower temple and place the stone you have brought on the tower. If it is indeed the missing stone, the universe will respond. Come."

***

38. Testing the Stone

The massed monks remain outside. The abbot, the two priors, Ju-Sin Junior, and Uss are inside the monastery building. In front of them is a stone table. On the table are nine stone towers of varying heights, each made up of small stones – about the size of flat river pebbles - piled one on top of the other. There are 1200 stones. The stones look almost identical to each other and to the one that Uss brought. A careful scrutiny shows that no two stones are the same size. In every tower the stones become progressively larger towards the base of the tower.

Armed guards watch from the four corners of the room to ensure no one tampers with the towers. Next to each armed guard stands a wooden statue of an armed guard in a ferocious-looking mask. These, according to Han-Bu tradition are spirit-guards that will also ensure the sanctity of the towers in the spirit world. The table on which the stones rest is massively heavy. Even an accidental bump against the table won't knock down any one of the nine towers.

Ju-Sin Junior has been selected to put the lost stone onto the fifth tower. He kneels in the doorway with the stone in his hand and says a short prayer under his breath. When he finishes he rises. Before he can advance the Abbot says, "Wait!"

The Abbot and the two priors bow their heads and each says a silent prayer. Uss watches from the doorway. He has no wish to approach more closely. The room is dimly lit by a single oil lantern hanging above the table. They are deep inside the monastery building where no stray draught can threaten the stones. The oil lamp burns steadily with a constant yellow flame.

The Abbot and the Priors finish praying. The Abbot signals Ju-Sin Junior to advance. Ju-Sin looks supremely confident that this is the missing stone, that the universe will send a signal to confirm it. Ju-Sin takes a step forward. Uss notices the flame in the oil lamp brightens, lengthens and gives off a puff of oily smoke.

Uss frowns. The others appear not to have noticed.

Ju-Sin takes another step towards the table. The room seems to sway in front of Uss' eyes. Is it the room, or just the oil-lamp that is swaying? This time the Abbot appears to have noticed. He is frowning too.

Ju-Sin takes a third step towards the table. There is an audible creaking noise from the wooden spirit guards. One of them falls backwards, propped now against the wall behind it. The nearest guard pushes the wooden statue upright.

Uss raises his voice, "We should leave the building."

Ju-Sin shakes his head. He wants to redeem his ancestor's reputation. The Abbot and the Priors seem too mesmerized to heed Uss. Ju-Sin takes another step. He's now up against the edge of the table. His hand reaches out to place the stone on the fifth tower. The towers sway away from his hands like dancing cobras. All four spirit-guards are swaying in crazy circles like slow motion spinning tops.

"GET OUT," shouts Uss. He starts to turn to the door. There is a grinding noise as though the whole building is moaning. Uss staggers as the floor under his feet moves like the deck of a boat. His last view of Ju-Sin is of a crack in the floor opening at Ju-Sin's feet. Ju-Sin is flailing his arms for balance. The missing stone is dropping out of Ju-Sin's hand. Towards the crack in the floor. Uss' final glimpse shows it suspended in mid-air, still falling. By then Uss is running to get out of the building.

There is stone dust all around him and the noise of falling objects. He makes it into the plaza and shouts to the assembled monks – "EARTHQUAKE! STAY CLEAR OF THE WALLS."

There is pandemonium. The Abbot and the Yellow Prior emerge from the monastery door. They are grey with stone dust. The Yellow Prior is bleeding from a cut on his arm. There is a pause then Ju-Sin bolts out of the doorway pursued by a hysterical Red Prior. Ju-Sin runs towards the portcullis and starts cranking open the door. The Red Prior stands on the monastery steps and shouts. You don't need to know the Han-Bu dialect to know what he is shouting. "STOP HIM. KILL HIM. HE DROPPED THE MISSING STONE. AGAIN, STONE GONE!! KILL HEEEEEEEEEEEEEEEEEEEM!"

There is a mass riot as red monks try to get at Ju-Sin and the yellow monks block them. Fists and sandaled feet are flying, punctuated by grunts, screams and very un-monk-like swearing. Torn bits of yellow and red robe are flung into the air above the rioting mob, like bright party balloons hovering over a carnival parade. There are fists waving in the air. Where monks have piled into a knot of wrestling bodies there are even feet waving in the air. There is a pitter-patter like first rain on dry mud. A puzzle for Uss until he sees sandals flying into the air and landing on the monastery roof. The monks are not very good at kicking at each other. Most of them merely lose their sandals. A scrum of red and yellow figures forms in front of the monastery steps. An overexcited red monk runs up the steps to gain height, then dives fist first onto the scrum below him. The scrum heaves open like a giant living flower and the diving monk is shot up into the air like a rocket. He lands on the lower roof of the monastery. He stands up shouting, "How do I get down from the roof?"

A sub-group of the mob is distracted by this. The portcullis stands open. Ju-Sin must have escaped. Those under the roof shout up to the hapless monk on the roof "You don't get down from a roof, you get down from a duck." He shakes his fist. "When I get down I will ..." The rest of his words are lost. The mob underneath the roof is variously shouting, "...be very warm" and "... make a quilt." Another large group makes quacking noises at him.

The earthquake aftershocks subside, but not the heaving mass of red-yellow combatants in the centre of the plaza.

Uss makes his way past the combatants, through the garden and finds the stables. His horse is still saddled. He mounts to leave.

Svalbaard appears and holds out his hand, palm up. "How about a tip for looking after your horse? I brushed him down, polished his hooves and shined the bridle." In fact, the horse, hooves and bridle look just as dusty as when Uss arrives. He smacks Svalbaard's open palm with his own in "high-five" style, shouts, "plant your corn early this spring" and canters out of the stables.

The plaza centre is still a battle zone blocking his way, but the earthquake has now brought down part of the wall at the rear of the monastery. There is no moat there. Uss and his horse canter out and back towards Gian Major. A quarter mile from the monastery, he can still hear the quacking noises.

He has to cross through the centre of Gian Major to get back to the farm field where Sal, Nyx and the wagon are waiting. The centre of Gian Major is in greater chaos even than the monastery. The earthquake seems to have collapsed at least one wall of every second building and people are milling through the streets in confusion. Miraculously, there appear to be no serious injuries, nor – as far as Uss can see – any trapped people. The masonry dust and general hubbub are cloying. Uss reins in his horse to look at the scene. A short, balding, barrel-chested, dust-caked figure steps out of the crowd and approaches him.

The dust-caked man says, "Overdid it again. No finesse. Couldn't just stop at one wall. Had to demolish half the town, did you? Give me a hand up."

Bach climbs up on the horse behind Uss. His voice is like sandpaper after breathing so much dust. "Home, Jenkins, and don't spare the horse."

***

39. The Miracle Worker

Sitting in the farm field inside the wagon, Sal and Nyx hadn't felt the earthquake. All they know is Uss has managed to free Bach. They ask Bach what happened.

"I'm asleep in my jail cell. Me and three dozen cats. Don't ask. I've no idea what they've done, but they're in jail with me too. And don't mess about talking about feline felons, I'm in no mood for word games. So I'm asleep. Which is not easy with the cats. Give me convicted murderers as cell mates any day. In Kiliman, I shared a cell with a serial killer, name of 'Fandu, Again'. 'Again' on account of the serial part of his crimes. A real gent. *He* never once tried to sit on my face when I slept. Not like them bleedin' moggies. Anyway. Where was I? I'm sleeping. Then there's one almighty bang. I wakes up, and I see half the rear wall of my cell is missing. The cats are out of there before you can say 'boo'. I follows. Blow me down. There's Uss standing waiting for me on his horse. Standing in the middle of the street right behind my missing cell wall. He's not only destroyed my cell wall, he's destroyed half the bleedin' town."

Sal and Nyx stare at Uss in silent wonder.

"So," says Bach to Uss, "how do you make such a big bloomin' explosion, Dom Bloomin' Genius Uss?"

Uss corrects Bach. "Not an explosion, an earthquake."

Sal and Nyx's mouths hang open. "How do you make an earthquake?" they ask.

Uss gives them no time for discussion. They need to get away from Gian Major before the MPs, Commander Zlod, the police or the military recapture Bach and arrest them all. They can't go west to Port Hamelin or south to Mersinia. Zlod will close off their obvious escape routes. The only option is eastward to the Sharan desert. Because not even desperate idiots would try to escape through the Sharan desert. There is some debate about whether to abandon the wagon and use horseback only, but they may need the wagon to carry water into the desert.

They hitch up and leave, with Sal and Nyx still staring awestruck at Dom Uss.

***

40. Burn Them

The Duke of Tarsis is angry. "Escaped? He escaped? Tell Zlod to round them up. Tell her it's their heads or hers. Send her a pigeon message."

The orderly bows and rushes out to send a pigeon message to Commander Zlod in Gian Major.

The Duke calls for Ham.

"Ham, I'm angry."

"With whom, Sire?"

"That damn travelling group of Illyrians. Their man Bach escaped. They've all escaped."

"I regret to hear it, Sire."

"Ham, I've been rereading some of my father's pre-EC texts."

"Yes, Sire?"

"There's one I don't understand."

"Yes, Sire?"

"It says if you're angry with people you should write them nasty letters, wait a day, and then burn them."

"Yes, Sire?"

"What does one do with the letters afterwards?"

***

41. Forced Detour

Nyx and Sal are riding ahead of the wagon. Uss, Bach and Chon are in the wagon. They're heading east on an increasingly dry trail.

Uss had shown them an old, rough map.

"We can't go west to Port Hamelin or south to Mersinia. Commander Zlod will have forces looking out for us. Northwards our path back to Illyria is blocked by the Blackrock Mountains. They're impossible to cross in winter. Snowdrifts so deep you can bury a house, ice coatings on every cliff wall and trail, crevasses so deep you can lose an army, freezing cold like you've never felt, and mountain storms that leave you no air to breathe. The only passable part of the range at this time of year is on the extreme east side of the mountain.

"The eastern part of the range is low. There are two formidable barriers to getting there, though. Firstly, to get that far east we'd first have to cross several days of Sharan desert. It's hard going, uninhabited, no water. If we manage to cross that, to get far enough east, the desert changes into very folded, hilly country. That's where the second huge barrier seals off access to the true mountains. There is a believe-me gigantic deep gorge, steep cliff faces on both sides, a white water torrent at the bottom. Most people believe that gorge is un-crossable, that you cannot get to the Blackrock Mountains from there. On the few maps that show it, it's named "Hell's Canyon". No one would expect us to go there.

"So, that's where we have to go.

"Here look, I'll show you on the map. East of us is the border between Celecium and Sharan provinces. There's an old wagon trail, barely used, but it's there. First, it goes through dense rainforest, right on the Celecium-Sharan border. We load up our wagon casks with water before we exit the rainforest. Then the trail goes into the Sharan sand desert for about two days. The trail used to be marked with stone beacons. Probably still is. The occasional prospectors, hunters, hermits and explorers keep the beacons going or leave a trail of their bones. Then comes one of the only watering points, a deep well. We can load up with water again there.

"From the well, we go about two more days into the desert. Then, there's a choice between a short-cut going north-east on more sand directly to Hell's Canyon, or a long curving way round on hard dirt. Both ways are difficult and dry. A wind that blow constantly too. Dries you out even quicker. The sand route is short in distance, but long in time. Sand is hard on the horses, they can't move fast. The dirt route is longer in distance but the horses will move faster. Either way we end up the north-east corner of the Sharan desert, we cross Hell's Canyon, cross the Blackrock Mountains, and then we're back in Illyria. Back home."

So now they're riding through ever-thickening rainforest on the Celecium-Sharan border. Sal and Nyx are riding saddle horses ahead of the wagon. Uss, Bach and a sleeping Chon are in the wagon.

Nyx is thinking about Sal. She's revising her view of him. She's made huge progress in learning how to read and write in Common Script. She's even started reading the simpler portions of Uss's notes. It's been exhilarating to have a whole new world of information open up to her after so many years. Like access to a once-locked treasure hoard. One she's only just beginning to explore. Sal was more than impressed with her speed of learning. He complimented her repeatedly. She has to admit he's an excellent teacher. He adapted his methods rapidly to her speed and style of learning. He made sure she was never held back, and that she never lost confidence by going too quickly. She suspects he's quite bright. But he has a lack of confidence that she's going to have to help him overcome. Probably because he's only Bach's assistant. And Bach still calls him Potato-Head. She'll have to choose her moment and tackle Bach on that. Put a stop to it. Build up the boy's confidence. Right now for instance, even though the trail is wide enough for them to ride together, Sal has very politely but firmly insisted she ride ahead of him. She's going to have to work on that. He has potential; he shouldn't feel inferior to her.

She glances back at him. He doesn't notice. He's riding a few paces behind her horse, his eyes intent only on the trees ahead and above the trail. His left hand is on the reins; his right hand is playing absentmindedly with the handle of a large machete tied to his saddle. Is he a birdwatcher? She'll have to ask him later about what he was hoping to see in the trees.

***

42. Bach and Uss in Conversation

Bach and Uss have been watching Sal manoeuvre Nyx into riding ahead of Sal.

Bach turns to Uss. "Look at him, the little scheming so-and-so. You told him about the pythons, didn't you? That's why he's got her riding ahead."

Uss grunts. "You planning on telling her?"

Bach considers it. "Nah. Not for now. Anyway, he'll probably do better than her at chopping at pythons if one does drop down."

Uss grunts. They follow on.

43. Well, Well, Well …

"Dragons take me, front and back," says Bach. They're crouched low on a sand dune to keep out of sight. Below them, on the other side of the massive dune the trail descends to the well. They've been crossing sand dunes like this for two days, longing for this water. The well is now in view. It's clear they're not going to get any water there. A platoon of about twenty Tarsis soldiers is camped at the well.

Bach looks at Uss. "Couldn't you … just get rid of them?"

Uss shakes his head. "I'm a physician, Bach. I don't do mass slaughter. And even in the old days, I don't know if I ever could take on twenty soldiers at once."

"So what now? Go back to Gian Major? Give ourselves up?"

Uss again shakes his head. "Let's go around this lot. Make sure they don't see us. We'll continue without reloading with water here. It'll be twice as hard, but it's doable. Quarter rations of water for us. Half rations for the horses, and full rations for Chon."

"Do we leave the wagon?"

"Not yet. It still has some water and food we want to haul. In any case, if we leave the wagon anywhere near here, the soldiers will find it. They'll come looking for us."

"You know what, Dom Uss?"

"What's that, Bach?"

"You're no longer fun to travel with."

"Bach, I blame you for all this."

"Me? How do you end up blaming me?"

"I figure the world is paying us back for your evil past."

Bach mutters obscenities and walks back down the hidden side of the dune to the wagon. Without waiting for Uss.

***

44. Not What They Expected

Two days past the well, Bach and Sal are driving the wagon. Uss and Nyx are on the saddle horses ahead of the wagon. The heat is relentless. The horses look gaunt. Their coats are matted, their eyes are dull. On reduced water rations, they refuse food. They're dragging their hooves. The humans have burnt skin and blackened lips. There's not much talking. Not much to say. They need to press on, get through this desert, and keep their mouths shut to preserve moisture. Until Bach halts the wagon and shouts in an urgent croak, "DOM USS!"

Uss' mouth is too dry to ask what the problem is. He merely turns his horse and has it plod back slowly through the hot, deep sand to the wagon. Bach points. Sal is slumped over in his seat unconscious. His face is red with heat. Uss dismounts. He spreads a tarp under the shade of the wagon. "Help me lift him down," he says.

Nyx looks on in alarm. She gets some saliva working and then manages to croak, "What is it?"

Bach growls, "Dehydration. The last two days he's been giving all his water rations to Duke and Farmer Joe."

Nyx is shocked. "All?"

Bach nods. "All. He can't stand seeing his two horses thirsty."

Nyx feels a lump in her throat. If her body wasn't so dry, it might form tears.

"Give me a cup," says Uss.

He leans Sal into a sitting position, then tries to get some water into him.

"WAIT," says a new voice.

They look up. A group of six men are standing next to them. They appeared so silently no one heard them approach. They're dressed in long sand-coloured monks' robes. Hoods pulled up over their heads have veils that cover mouth and nose leaving only the eyes exposed. The hoods jut out over their heads like hat brims, casting shade onto the eyes. Strangest of all they're barefoot. Their heavily calloused feet seem impervious to the heat of the sand. The speaker is holding out a large canvas water bag to Uss. "Hold his mouth open and squirt water from the spout into the front of his mouth. Small amounts. Not into the back of his mouth or he'll choke."

Uss gives Sal several squirts of water. He notices that the canvas bag and the water are cold, almost frigid, from evaporation through the canvas. The boy appears to breathe more easily now.

"Lay him back down to rest," says the water bag owner, "squirt water over his hair, face, shirt and neck. Soak him thoroughly. Lots of water. He needs cooling. Good. Now give me back the water bag. It is not for the rest of you."

Uss hesitates. Looks longingly at the bag. Then hands it back.

"Please stand up," says the leader of the strange group to Uss. "Which one of you is Master Bach?"

Bach steps forward.

"Me," says Bach.

"Ah," says the stranger. "Please stand still."

Bach does.

"Very good," says the stranger and smacks Bach very hard.

Bach staggers. He's caught unawares; he is sluggish with the heat and dryness. He raises his fists. Dom Uss holds him back. "Wait, Bach," he says. "My turn."

The stranger turns to Dom Uss and bows low.

"Dom Uss?"

"Yes."

"Please stand still," says the stranger who bows a second time, then smacks Uss even harder.

***

45. Scones with Tea

"Please try some of the hackberry jam. We make it ourselves. The bushes are hard to find in the desert, but the jam is delicious."

Herman is the name of the monk who assaulted Bach and Uss. A surprisingly innocent name for a monk who hunts down dying strangers in the desert and smacks them.

Herman is now sitting companionably with Bach, Uss and Nyx inside the Monastery of St. Ephebius serving them scones with cream, hackberry jam, and an assortment of drinks.

The central teaching of the Monks of St. Ephebius is that the powers of darkness and light are precariously balanced. They spread this knowledge by practical example. They smack random strangers and then shower them with precious gifts.

The monastery, to which Herman has led Uss' entourage, is carefully camouflaged between the sand dunes, sandstone cliffs, ancient waterways, and dry wadis of the Sharan desert. The room that they are seated in has a magnificent view of the sun setting across the dunes. A fine dust cloud hangs above the desert. Sand stirred up by the constant winds. The windows they look out of are set in small vertical cracks in a cliff wall. From outside it's impossible to tell that a spacious comfortable monastery sits behind the cliff wall.

Herman has provided the most precious gift of all to Uss and his crew. Water. And milk for Chon. From who knows where. Somehow, Herman knew about Chon.

Now they've moved on from water. Uss is drinking juice and nibbling scones with jam, Nyx is drinking tea with a plate of sandwiches. Bach has a large beer stein in his hands.

Sal was in the stables apologizing to Duke and Farmer Joe. Ensuring they drink their fill at the stable trough. He waited with them until they perked up and nuzzled him. Forgiving him for the long trek with not enough water. The big draft horses suffer in the heat far more than the little saddle horses.

Sal is back with the group now sitting next to Nyx, picking at her sandwich plate. She's dividing her attention between talking to Chon on her lap and scolding Sal for giving up his water ration. She strokes Chon's cheeks. When she talks to Sal, she grabs his hand to emphasize her scolding and to ensure his attention. Neither Chon nor Sal appears to be listening too closely, but both seem to enjoy her touch.

Sal realizes with shock that, if you tune out her scolding, she is every bit as attractive as Alyx. In a different way, of course. Alyx is blond haired, blue-eyed and merry. Nyx is serious, black-haired, black-eyed, with the slit-shaped eyes that are common in Mersinia. Her skin is flawless, almost radiant with health, and her face is beautifully proportioned. Since Nyx merely thinks he's paying deep attention to her scolding, he has time to look at her face at length without embarrassment.

On the other side of the table, Bach still has a red palm mark and an annoyed look on his face. He seems to have put off vengeance, though, at the very least until the beer runs out.

Herman is talking to them about their route onwards. "The Duke's militia have started a search of the desert now. Under direct orders from Commander Zlod. You'd best move on in the morning. You mention the fork in the trail. I know it well. Both sides of the fork eventually end up at Hell's Canyon. One side of the fork sand, the other side dirt, but longer. That fork is a good day or two away. Once you get there, I cannot advise you which side to take. We can give you some water for the casks in your wagon, but even so, you will run short again before you reach Hell's Canyon. There is no water before you reach it. Also, I do not advise going to Hell's Canyon. No one can cross it. Or get down the cliffs to the water in the gorge. Once there you'll be stuck without water. And not enough water to return here. Hell's Canyon is a dead end. I mean the dead part."

Uss and Sal both speak together.

Uss says, "I will get us across Hell's Canyon. And I can get water from the bottom."

Sal says, "I know how to speed up our travel to Hell's Canyon. If we can fill our water-casks before we leave, I will get us to there before the casks are empty. With all of us on full rations of water."

All except Uss stare at him. Nyx was in the middle of again scolding him. She's so surprised by his claim that she falls silent and forgets to let go of his hand.

Uss already knows what Sal plans. "I'll show you when we get to the fork," is all Sal says to the others.

**

46. Bach, Diplomatic As Ever

After dinner with the Ephebians, Nyx passes Bach in a corridor of the monastery. He's on his way to fetch something for Uss but has time to say briefly in passing, "Remember not to handle him too much if you want to release him to the wild."

"Good point," she says. "I hadn't thought about that. Still, I have to hold him so that I can give him his milk and meat."

Bach mumbles something. He's already part way down the corridor and facing away from her. She's not sure what he said. It sounded like "I didn't mean Chon."

She shakes her head. What does that mean? That makes no sense. She'll have to ask him in the morning, if she remembers, or let it go. It probably wasn't important."

**

47. Leaving the Ephebians

The next morning they rise early. The sun is already baking the dunes, and the usual wind is creating a white layer of mist-like sand blowing knee deep over every dune. Herman supervises the filling of their water casks. He brings a sealed jug of yoghurt for Chon. "Milk goes sour too quickly in this heat," he says to Nyx. Try him on this. Small amounts first to make sure he tolerates it."

When the water tanks are full, he gives Bach a small wooden cask. "A little present for you, Master Bach. A batch of our best beer."

Bach smiles broadly. "Ta, Herman. That's very thoughtful. Truth is I'm sorry to leave. I've learned a lot from the Ephebian philosophy."

"Really?" says Herman.

"Yes," says Bach and smacks him hard.

Herman stares in shock.

"See, that's the first part I learned from you," says Bach, "Now for a gift for you."

He reaches into a shirt pocket and pulls out a piece of lettuce leaf.

"This was in my sandwich yesterday. I wanted to give it to you this gift. An object for meditation."

Herman is still trying to catch up with events. He rubs his cheek, splutters, then gets his words together.

"For meditation?"

"Yes. If ever you find that your teaching strategy isn't reaching people, maybe because things go south after you smack them, then this lettuce leaf will tell you that all religions can evolve to new strategies."

"How does the lettuce leaf tell me that?"

"Ah Herman, shillings to shekels, you don't know the history of the cult of the Great Green Lettuce Gods?"

"No ... I haven't heard about them."

"My father worshipped the Great Green Lettuce Gods. He was a certifiable loony, of course. That's not the point. The point is the cult of lettuce worship evolved from a bunch of even greater loonies who worshipped lightning on mountain peaks."

"From afar?"

"No, no. Right up there. On the mountain peaks. During lightning storms."

"That's ... that's crazy dangerous, Master Bach."

"Yup. Killed an awful lot of them. Would have killed many more. But they changed. Evolved. Decided they could worship the power of nature just as well in a field of lettuce during a mild rainfall. See? The big brains in the Tectis Monastery call that evolution. Evolution of religious strategy. You with me?"

"Er ... yes. Very instructive, Master Bach."

"Anytime you need it, just meditate on Master Bach's lettuce leaf. You might want to dry and press that leaf. Give it pride of place in the Abbey. Upon the altar, in a glass case, with the other religious artefacts, bones of saints and what have you. Well, thanks for everything. Almost everything. I mean the food and water part of your instruction. Thanks for that. The beer isn't half bad, neither. You take care, Herman."

Bach swings himself up on the wagon. He and Uss are driving. Sal and Nyx are already moving out on the saddle horses.

Nyx and Sal are chatting. She needs to keep an eye on him, ensure he doesn't do something stupid again, like foregoing his water in the desert. She is also curious about the boy. He's holding something back from her. He won't talk about his family or where he comes from. There's a mystery there she intends to get to the bottom of. Mind you, she's not ready to tell him too much yet about her own father either. The boy only knows her father is part of an underground movement. She'll decide what else she can share with him once he's revealed more about himself. An image comes to her mind of herself prying open a reluctant oyster. She's good at getting people to talk and unwittingly reveal things. She smiles to herself. She's just found a nice little project to work on as they ride together. "Boy," she thinks, "you don't know it yet, but you're my oyster for the next couple of days." She smiles again.

***

48. Evolutionary Blind Alley

It would be gratifying to report that the Ephebians subsequently adopted a gentler approach to teaching the world about the forces of dark and light.

In fact, three centuries after Bach's conversation with Herman, the Monks of St. Ephebius did adopt a new strategy. This was under the stewardship of an Abbot called Genghis-Hum. Genghis had been treasurer for the monastery and rose to the position of Abbot after introducing various cost-cutting measures.

As Abbot, Genghis was tired of seeing Ephebians beaten after smacking their intended pupils. This interfered with the Ephebian gift-giving sequence, and with what Sal three centuries earlier called 'pedagogically sound practices'.

Genghis decreed that instead of smacking people, the monks should decapitate their intended pupils with sanctified swords. The monks could then offer gifts to the souls of the recently decapitated. The souls were free to accept or reject the gifts and teachings. Without retaliation against the monks.

The advantages, Genghis said, were not only a lack of retaliation against the monks but a reduction in expenses for gifts.

Within twelve months, this led to a mass citizen uprising and the murder or exile of every Ephebian monk. After this, the monastery gift-giving expenses dropped to zero. Had Genghis survived the uprising, he would have been pleased by this final cost reduction.

Genghis-Hum's changes are often quoted as an example of a socio-evolutionary blind alley, and of how random mutations in social customs do not always benefit the host society.

***

49. Desert Speed

The boy is annoying. Nyx has not been able to open the oyster yet, has not gotten the details of his family background. He's been fun to chat with, even likeable and sweet, but he has withheld much from Nyx. The more they talk, the more difficulty Nyx has in assessing him. He claims that he's a student at the Tectis Monastery. Nyx is sceptical. When she asked him which satellite school he'd been selected from, he said 'none'. He claims he gained admission just by arriving at Illyria and answering some test questions. Nyx knows you don't gain admission like that.

Probably he's just Bach's assistant wagon driver, trying impress her with talk of being a student. Which isn't necessary. There's nothing wrong with being an assistant wagon driver. She was impressed by his affection for Duke and Farmer Joe, by his idiotic willingness to give them his water ration. Even if it came close to killing him. Then again, she gets fleeting glimpses of strange twists to the way his mind works, glimpses that she can't reconcile with a straight forward wagon driver's assistant.

Now he's doing something with the wagon. They've reached the fork in their path. To the left more desert sand, the direct route to the giant gorge. To the right the longer curve of hard pack dirt, ultimately leading to the same gorge.

He's wheeled the wagon onto the dirt and asked the rest of them to climb down. This is where he'll show Bach and Nyx his speed trick, whatever it is. Uss apparently knows and approves. Something the boy claims to have worked on back at the Tectis Monastery with the Tectis artificer, Dom Taane.

Sal has stripped the rear two-thirds canvas cover off the wagon. To still protect Chon from the sun he's put a special net and small canvas over the wagon floor where Chon is.

Now Sal removes the wagon shaft, the long wooden pole that normally sticks out in front of the wagon, between the two draft horses. He removes a hatch from the wagon floor to reveal the kingpin. Nyx knows that's the pin around which the front wagon axle swings left or right, to steer the wagon. He locks an L-shaped wooden piece onto the kingpin from above. Then he erects the wagon shaft, minus the doubletree, pointing up at the sky, near the back half of the wagon, supported by various ropes that he tightens.

Nyx is not enjoying having to stand in the hot sun while he fiddles. Her attention wanders. Next to her Master Bach is nodding in appreciation of whatever it is that the idiot boy is now doing.

Bach is another confusing note in her attempts to categorize the boy. She had thought Bach was his master, Sal the assistant. Watching Bach, it's clear to her that Bach has no idea what Sal is doing. Bach is watching Sal like a bystander watching a painter filling in background, watching and waiting for clues to what the foreground will be.

She looks back to Sal. He's lacing one edge of the loose canvas to the vertical wooden shaft. Now Bach is nodding again and shouting, "I like it, Carrot-Head. A sloop rig."

She turns to him, "What?"

"A sloop-rig is a triangular sail rig, Young Cabbage."

Nyx understands now. Sal intends to drive the wagon using the ever-present desert winds. She sees that the L-shaped piece of wood from the axle will act like a boat's tiller. She likes how there is still a canvas cover on the front third of the wagon to provide shade for them. She's impressed in spite of herself. The idiot boy is creative.

"Will it work?" she asks Bach.

"We're about to find out," he says.

The boy has hoisted the triangular sail on the wagon shaft that's now doing duty as the mast. The sail snaps back and forth in the strong wind for a moment, then he hauls in on some ropes and the flapping quietens. The wagon is not moving.

"Why doesn't the wagon move, Master Bach."

"Because the sail isn't powered up yet, it's streaming back with the wind, like a flag. When he sheets in the sail at a tighter angle, that's when it will power the wagon."

Sal checks that the wheel brakes are on. Then he jumps down and says to Uss, "She's ready. Please remember to always put the brakes on and loosen the main sheet or the wagon will run off without us."

They gather round Uss. He's smiling in approval. "Very good. What do we do with the horses, Sal?"

Sal seems to have anticipated this. "We tether them loosely behind the wagon. We'll move at a fair pace. Not an issue for the saddle horses. For Duke and Farmer Joe, normally this would be too fast, but this time they're not pulling a wagon, they're trotting free. They should be fine."

Uss nods. Bach is more cautious. "Did you and Dom Taane test this back in Illyria? At all?"

Sal nods. "We did, Master Bach. She handles beautifully."

They climb on. Nyx isn't sure what to expect. Sal asks them to sit on the windward side of the carriage. To counterbalance the sideways force of the wind. She watches him release the wheel brakes and pull the sail tight, what Bach called 'sheeting in the sail'.

She watches the sail with some disappointment. She's about to say, "How long until something happens?" Then she glances to the side. It's the lack of hoof-clatter from up front that has deceived her, the lack of jingling harness. The carriage is almost silent, but already they're moving faster than ever the draft horses pulled it. The dirt plain is zipping by them. The speed of the carriage adds a cooling effect to the breeze. She would let out a whoop of exhilaration, except it would go to the damn boy's head. And she still feels annoyance at his air of mystery.

She looks back. The horses are trotting steadily without effort. The hard dirt under their hooves is easier going than plodding through sand. They look like they want to whoop too.

The only one looking grim is Uss. He pats Sal on the back and says, "Just in time too. Give us more speed." He points backwards. There is a dust cloud on the furthest visible sand dune. Riders in formation cresting the dune. Judging from the way they keep rank, it's a platoon of Tarsis soldiers.

Uss watches carefully. "We're pulling away from them. Plus they've miles of heavy going through sand still. It will wear them out. Barring any accident, we'll get away."

***

50. Hell's Canyon

Nyx's stomach lurches. She had no idea the gorge would be so deep, so sheer or so forbidding.

The ground drops away so vertically, and so suddenly, that she didn't see the gorge until she was half a dozen paces away. The only hint of change in landscape had been a sudden cluster of large boulders. When Uss stopped their wagon 100 feet back, she even asked, "Why are we stopping?"

It looks like some giant being has struck the rock they're standing on with a titanic cleaver. One blow only, leaving a clean cleft in the rock, perhaps 500 feet deep and 30 feet across. And stretching for several miles left to right.

At the bottom of the gorge, there is a ribbon of boiling white water. Nothing can live in that violent tumult. There is clearly no way down. The cliffs are smooth like wet glass, wet from vapour boiling up from the raging current. The drop sickens her. It frightens her. She wants to say, "Whatever your plan, I'm not climbing down there. I'd rather give myself up to the Tarsis troops."

She keeps quiet though, her heart thudding, her stomach nauseous.

She looks at the others. Bach and Sal are as pale as she feels. Only Uss is calm. "About twenty years ago, I built an escape route here. I built it to last. It took three of us several weeks. It will still be good."

She can't see what he's talking about. He points to the other side of the gorge. It's equally steep and smooth. The blackness of the rock looks like it wants to actively repel anything and everything. It looks hostile.

"See the two giant boulders on top of the cliff, on the other side, there, 20 feet back from the edge?" He points.

They all nod.

"Can you see the small white disk midway between the boulders?"

They nod again.

"What is it?" asks Sal.

"Watch," says Uss.

He goes to the wagon and pulls out a package wrapped in oilskins. He removes the oilskins. Underneath is a longbow, a quiver and a smaller packet. He strings the longbow, flexes it and puts it aside. He opens the smaller packet. There is a reel of cord in the smaller packet, very fine, like fine fishing line. The reel has an axle through the middle.

"Here," says Uss to Sal. "Hold each end of the axle. On your life and ours, do not let go."

Sal grips the axle. The reel can spin freely around the axle to pay out cord.

Uss looks at his quiver. He carefully selects an arrow. It has the usual goose feather on the rear end. Behind the goose feather though, another inch of arrow shaft sticks out backwards, with a small eyelet in the wood. Uss carefully threads an end of the cord from the reel through the eyelet. He ties it off with a complicated-looking knot, tugs on the knot twice, then nods to himself in satisfaction.

Nyx has no idea what he's planning. Bach is smiling at her and Sal in anticipation. "The good doctor and physician, here," he nods at Uss, "had a very naughty past before he became a healer. No one could touch him for precision archery."

Uss frowns. "Don't jinx me, Bach. It's not an easy shot. I have to allow for the drag of the cord on the arrow. And the wind. Quiet now."

He stands facing across the gorge. The bow is held loosely in his left hand. His hand is at the level of his waist. The bow slants diagonally across his body, more horizontal than vertical. His right hand has nocked the arrow on the bowstring but left the string un-tensioned. He's staring at the white disk. It seems impossibly tiny to Nyx. She's one of the best competitive archers in Mersinia. It's her sport. But she knows that neither she nor any of her competitors would ever consider such a shot possible. The bow he's using is huge. Probably a one-hundred-pound draw. The left side of his body is forward towards the target. The right side is back. She notices with a shock how lopsided his body is. The muscles on his right shoulder and right forearm are huge compared to the left side. She wonders how she could have missed that until now. He's looking completely relaxed. Breathing slowly.

Then his breathing slows even further. Finally, it stops.

She expects him to draw the bow and sight long and carefully along the shaft before releasing the arrow. None of that happens. What happens is so quick, so fluid, her brain has to do a replay after the event to assure her of what her eyes just saw. In one fluid motion, he raises the bow to the vertical; at the same time as the bow is rising, the right hand is pulling back the bowstring to a maximum draw, the two actions flowing together in perfect timing. As the bow reaches its vertical position and the string reaches full draw, he releases without pause and lowers the bow again. She gasps. Just one smooth uninterrupted cycle. She hears the reel in Sal's hand screaming as it spins. There's a hard wooden thump from the other side of the gorge. The arrow is firmly lodged in the white disk. Her head is spinning. He aimed BEFORE he raised or drew the bow. He didn't sight along the shaft. Couldn't have. The shaft was only at eye level for a fraction of a heartbeat before descending, never stayed there long enough for sighting along. The bow and his hands are back to his starting position, left hand at waist level, bow tilted across his body diagonally. By reflex, he already has another arrow nocked. Not that he needs another arrow. No one she has ever shot with does it this way. And he seems unsurprised that he's hit the disk.

She notices that his breathing has resumed. The tempo is barely elevated.

"Don't let go the reel," is all he says to Sal.

To Bach he says, "Pull that white disk across to us, VERY GENTLY. Do you hear me you evil water-rat?"

For the first time, there is tension in Uss voice. He's looking hard at Bach to make sure Bach understands him. "We get one chance only to do it right. I don't want the cord to snap or the arrow to pull out of the disk."

"Aye-aye, cap'n," says Bach, touches his forehead with two fingers and gently reels in the disk. He winks at Sal and Nyx. "Just like old times, 'cept he wasn't target-shooting back then."

The little white wood disk is now suspended across the gorge. On the one side is Uss' arrow and the cord attached to the arrow. The rear of the disk is attached to a matching thin rope that runs back between the boulders on the far side of the gorge. Bach continues to reel it in. When the disk is in Bach's hands, they see that it is a slice from across a tree trunk, the growth rings still visible, all painted white for added visibility. Uss removes his arrow carefully. He unties his arrow cord, recoils it and puts arrows, bow, cord and quiver neatly down on the oilcloth.

"What now?" says Sal.

"Well," says Uss, "There's a giant iron drum anchored between those two far boulders, on the far side of the gorge. We'll pull in this rope, which will pull across a thicker rope, and then a thicker rope still. As we pull the thickest rope, the giant drum on the far side will unwind. That will let us pull across a rope footbridge with wooden foot planks and supporting ropes. The bridge will be too heavy for us to pull. We'll need to harness Duke and Farmer Joe. The wood is an SI variety of camelthorn. It's good for another hundred years before any rot or insects will touch it. The rope is greased against rot and will be good as the day I wound it onto the iron drum. Once the bridge is pulled across the gorge, we can anchor this side to six iron stakes that I hammered into the rock twenty years ago. They're just back from where we're standing now. The far end remains anchored by the big iron drum on the other side."

By the time they've harnessed Duke and Farmer Joe, and then by the time they've pulled the bridge across and staked it down, it's twilight. They straighten up, ease their backs and stare in satisfaction at their work.

"Well done," says Uss.

"Indeed," says a new voice.

Commander Zlod steps out from behind a jumble of rocks. She's on foot leading a camel behind her. Uss' oilskin with bow and quiver are in front of her. She puts one foot on Uss' bow.

"I watched you pull across the bridge with great interest. Uss' archery is as extraordinary as ever. Well done indeed," she says again. "I would applaud, but my hands are full, at least this hand ... "

A wicked looking crossbow, fully drawn and loaded dangles from her right hand.

***

51. Zlod

"Commander Zlod," says Uss calmly, "Welcome. How did you get here so rapidly?"

Zlod points to the camel behind her. "The camel, across the sand route. Much quicker than a horse across sand, about the same time as your very clever sail-wagon took across the dirt route."

She pauses, then continues. "Walk with me a little away from the rest of the group, please Dom Uss. And please take your bow with you. We know each other. I trust you with the bow. The others might be tempted to do something rash if you leave it lying there."

Uss picks up the bow. The quiver with the arrows stays on the ground. They walk away from the others.

Nyx watches the two of them. She can't hear what they're saying, but they're having a very earnest discussion, looking at each other intently.

"What do you think will happen, Master Bach?" Nyx asks while still keeping her eyes on Zlod and Uss.

"Hard to say, Young Cabbage. Uss and Zlod have known each other a couple of your lifetimes. They're both SI, so when I say they go back a long way, I mean it. Uss cured her dad and brother of coal miner's lung. They have a lot of respect for each other. She's a lady with a lot of backbone. Very good at what she does, and straight up honest. Which is why she hasn't hanged me. Probably can't stand the new duke."

Nyx snorts at Bach's comment and continues to watch the earnest discussion between Uss and Zlod. Uss seems to be giving Zlod some kind of assurance. He has his hand on his heart to emphasize some point he's making. They both fall silent, just looking at each other for a space of time. Then Zlod nods, and carefully uncocks her crossbow. Uss gestures for her towards Bach, Sal and Nyx. He starts to walk towards them. Zlod doesn't move. Uss stops. He looks confused, then embarrassed. It's the first time Nyx has seen anything less than total assurance on his face. Now he's blushing. He turns back to Zlod. He seems to be apologizing to her. She has a slightly amused air, as though being patient with a young child who is trying on a new task and making a hash of it.

Nyx makes a mental note. That would be a very useful look for her own armoury.

Now Uss holds out his right forearm as though he's about to escort her into a formal dinner. She lays her left forearm on his forearm and they walk in a solemn, stately way back to where Nyx and the others are waiting.

Zlod looks at Uss and waits. Uss clears his throat. He still seems less than his usual assured self. He hesitates as though not sure how to approach a topic. Then he says to them, "May I introduce the Lady Clara Zlod, Baroness of North Sophenia Province, retired Commander of the Tarsis Police Force. Lady Clara has decided that after a long career in ..."

Zlod clears her throat.

Uss is looking miserably nervous now. He tries again, "... after a long and honourable career as Commander of the Tarsis Police Force she is retiring, effective immediately. She feels that the recent ascent to the throne of the new Duke of Tarsis is the perfect time to announce her retirement. The times call for a new commander with ethics that better match the new rule. She has expressed an interest in several retirement pastimes, including travel. She has been kind enough to accept my offer to be her guide to Illyria. She will travel with us. Lady Clara, may I introduce your fellow travellers. First off our Illyrian Ranger, Master Bach."

To Nyx's surprise, Bach bows deeply and merely says, "Honoured to have you travel with us, Your Grace."

Zlod smiles and says, "I'm particularly glad to see your feline jail mates escaped the Gian Major cells, Master Bach."

She pauses, still in apparent amusement, lets the pause hang, then continues, "You too of, course. Would this be the third or fourth time you've escaped a death cell?"

Bach bows again, "Only the third, Your Grace."

Uss is continuing introductions. "May I present Mistress Nyx, Lady Clara Zlod."

Zlod smiles at Nyx. "You'll be pleased to know that your father is in good health and still at liberty. I did my part to ensure that. When we're at leisure during our journey, I can tell you more."

Nyx's heart beats faster at the news. To her renewed surprise, she finds herself bowing as well. "Thank you, Your Grace."

Uss interjects again. "May I also introduce Master Sal, a student at our Tectis Monastery?"

Zlod looks at Sal with great interest. "One hears unusual stories about your high-diving feats in Kiliman, Master Sal. Mere rumours of course, which I wouldn't pass on, but when we're at leisure on our journey together perhaps you'll tell me more?"

Nyx pricks up her ears. So, Sal really is a student? And he comes from the Kiliman islands. She will have to talk to Lady Clara at greater length and see if she can find out why Sal has made such a mystery of his background. Sal meanwhile is bowing wordlessly with a look of sullen shock on his face. The kind of sullen shock that an oyster might express, if it could, on being opened against its will.

Zlod looks at them all. "Thank you, Hugo, for that nice retirement speech and introductions. After so many years as Commander, I thought a formal retirement ceremony and speech were appropriate. Now that the formalities are nicely taken care of, I hope you will all please call me Clara. We're going to be together for too long a journey to bother with titles. Also, I should tell you that the nearest platoon of soldiers might arrive by early morning tomorrow. Perhaps, Hugo, we should continue with crossing Hell's Canyon and then destroy the bridge?"

"Hugo?" Nyx thinks to herself, "Dom Uss is a 'Hugo'?" Interesting. She has much to learn from Lady Clara Zlod, not least how effortlessly she has gained some kind of upper hand on Uss. Uss meanwhile has the confused look of a drunkard picking himself off the road after falling off both a literal and figurative wagon.

"Right," says Uss. Then gathers his thoughts and says "Right" one more time. Finally, his brain snaps into gear and he issues instructions.

"Bach, Sal, Nyx, the wagon can't go over our footbridge. Unpack the essentials we need, transfer them into our backpacks. Nyx, could you please take Chon?"

Nyx notices that Zlod is still watching Uss with amusement. Maybe a hint of affection too.

***

52. Can You Lead a Horse to Water?

They unload the wagon and ferry their backpacks to the opposite side of the gorge. A nearly full moon provides enough light to walk back and forth across the rope bridge. They all gather back at the wagon.

"Dom Uss, what about the camel and the horses?"

"The camel will get itself back to water once Lady Clara releases it. For the horses, I'm hoping that the soldiers will see the wagon here, come to investigate and take the horses back with them. We can leave some barrels of water from the wagon for them to drink while they wait. They shouldn't have long to wait. Thanks to your wagon-sail, our desert crossing was so swift that we have water left."

Sal shakes his head. "I want to lead Duke and Farmer Joe across the bridge."

Uss raises his eyebrows. "The bridge will hold their weight but it will sway under them. What if they take fright and bolt?"

Sal says, "I can lead them across. They trust me. The wooden planks are close enough together. There are no big gaps for the hooves to fall through."

Uss tries again. "Sal, they're huge draft horses, their centre of gravity is too high. Once the bridge starts swaying, they'll panic. If they rear up on their hind legs, the whole thing will go sideways like a child's swing in the wind. Either you'll fall off with them or they'll get caught in the ropes and kick holes in the planking."

Sal considers. He replies calmly. "With respect, Dom Uss, Duke and Joe are my responsibility. I will not abandon them. I suggest you all cross first. That way any problem affects only the horses and me. Or you can leave me on this side of the gorge and I will attempt to drive the horses and wagon back to the soldiers or to Gian Major."

Uss considers. "If the horses become trapped on the bridge?"

"Then I will help you to cut the bridge loose. They will have a quick death below, rather than dying of thirst if the soldiers don't reach them, or don't have enough water to help them return to an oasis."

"And if a panicking horse kicks you both off the bridge?'

"Then I ask you to inform my father. Tell him it was my will."

"It's that important to you, Sal?"

"Duke and Joe trust me. That matters. On Kiliman, trust is everything."

Nyx regards him narrowly. There is a dignity and earnestness to him she hasn't noticed before. He's speaking to Dom Uss as an equal; he's no longer a student talking to a teacher. He's focused and confident. And why doesn't he speak of his mother?

"Very well," says Uss. "I cannot argue against keeping trust."

The others cross over. They watch Sal. He takes two of the wooden arches that normally support the wagon cover. He harnesses one each to Joe and Farmer's back. The long ends drag backwards on the ground on either side of the horses. Then he carries four barrels of water to the edge of the bridge.

Dom Uss is watching with intensity. "Bach," he says, "Get the rope ready that releases the slip-knots holding the bridge. If we have to drop the bridge into the gorge, let's make it quick and humane."

"Ready aye," says Bach. His eyes too are glued on Sal. "What's he doing with those arches?"

"He's using the same trick that he used to get across the footbridge at the Illyria Monastery," says Uss.

"What trick?" says Nyx.

"He's using what tightrope walkers call a balance beam."

"What does it do?"

"As long as you're standing perfectly vertically above a tightrope you don't fall off. If your body tilts away from the vertical, sideways, left or right, then you fall. The beam adds resistance to tilting. Slows it down. Gives you a chance to recover."

"How?"

"Think of a wheel. The heavier it is, the harder it is to start it rolling. Adding a heavy balance beam makes it hard to roll or tilt the horses off the bridge. They tilt only slowly, they have time to recover. If you get the weights low enough they even help the recovery."

"Is it foolproof?"

"No. Nothing about giant horses on a tiny, swaying rope bridge over the world's deepest canyon is foolproof. One day they'll sleep through an earthquake, the next day a fly, a mosquito, the sound of their own breathing will have them panicked. Sal is taking his life in his hands. We may well have to cut the bridge away if he's kicked off and a horse breaks a leg."

They watch.

Sal is putting blinders on Farmer Joe, leather eye patches that prevent him from being distracted by objects to the side of him. Sal wants Joe to see only the bridge in front of himself, not the drop to the side.

The two of them, Sal and Joe, stand together for a long moment. Sal is holding Joe's rein. Joe has his head bent down, nuzzling Sal. Sal is whispering something in Joe's ear. Then Sal leads Joe to the bridge. Joe follows, his head bobbing up and down. Joe hesitates briefly at the edge of the bridge. The watchers hold their breath.

Then Joe advances. Four feet onto the bridge, Sal stops Joe. At this point, close to the land, the bridge is still relatively stable. Sal fiddles with the water barrels squeezing to first one side of Joe, then the other, hanging the barrels from the arched balance beam. The beam and the barrels protrude over and beyond the flimsy side ropes of the bridge. Joe stands patiently waiting for Sal to finish. His neck is arched sideways, his head turned back watching Joe and the barrels. Sal walks back to Joe's head, takes the rein and starts walking. They're going very slowly, four feet forward, pause, four feet forward, pause.

Bach mutters, "He's trying to minimize the bridge movement."

Nyx realizes she's biting her lower lip. She's too distracted to do anything about it.

Halfway across the bridge, Joe balks. Sal tightens the rein to encourage him forward. Joe throws his head up, away from the tug of the rein. Even from a distance, it's clear to the watchers that just Joe swinging his head makes the bridge move under him. Sal freezes. And waits. He makes no immediate attempt to coax Joe further forward, no further tugs on the rein. He reaches very slowly into a pocket, no sudden movements that could frighten Joe, then holds out something to Joe.

At this distance, Nyx can't make out what it is. Joe puts his head down and daintily nibbles whatever Sal is offering. The two of them have a conversation, a pat on the muzzle and then they're moving again. They're on the uphill curve of the bridge. Somehow. Paradoxically, this seems easier for them; they're walking with fewer stops. Still it's a good two minutes before they reach the rim of the gorge and step off the bridge.

Nyx wants to run up to Sal and say something to him, some word of encouragement, a pat on the arm, but she hesitates. He's concentrating too deeply on Joe. And on what still lies ahead. Nyx doesn't want to break that concentration. He'll need it. All of it. Now he's talking to Joe, giving his sides a rub with the flat of his hands, undoing the barrels and the balance beam, tying Joe's reins to a small stunted bush. Then he heads back over the bridge for Duke. He hasn't said a word to the watching group. Too focused. Too consumed by the unfinished work.

Nyx sees how the bridge is swaying under his tread alone. She remembers the sickening swaying as she crossed over it, trying not to look over the side.

The routine with Duke is similar. Duke is less placid though. He tries to look sideways several times, over the side ropes of the bridge. Sal keeps pressure on the reins, pulling Duke's head into looking ahead. Two thirds of the way across, Duke sees something on the bridge bed that startles him. He snorts, stops and backs up several paces. The bridge is swaying more than when Joe came over. Again Sal soothes the horse, spends time talking to him, then puts his foot over the object on the bridge bed and guides Duke forward again. His foot remains on whatever he was covering up until Duke's head is almost past it.

Ten feet further and somehow, one of the barrels on the balance beam is caught on the side rope. Sal stops. Nyx sees that he's considering his options.

She puts herself in his shoes.

If he unties the stuck barrel then he unbalances Duke and the bridge. That's not an option. If he squeezes along Duke's side to loosen the barrel then his weight unbalances the bridge. Or Duke will step to the other side to give him room. That unbalances the bridge even more. If he crouches underneath Duke's belly, Duke will panic and trample him. The options don't look good. Maybe the best Sal can do is leave Duke stuck on the bridge and walk away from him. Walk away for his own safety. Hope that when he walks away Duke doesn't try to follow. With the barrel caught, Duke would pull the bridge off kilter and dump them both into the abyss.

Nyx can almost see Sal's mental gears grinding through the options.

Then Sal speaks gently to Duke softly and backs him up several paces.

Nyx holds her breath. The barrel frees itself from the side rail and they move forward again.

When they climb off the bridge, Nyx notices Sal's shirt is wet with sweat.

"What was on the bridge?" asks Bach. "The first trouble spot you hit."

"A stupid moth," says Sal. "Would you believe it, a one-ton horse having a schoolgirl fit because there was a moth on the bridge? I had to keep a foot on the moth to hide it before the idiot horse would move again."

"Well done," says Zlod.

"Thank you," says Sal. He leans forwards, hands on his thigh, and breathes hard. Like a runner at the end of a long race. Once he's breathing easier, he straightens. "Would anyone like me to bring a saddle horse over? I'm willing to try. Probably be easier than dealing with Duke and the Moth. Nyx? How about I bring Socks over?"

"Enough," says Uss. "I saw how badly that bridge swayed when Duke came to the moth. I saw the whites of his eyes. From here. Another moth, a more high strung horse than Duke, and you'd all have been lost. No more horses."

Nyx is relieved. Much as Socks is dear to her, she remembers how skittish he was on the cliff trail to Elsin's cabin. On a swaying bridge, he'd kill himself and Sal.

They slip the knots holding up the bridge. The far end falls into the gorge. Then they use Duke and Joe to haul and wind it all back up onto the iron drum.

"Might need it again in twenty years," says Uss. "Now let's move out of sight of the rim walls before we camp. If the soldiers get to the other side tomorrow, I want them to see nothing but our abandoned wagon and saddle horses. I want them puzzled. They'll spread the right kind of rumours about us. They'll say that Bach is the Devil in earthly form. They'll say we traded our souls to him in return for wings to fly. Of course, the part about Bach being the Devil incarnate may be true."

Bach spits. "All these years you've known me, and you're still rude. I do most of the work for this stupid trip you've taken me on, I get put in jail with 30 flea-bitten cats for sod-all, and then you talk like that about me. That's disrespectful that is, Dom Uss. It's not right. I don't think Brother Herman smacked you nearly hard enough. Might have done you some good if he had. You know what I think? I think you're the one with the nasty mind."

Uss bows to Bach. "I apologize, I take it all back; forgive me Great Prince of Darkness."

Bach huffs, but he's mollified, "All right then, that's more like it. A bit of decent respect. We'll say no more then."

They load the bulk of their food and equipment onto the two draft horses and start walking.

***

53. Verbosity

The morning after crossing Hell's Canyon the group is walking into the Blackrock Mountains. It's a steady uphill slog. The path switchbacks up and up. On the exposed rocks there are occasional patches of ice or old snow. Bach is leading Farmer Joe by the reins; Duke is following tethered loosely to Joe. Nyx and Sal are further back. Nyx is trying to talk to Sal and getting nowhere with it.

Uss and Lady Clara, the former Commander Zlod, are walking at the rear of the group. They're far enough back that their conversation can't be heard by the others.

"When we get to Tectis," says Clara, "I need to talk to your Abbess. Illyria and the monastery are in danger."

"How?" says Uss.

"The Duke and Ham have sent trained assassins into Illyria. They will gather information on how to best invade Illyria, perhaps looking for charts for a naval approach. They may also try to destabilize and take over Illyria by simply assassinating your abbess."

"Not much we can do from here," says Uss. "We'll get back as quickly as we can and then talk to the Abbess."

They walk a while in silence then Lady Clara switches topic.

"Interesting youngsters," she says. "Sal and Nyx."

Uss grunts.

"That's all you have to say about them?"

"I don't like travelling with youngsters."

Clara nods. "I know. I know the history."

"Still, these two are not the worst."

"Don't know if you were awake to see it. Nyx was up early this morning, borrowed one of your smaller recurve bows. Said she needed meat for Chon. Took just one of your arrows, was gone an hour and came back with a rabbit. Said she doesn't like killing but will do it for meat."

"I didn't see her leave, but I saw her come back."

"You know, in Mersinia she's an archery champion."

"Ah."

"Not in your league, of course, but still she's reckoned to be very good."

"Oh, yes."

"I watched yesterday. She was watching you. When you shot the cord across Hell's Canyon. I could see on her face she was shocked by your accuracy and technique. She'd probably welcome being mentored."

"I don't work with youngsters."

"No. Of course. I wonder where she gets her skill from. Part of every good athlete – archer, sprinter, horsewoman or mountaineer - is genetic. Her father is no archer, no athlete of any kind. Her mother's family I don't know much about. The mother died when the girl was very young."

She pauses, when she sees Uss is not commenting, she continues, "Sal is quite exceptional. You say he's a student at the Illyrian monastery?"

"Yes."

"You can't leave him as a student much longer."

"Because?"

"Because, Hugo, there's not much anyone can teach him."

"True."

"In some ways, what he did yesterday with the horses was a childish, dangerous act. In other ways, it was a very grown-up assessment of responsibilities, risks and his own capabilities. Don't you think?"

"He did well. He was scared but handled it."

Lady Clara looks up the path ahead at where the boy is walking. "He's feeling the after-effects right now. Strung tight like a bowstring from the adrenalin and wanting to be left alone. Probably didn't sleep much last night while we slept. Nyx is choosing the wrong moment to chat to him. She's too green to know it. Maybe I'll distract her with some conversation. Tell her about her father."

"That would be a good idea, Commander."

"'Clara'. No longer 'Commander'."

"That would be a good idea, Lady Clara."

"Just 'Clara', Hugo."

Uss nods. It will take getting used to. Truth to tell, *he's* still feeling strung like a bow after all that tomfoolery with the boy, the horses and seeing the bridge swaying wildly under them. Wondering if the swaying would panic them. A vicious circle, more panic, wilder swaying, until they all fell off the bridge. Uss doesn't feel much like talking either.

Lady Clara seems to have sensed that. She says, "Well, I'll give it a go. Chatting to Nyx, I mean. Don't know if I have the energy though, after such an exhausting conversation with you, Hugo. You really must learn to be less verbose."

Uss considers that. "I suppose," he says.

Clara moves off to speak to Nyx.

***

54. Woman to Woman

It's the second day after crossing Hell's Canyon. Nyx is feeling irritated. Yesterday she tried talking to Sal about how it felt crossing the swaying footbridge with Duke. The boy *is* an idiot. He had nothing to say. Just clammed up. Would only answer 'yes', 'no', 'I don't know'.

Bach and Uss are just as annoying. She asked Dom Uss about his archery technique and he's barely responded. Later she had tried to explain to them both a better, organized way to pack cooking equipment. They seemed uninterested. Bach even tried to pack unwashed plates on the horses. In exasperation, Nyx washed them.

Thank goodness for Lady Clara. Nyx is drawn to the woman. Nyx had thought a police commander would be dour. Just the opposite. Lady Clara is amazingly easy to talk to. Yesterday Clara told her the Duke had ordered both Nyx and Sri, her father, arrested and tried for treason. It's thanks to Clara's deliberate inaction that her father is still at large. Clara had even known about Sri's trip to take Nyx to Elsin.

Clara assures Nyx that whoever her successor is, he or she is unlikely to find out about Elsin. Clara deliberately has not put this information into any written notes. Nor has she made written notes about Sri's various hiding places, which she also seems to know about.

Now Nyx and Lady Clara are walking up the mountain path. They're in the middle of the group. Far enough from the others for a private conversation.

"Why did you take the tea away from Dom Uss last night, Clara?"

"You know that he and I are SIs, right? Silicon-based life forms. Mutations coming out of the gene-altering virus weapons of the second EC."

"Sure," says Nyx. "Not that there's much difference. I mean SI's and carbon-based humans live together so well, half the time you don't even know which is which. There's never been friction between the two groups. I can't tell one from the other."

"True," says Clara. "Well, tea is a drug for SIs. A bit like alcohol for carbon-based humans. In quantity, it's both a sedative and an antidepressant. Bad for the liver and heart. Quite dangerous if taken for long periods. Uss should not be taking it."

"Why does he take it? What's he depressed about?"

Clara sighs. "It's an old story, but no secret. About – oh maybe - one hundred and twenty years ago or so, Uss fell in love with a C, a carbon-based woman, what you would call a normal woman. He married her and they had a daughter. A big mistake."

"Why?" asks Nyx.

"Because," says Clara, "an SI, a silicon-based human like Uss, lives for centuries. The C-woman he married would age and die while Uss was still a young man. What they hadn't expected was that they'd have children. Their biology makes it rare for an SI and a carbon-base to have children. And when they do it's a toss-up whether the child will be SI or carbon-based. In fact it's almost impossible to tell for years."

"What happened?"

"His wife saw how Uss doted on the child, more and more each day. She was convinced the child was a carbon-based child, not SI. She saw how much it would tear Uss apart to raise a child and have it age and die while Uss was still young. Having your child age and die is very different to having a wife die. She didn't want him to go through that. She took the child and left. Uss came home one day to an empty house, to a long, loving, tear-filled, apologetic, good-bye note. He had no idea where to look for his wife and child. He tried, but never succeeded. They had vanished completely."

"Oh."

"Sometimes when the memories come, he drinks tea."

"Do you think his wife did the right thing?"

"Who knows?" says Lady Clara. "In any case, the wife and child are long dead now. That's why he drinks tea, and that's why I stop him."

Nyx sees that Clara wants to say more. She's arranging her words before speaking. Nyx keeps silent. At length Clara says, "Another thing. I heard you asking him about his archery. You didn't get much reply. Don't take it to heart. Sometimes it's hard for Uss to be around young people. Like you and Sal. He gets to thinking 'is this how my daughter would have been at that age?' But it's good medicine for him to be with younger people. Don't stop asking. Don't let him put you off. Act like you would act if you hadn't heard his story. Neither extra pushy nor extra reticent."

Nyx feels a lump in her heart for Dom Uss and his missing family, now dead.

It reminds her how her own orderly life has turned upside down since leaving Mersinia. So much misery for her at every turn. Parting from Sri. The horrible cliff climb. Parting from Elsin. The bitter cold climb over the Great Cold Range. Being forced into thievery in Brackwater Lake. Thinking Bach would be executed in Gian Major. Fearing they might die of thirst in the desert. Believing Sal and the horses would fall off the swaying bridge and having to leave Socks behind.

She's also worried about going to Illyria. It will be hard to set Chon free. Much as she's pleased for him, they're very attached to each other. He's been the one living being she can confide her worries to. She talks to him and he purrs. He curls up against her stomach at night, a little friendly warm ball of fur. He yawns at her and shows her a little pink tongue. She plays with him and he pats at her hand with his baby paws. And once she's returned Chon, where will she go? She doesn't belong at the monastery. She can't go back to Elsin or Mersinia. Her father is in hiding. She has no one.

Now this horrible story of Uss. Misery upon misery. It makes her angry.

"That's not fair. Dom Uss is a good person. In the villages we pass through he cares for anyone sick who comes to him. Without any request for payment. I've seen how everywhere we go people remember and revere him. To have something like that happen to a good person is not right."

Clara wants to smile at this idealism of how life "should" treat people. But she sees how passionate Nyx is, and stifles the smile. She simply says, "I've known him a long time. You're right. He has never changed. He was always, and is still a good person."

Nyx looks at Clara. A sudden change of mood. "You like him, don't you."

This time Clara does smile. "He's got a few rough edges that need work, but yes I like him. He reminds me of an old chair I had planned to re-varnish, re-glue, and upholster in my retirement. In the Duke of Tarsis' office."

They look back at where Uss is trailing them.

Nyx starts to giggle, "I'm imagining him as a chair. Nothing frilly or delicate. Not a collapsible garden chair. Not really a decadent club chair for sinking deep into, either. Maybe a simple wing chair. Very upright. Something in a very dark heavy wood. Solid, like what you'd find in an old farmhouse. Maybe oak or walnut. With a good but worn leather upholstery. In neutral colours that blend into the background. But I shouldn't laugh. That's not very flattering."

"Oh, but it is," says Clara, "the chair was the only decent, likeable, honest thing in the Duke's office. There was no deception in that chair. It told you straight off what it was, what it could do, and then you could rely on it to do exactly that, no matter what horrors the Duke was spouting. I was very fond of it."

She pauses, then adds, "You needn't tell Uss any of that."

"Do you plan on re-varnishing, re-gluing and re-upholstering him?"

"Hmm," says Clara. "Interesting thought."

***

55. Crossing Blackrock

After two more days they've crossed the high point on their march. They're now descending the eastern edge of the Blackrock Mountains into the Illyrian caldera. Tectis is not yet in sight. They'll need to get lower down, away from the steep inner cliffs, then angle westwards. Bach and Uss say they should be in sight of Tectis and the monastery in another two days.

They've found flat ground for camping for the night. A circle of boulders provides some shelter against the wind. There is reedy grass for the two draft horses to graze. Some stunted trees have provided enough wood for a cooking fire. Bach has promised to make bannock bread for them tonight. Bannock bread, he says, is campfire bread. In a nearby sheltered gully he found some blueberries to add to the dough. He promises them the bannock will be excellent. After days of living off dried meats, hard tack, rusks, rice, oatmeal, and the occasional rabbits that Nyx has shot for them, the thought of fresh bread has them all drooling.

They gather in a circle around the fire. Bach mixes flour, lard, baking powder, blueberries and water thoroughly.

"Now," he says, "pay attention, Young Cabbages. There are two ways to do this. We either fry it in a pan on the fire. Or spike lumps of dough on sticks we hold over the coals. Not a lot of wood to waste up here so I'll grease a pan and we'll fry up the bread in a pan."

Darkness falls abruptly. The sun has sunk behind the western rim of the Blackrock Mountains. The temperature drops just as abruptly. The horses, who were grazing, suddenly lift their heads. They're staring at something out there in the circle of darkness. Farmer Joe has drawn his lips back from his mouth. He's showing his teeth in what looks like an idiotic grin. It's really a way of drawing air past the special scent organs on the roof of his mouth.

Sal and Nyx are too focused on the frying bread to notice. Bach, Uss and Clara glance at each other. Uss nods at Clara while Bach watches. Bach gives them both an answering nod. Uss and Clara quietly get up and move away from the firelight.

Bach looks completely relaxed, as though his only care in the world and all his attention is on the bread. He's on the opposite side of the fire to Sal and Nyx. All three have their night vision curtailed by gazing into the fire.

"Master Bach," whispers a voice into his ear from behind, "if you were poacher, I'd have knife to your throat. Like this."

The whisper takes on normal volume as it addresses Nyx and Sal. "You two sit quietly so Master Bach doesn't get hurt."

Bach feels something pressing against his throat.

Sal and Nyx stare in confusion.

Bach shakes his head, but keeps the movement very small. "It's alright, Cabbages," he says to Sal and Nyx. "Just Vlad, one of my rangers, on poacher patrol."

Then to Vlad he says, "Stop messing with my throat and sit down. We'll give you some bannock if you behave."

Vlad sits next to Bach. He sounds disappointed. "How you know it was me?" He speaks in a North Sophenian way. Their grammar is odd.

"Who else would show up just when I'm cooking bannock? And we heard you coming."

"No, you didn't. No one hear me."

"Want to bet?"

"Sure. What we bet?"

"A cask of beer when I'm back in Tectis."

"Hokay. Now prove you hear me coming."

A voice from behind him says quietly, "Here's proof number one. And don't lean back. My sword point is right behind you."

Vlad stiffens. The voice chuckles. "Now you can lean back." Lady Clara steps into the firelight and sheaths an ugly-looking short-sword. No gold, no inlays, no curlicues, as plain as a workman's hammer, but sharp and ugly.

Bach shakes his head. "Vlad, how many times must I tell you to count the opponents before you engage?"

Vlad is upset. "So, I miss one. It happen to anyone."

A second voice from the darkness says, "You missed two." Uss steps into the firelight and sits down beside Clara. He puts his bow down next to him and puts an arrow back into its quiver.

Vlad stands and bows low to Dom Uss. "I was quiet. What give me away?"

Bach points to the horses. "They smelled you. Next time crush leaves from whatever is growing nearby and rub it onto your clothes, hair and skin. No poison ivy, poison oak or poison sumac, please Vlad. Pine needles, cedar leaves, balsam all work. If you're above the tree line, rabbit droppings will work too. That's a lesson worth paying a cask of beer for."

"Rabbit droppings?" says Nyx, "Master Bach, I hope you washed your hands before mixing that bannock dough?"

"Probably did," says Bach. "If you ask 'when', I think it was when we were in Gian Minor. I had to wash to impersonate his nibs there, Dom Uss. For the big, fancy banquet with the mayor. Anyway, whatever was on my hands will be cooked clean in the pan. If you decide not to have your portion of bannock, let me know. The rest of us will eat your portion for you."

Nyx wrinkles her nose in disgust. Sal leans over and whispers quietly, "It's OK. I saw him wash in the stream before cooking; he's just trying to talk you out of your bannock portion."

Nyx is startled. After yesterday's failure to talk Sal any better than she could talk to a lump of wood, she hadn't expected this. In some ways, it's a ridiculously tiny conversation, but the prospect of fresh bread after so long has assumed huge importance to her, beyond all normal proportions. It's now wound up with all sorts of expectations, like a cake at birthday parties when she was very young. It has all that nostalgia too. Bread is associated with a normal lifestyle, something she hasn't had for weeks and weeks. It's associated with being home with her father, with a placid daily routine, with watching her father bake bread in their oven at the end of his work week, with being warm and comfortable together in their kitchen on cold winter nights, with having a routine and the same roof over her head every night. Just the smell alone is bringing back memories of sitting at a dinner table, with a crisp white linen tablecloth, with her father sharing a newly baked loaf. The smell of baking bannock has brought back the image of her father cutting bread. Brought back the image so clearly she can see the cracked handle of their old bread knife and every steaming crumb of bread as the slices are cut. She'd give the world to be transported back to that. It was meaner than Bach knew to try talking her out of her share, and generous of Sal to notice her distress. Generous of him to speak up. Strange how a little thing like this can matter so much.

She touches his arm and says, "Thank you, Sal." He's startled. His arm flinches, almost imperceptibly. He wasn't expecting any reply. Probably doesn't realise what this meant to her.

She shifts closer to him. "It's uncomfortable not having a chair. Can I lean my back against you?"

"Sure," he says and shifts closer. She half turns her back to him and leans against him. He adjusts and leans his back against hers.

"OK?" he asks.

"Good."

They sit quietly. Nyx senses that Sal too is enjoying the backrest and the mutual warmth. The evening is chilly. She has no wish to talk right now. Just wants to relax. She's been carrying a heavy pack ever since they crossed Hell's Canyon. Carrying as much as the others. Determined to keep up and not complain. The warmth against her back is like a spa. Relaxing the aching back muscles.

Meanwhile, Vlad is curious to know which route they took to get here. Bach shakes his head and is cagey. "If I told you, you'd focus too much on that route. Then poachers would get by you on other routes. Just know that you have to cover all the possibilities."

Vlad nods. "Hokay. Give some bannock, though."

The bannock is delicious. A fresh dough after so long is a feast. Sal has one more surprise left for her. He notices her finishing her bannock in record time. Before he's quarter way through his.

"Here," he says, breaking his in half, "take some of mine."

"No," she says, "you eat it. It's good." Meaning it's good for him too. They bicker a bit, she continues to refuse, and finally he finishes his bannock. She's touched, though. Again. She lets more of her weight lean against him and thinks, tomorrow, tomorrow I will restart the oyster project. Lady Clara may have started to pry you open, but I will finish the job.

The next morning they leave Vlad to his patrols and continue down the mountain, north and west towards Tectis and the monastery. ."

***

56. Poacher Turned Gamekeeper

Even the longest journey finds its end.

Uss and Lady Clara are sitting with the Abbess in the monastery at Tectis. She's interrupted her meditation briefly for their return. Given them time to wash, eat, find fresh clothes, and then called for them. An unusual interruption to her meditation. But warranted.

Uss has just finished his report on his trip to Tarsis.

The Abbess is counting on her fingers once more. As she had done when she first gave Uss his marching orders. Summarizing now what Uss has told her.

"Number 1. You delivered the coronation gift to the Duke, then?"

"I did."

Lady Clara smiles. "I hear he is incensed that there are no plates. He believes it was a subtle insult."

"Just so," says the Abbess, holding up finger number 2. "You destroyed the Illyrian lynx pelt also?"

"Yes," says Uss. "We left the Duke with a cloak made up of skunk pelts. I doubt he'll wear it. And Nyx, daughter of the rebel Sri, has brought back a lynx cub that was stolen from Illyria when its mother was killed. In a week or two, the cub will be old enough to release back to the wild."

The Abbess holds up a third finger. "I understand she is the only student from Brackwater Lake that elected to come here this year. Although whether she wants to stay here is another question. I would like to speak to Nyx in a week or two when my meditation period is done," says the Abbess. "Until then Uss, please ensure her every comfort. Let her know my intent to call for her in no more than two weeks."

"Very good," says Uss. He anticipates the fourth finger. "And we returned the missing stone to Han-Bu."

"And was it the real, missing stone?" asks the Abbess.

"It appears so. And, as you foretold, the universe resisted the return of the stone. With a vigorous earthquake. The stone is lost. Again. During the quake."

"Yes," says the Abbess. "I'd heard. Oddly, Abbot Yan sent me a thank-you gift in return. It appears to be less of a gift than a piece of revenge for the earthquake, disguised as a gift."

"What did he send?"

"A nasty old monk called Svalbaard. Yan suggested he would be infinitely useful to us. Which Svalbaard clearly is not."

"Oh."

"Yes, Dom Uss, 'oh'. It seems you've already met Svalbaard."

"Yes."

"Fortunately for us, Svalbaard has lost interest in being a monk. He came here with a defrocked monk from Han-Bu. That monk goes by the nickname 'Duck-Man'. He's buying up Illyrian duck down for making quilts and jackets. He's hard to understand. Makes lots of quacking noises when he speaks. He's obsessed with ducks to the point of being deranged.

"He and Svalbaard have formed a business partnership here in Illyria. They buy ducks. Duck-Man makes quilts and jackets for sale, stuffed with duck down. Svalbaard uses the duck meat to manufacture a food item he calls duck dogs. It's ground up duck meat, rolled into a sausage, grilled on a brazier and sold in the streets and taverns of Tectis. It's disgusting. But most of our students, our dockworkers and sailors love it. Even our monks like an occasional duck dog. It's cheap, spicy and served hot. It seems Duck-Man and Svalbaard will be successful merchants."

"Oh," says Uss. "I can suggest a gift we could make to Abbot Yan. In return for Svalbaard."

"I'm ahead of you," says the Abbess. "I've sent Dom Bal as a gift to Abbot Yan and his monastery. His ship is underway."

Uss and the Abbess look at each other and chuckle.

"Incidentally, Uss. You'll be my stand-in until my meditation is over. Now that Dom Bal is gone. I had put him in that role, hoping to see proof of treachery and abuse of power. Giving him rope to hang himself. There had been suspicions that he had supplied a nautical chart to a ship from Tarsis. However, we found no proof of collusion with Tarsis. He's just an unpleasant personality."

The Abbess holds up a fifth finger. "As for Bal's petty dislikes, Bach and Sal, they can return to the monastery with an easy heart. I assume they acquitted themselves well during your trip."

Uss nods without meeting the Abbess' eye.

She misses nothing. "I will be more specific. Did Master Bach get into trouble on your travels?"

Uss clears his throat. "Er ... no. He was a great help. Though the trip was quite routine. No troubles."

"Really," says the Abbess. "How nice. Of course, it would be better, Uss, if you could look me in the eye while saying that. Well, let's move on. Now we come to Lady Clara, formerly Commander Clara Zlod. Welcome with all my heart."

The two women smile at each other with genuine warmth. They've already sized each other up. Respectfully. And seen kindred spirits. Triple layered. Satin coverings with steel cores. And a large heart inside the steel.

"Uss hinted you had concerns for Illyria, My Lady?"

"Yes, Abbess. The Duke has sent assassins to Tectis. They pose as merchant traders visiting Tectis. They will either gather information for an invasion, or destabilize Illyria by assassinating you. If they can."

"What are your plans, Lady Clara?"

"I am retired. I had thought to take on some small hobby projects, perhaps to rebuild one or another ancient furniture piece in my retirement. I'd like to stay in Illyria. I cannot return to Tarsis."

The Abbess looks thoughtful at this. An almost sly look of conjecture crosses her face. Clara knows better than to look away, but her face takes on an uncharacteristic and slight rosy hue.

Uss interrupts their silent exchange. "We would not be here if it was not for Lady Clara. She saved us from imprisonment and hanging in Tarsis several times over. We owe her our lives and the success of our mission."

The Abbess regards him with raised eyebrows. "Interesting that on a ... what did you say earlier ... 'a quite routine trip' ... you needed your lives saved several times over."

The Abbess turns back to Clara. "Do you know how many assassins were sent? Would you recognize these assassins?"

"Two assassins. And no, I would not recognize them."

The Abbess continues to gaze at Clara. "You were widely known as the most competent police officer in all Tarsis. Perhaps anywhere on the known globe. If you put your skills to it, do you think you might be able to unmask the assassins for me? Putting off your retirement project temporarily. I would give you every support you could ask for. Any title you wish and a generous salary."

Clara looks doubtful. "I can try," she says.

"Deal," says the Abbess. "Let me know what you need."

***

57. Butterfly of Chaos and Moth of Stupidity

Dom Uss spends a late night with his friend and colleague, Don Smuel, reviewing the details of Uss' trip to Tarsis. Smuel has long thought to produce a book based on Uss' various travels, including this latest one. They are seated over a meal of lamb in a quiet corner of the King's Hand. Smuel has a notebook open and is recording the facts of the trip in a precise script. After three glasses of Bacchan wine, Smuel's handwriting becomes noticeably less precise. The notes turn to doodles. He becomes obsessed with the crossing of Hell's Canyon. In particular with the moth on the bridge across Hell's Canyon.

"Was it the Moth of Stupidity, Uss?"

"Was it the what?"

"You know about the Butterfly of Chaos, Dom Uss? Yes? It has a fractal wing edge, which makes the edge infinitely long, and powerful; powerful enough to create storms on the far side of the globe, yes?"

"OK."

"Hokay, listen now Uss, there are two lesser-known but even more powerful species."

"Yes?"

"Yes, Uss."

"What?"

"What 'what', Uss?"

Bacchan wine is notoriously unpredictable. It seems to be making Smuel's lines of thought unpredictable too. Uss looks at him carefully and then asks again, "What are the two more powerful species, Dom Smuel?"

Smuel stares at his neatly written notes about Uss' trip, looks frantically for a blank page, finds one, tears up his written notes, and scrawls a rapid picture of a moth on the blank page.

"Nu, the second species, my revered friend, is the 'Moth of Stupidity'. I have deduced it from first principles. It has a fractal wing surface, which makes the surface infinite. And of course, even such a tiny moth has huge influence on the world, because its wings have infinite area."

"How did you deduce its existence, Smuel?"

"Because of history, Uss. I teach history, you know."

"Yes."

"What?"

"Yes, I know you teach history."

"Good."

Uss stares at him patiently. Finally, he says, "And how does history let you deduce the existence of the Moth of Stupidity, Dom Smuel?"

"Because, friend Uss, if you teach history, you see that chaos is not the driving force in the world."

"No?"

"No, Dom Uss. The driving force of history is mass stupidity. And if chaos is caused by a mere butterfly with a fractal wing edge, then global stupidity is caused by ... and I have spent years refining this argument, I won't bore you with the intermediate proof steps, but the conclusion is that ... did you say something? No, well global stupidity is caused by a moth with an infinite wing surface. There. Nu, I'm sure you never thought of that, my clever friend."

"Astounding, Dom Smuel. The leap of logic from a fractal wing edge to a fractal wing surface."

"Thank you, friend Uss. Another glass? And a toast to my theory?"

He pours.

"So, Uss, was the moth on the bridge a Moth of Stupidity?"

Uss considers. "By appearance, I placed it in the moth genus Tegeticula."

"The horse behaved stupidly, though?"

"Horses behave stupidly for moths, mosquitoes, explosions, other horses, the absence of other horses, gunshots, goats, a falling leaf, a leaping cat, the absence of leaping cats, and, depending on the day of the month and some complicated internal horse calendar of their own, even the colour blue."

"Ah. So, not Tegeticula Stupiditas, Dom Uss?"

"I don't believe so. Does your theory explain why no specimen of The Moth of Stupidity has yet been captured and catalogued, Smuel?"

Smuel smiles and shakes his head indulgently. "Uss, old friend, an obvious question with an obvious explanation. Anyone capturing The Moth of Stupidity becomes too stupid to recognize it."

"Brilliant, Dom Smuel. I should have thought of that."

"My work is like that of an astronomer looking for black holes, Dom Uss. I do not expect ever to see a live specimen. I have to infer it from behaviour. I research accounts of groups like yours whenever they encounter significant moths. For years I have gathered accounts of travellers and moths they encountered. How did the boy behave when confronting the moth?"

"Sal did not behave stupidly. Nor did the rest of us. Your theory of the Moth of Stupidity is brilliant, Dom Smuel, but this moth was just a Tegeticula Ordinarius. You haven't told me about the other species, though. The other species that is more powerful than the Butterfly of Chaos."

Smuel smiles. "After I tell you, you may see it is obvious. But gravity too became obvious only after Newton."

"True. Tell me, Smuel."

"Think, my friend: first we have a butterfly with a small wing of which the edge is nevertheless infinite in length, we're talking infinity along a curve; then we move to a moth with a small wing which nevertheless has an infinite surface area, here we have infinity on a two dimensional scale. From this, I infer the existence of a small creature, which nevertheless contains an infinite three dimensional, interior volume. I have reasons to believe it may be a small bird with a fractal stomach of infinite volume. There. What do you think of that?"

"Truly astounding, Smuel. The butterfly with the infinite wing edge is responsible for chaos, and the moth with the infinite wing area is responsible for stupidity. What is this small bird responsible for?"

"That I am still pondering. This is my work for many years still to come, Dom Uss. Something that momentous does not reveal itself at once. It will be the defining work of my life. Another glass of the St. Bacchan?"

***

58. Freeing Chon

Hard as the journey through the Sharan desert and the Blackrock Mountains was, Nyx is finding the monastery life just as difficult. Uss provides a room and meals for her but keeps his distance. Bach and Clara seem preoccupied. Sal is back in classes, which hold little interest for Nyx. She sees him at dinner time, but usually together with a group of other students. They're friendly enough, but she is an outsider.

Her main companion is Chon. Which makes the prospect of setting him free even more difficult. He's grown enormously. She walks him along wild stretches of waterfront every day. He's becoming increasingly reluctant to return to the monastery. He still purrs at her company but tolerates being in her monastery room less and less. She no longer uses the leash and collar outside the monastery.

Four days ago, Chon caught a partridge. The bird exploded out of the grass and took flight. Chon leaped. Swatted it out of the air. Five feet above the ground. The bird accelerating upwards in takeoff, Chon in an effortless leap. Hind legs grown huge launched him like a spring. Oversized front paw stretched high to swat the bird out of its element. Brought it down with a swipe of his paw. As effortlessly as a house cat hooking a goldfish out of a bowl.

Three days ago, they startled a rabbit as they walked through some scrub. Chon caught it easily for all the wild zig-zags the rabbit tried. Chon ate most of it there and then. Growled slightly at her when she approached before he had finished his meal. A sign of growing independence. And pride at his prowess.

Yesterday he added a new hunting tactic. He lay hidden in a clump of reeds. She drew back and waited. A gaggle of witless guinea fowl approached his hideout. He had one in his jaws before they'd even seen him jump. Again, he wouldn't let her approach until he'd finished his meal. Growled at her if she tried. Afterwards, it was touch and go whether he'd come back to the monastery or stay in the wild.

She'd told Sal at dinner afterwards that today would likely be the day. The day Chon would choose to stay in the wild, to not come back to the monastery. The thought choked her. Sal touched her arm and said, "Do you want me to be with you tomorrow, when you walk him? In case he doesn't come back."

It was kindly meant, but she declined. She knew she'd be better alone when it happened.

And now it's happening. It's twilight. Time for them to go back to the monastery. Chon has scared up a rabbit, and again caught it effortlessly. His speed and agility far exceeding that of the rabbit. He shows no inclination to eat it on the spot. He's loping away from her with the rabbit in his mouth. Away from the monastery.

She calls to him. He looks around briefly, twitches the tips of his ears, growls low, and disappears into a grove of trees, still carrying the rabbit. As usual in the shadow of the Blackrock Mountains, darkness falls like a knife. She sits in the same spot and waits, feeling an empty pit in her stomach. She doesn't want to go back to the monastery until the crowds have settled down for the night. Doesn't want to have to face people. Doesn't care about supper either. Can't imagine eating. Half of her hopes Chon will come back. The other half says, "be happy for him, even if it's hard."

She thinks about the twitch of his long, tufted ears. The way they twitched briefly at the sound of her voice as he ran into the trees. His ears were always comically oversized for his body. Even when she first carried him as a tiny kitten. She used to rub the tufts gently when he lay in the sling across her chest. It felt like rubbing silk. Chon used to shut his eyes and purr when she did that. She tries her fingertips against her sweater, then her shirt. Even her scarf feels coarse compared to those ears. She wonders if she'll ever feel anything as soft again.

She puts her head in her hands and closes her eyes. In the stillness, she can hear her own heartbeat. It's a surprise and disappointment to her, still beating like a steady metronome, as though nothing in the world had changed.

Later, the cold forces her to raise her head. She watches Orion climb from the horizon to overhead. Then she stands, stretches, calls to Chon. Just in case. Her heart already knows. There is no answer. She goes back to the monastery, avoids the common area where a few late-owls may still be lingering, chooses side passageways and out of the way stairs to get back to her small room.

"Now what?" she thinks to herself.

***

59. What a Difference a Day Makes

In the second century after EC 3, before Tarsis became a nation, Celecium was invaded by troops from

Sophenia. Things looked bleak for Celecium, their troops outnumbered, their situation desperate. Dom Smuel relates how the Celecian general consulted the Oracle at Om.

"Should I flee to Sharan?" he asked the Oracle. Fumes from the sulphur well surrounding the Oracle drifted upwards like a veil. The Oracle replied in a deep, echoing voice, "What a difference a day makes," and then added in a normal voice, "pay on your way out. We accept gold, silver, and amber."

Encouraged by the first part of the message, the general did not flee. The next day his Celecian army was defeated and he was executed. Which all goes to show what a difference a day makes.

It also shows, for the hundredth time, how people will blame defeat in battle on any available oracle. Which is why the Oracle at Om has extended its limitations of liability wording to specifically exclude consequential damages.

Short-sighted historians are among the foremost to blame this or that oracle for this or that general's defeat. Throughout history, they have rushed to point to the ambiguity of one or another oracle's advice. All of which is gratifying to the generals' surviving family and heirs. They can say he was a great man, a great general, misled by an oracle. Which is wrong on all counts. The smarter historians ask why the dolt of a general abandoned a field of battle to waste time with an oracle. Why wasn't he fortifying his defences or launching a counter-attack?

Historians are also still debating the lawsuit brought against the Oracle at Om in the fifth-century post-EC 3. The up-and-coming barrister of the time, Hywell Glynn, brought a class action lawsuit against the Oracle. He accused it of fraud. In its only statement of defence, the Oracle foretold that Hywell would win his case.

This presented the judges with a delicate problem. If they found the Oracle guilty of fraud, its latest prediction would be proven reliable and their judgement would be seen as faulty. If they found the Oracle not guilty, its latest prediction would be proven wrong, and, again, their judgement would be seen to be faulty.

The judges solved the dilemma by finding the Oracle guilty of fraud. They immediately appealed their own verdict and found the Oracle not guilty on appeal.

They awarded punitive damages of 1000 mohurs, to be paid by Hywell to the Oracle. Since judges abhor lawyers who present them with legal paradoxes, they fined Hywell another 1000 mohurs and permanently barred him from practice.

In the case of Nyx, the day following Chon's return to the wild brought no change. All day she looked for Chon near where she'd last seen him. She found feathers from two freshly killed guinea fowl, and that was all. For her, the answer to 'what a difference a day makes' was precisely 'none'.

Which also goes to show that any oracular advice that has passed its best-before-date, and for which you did not pay on your way out, should not be reused. Oracular sayings, like disposable medical supplies, should be labelled "single use only".

Back at the monastery for dinner, Uss alerts Nyx that the Abbess will see her the next day. Nyx knows what that will be about. The Abbess will thank her for bringing Chon back and will ask if she wants to be a student. Nyx will say no.

***

60. What a Difference another Day Makes

The next morning Nyx is packing her meagre belongings. She has decided to leave the monastery right after her talk with the Abbess. There is nothing here for her. She will go back to Tarsis, seek out her father if she can, and join the underground.

Even if she does not have much to pack, she likes things to be washed, dried, folded and neat.

Uss arrives, escorts her to the Abbess, then leaves.

Nyx finds herself in a small office on the second floor of the Abbess' quarters. Lined with books and a desk.

"Please sit," says the Abbess. "The monastery and I are very grateful for your return of Chon. You've endured many hardships to return him. What can we do for you in return?"

"Nothing, thank you," says Nyx.

"Well, I have something for you," says the Abbess. "A letter arrived this morning for you. Please take your time to read it. I will get us something to drink and eat while you are reading."

Nyx recognizes the handwriting immediately. Her father's. She opens the envelope. He has again written in a very cautious style, making sure that the letter will not give names or locations if intercepted.

> My Dearest,
> I have moved around much in the last few weeks, but always my thoughts are with you. This week I am with E. She misses you greatly. She tells me she thinks of you as the daughter she always wanted and

never had. *Much as she tried to hide it, in order not to burden you further, I think a piece of heart broke when you left. If ever you wish to return, she says, your room will be ready and waiting for you. As will she. I hope by this time you are safely and happily at the Tectis monastery, along with the object I asked you to carry. Not only would this mean you are safe, but, I am thinking of travelling there myself in a month or two. I hope we can meet up there. If I get definite word that you are there, I think E. may be willing to temporarily put her responsibilities on hold and travel with me. I may have to move again soon, but send word to E. if you can. I will stay in touch with her and hear if you do write.*

E. and I both send much love.

Your loving father. Always.

The letter takes her breath away. He's safe. Elsin *does* miss her. Maybe she can complete her training as a herbalist, after all. Her plans to leave the monastery need further thought. She would love to go back to Elsin, if she can slip into Tarsis undetected. But if they are coming to Tectis, it makes sense to wait.

The Abbess comes back with two glasses of juice and some sandwiches. "Good news, I hope," she says pointing at the letter.

"Very," says Nyx. She looks at the date on the letter. Two weeks ago. "My father is travelling to meet me here. He may not have left yet, or he may already be underway. Would you be able to give me lodging at least until he arrives?"

"You are welcome here. As long as you are able to stay with us. Of course, food and your room too. If you need clothes or something else, we'll be happy to provide that."

"Thank you, Abbess. Dom Uss has already given me some money for clothes and everyday items. I thank you for the help."

Nyx pauses in thought. "In a previous letter to me, my father asked that I should see you when I arrived here. You were in a meditation retreat, so this is my first opportunity."

"Yes?"

"He asked me to show you this. It has been in the family on my mother's side for several generations."

Nyx pulls the chain off her neck and passes the amulet to the Abbess. The black stone glints, showing off the dragon claw, the arrow and the heart in a rainbow sheen of reflections. The Abbess puts on reading glasses. She stares at the inscription and reads aloud, "The Hand of God."

The Abbess puts down the amulet. She slowly puts down the reading glasses, hesitates, puts them on once more and rereads the inscription. She puts away the glasses. She steeples her forearms on the table. At the point of the steeple, her two hands clasp. Her right hand forms a loose fist, wrapped up by the open left hand. Paper wrapping rock. Or one hand wrestling the other into immobility. Both hands are white at the knuckles. She tilts her face forward until her mouth is resting on the steepled hands. Those hands are now masking her mouth, masking whatever expression her mouth shows. Her eyes are shut. Another way of hiding whatever emotions they might show.

Nyx can hear the Abbess breathing out, a long slow sigh through the two hands in front of her mouth.

Then the Abbess sits up and opens her eyes.

"This belonged to your mother?"

"Yes. And her mother before her, and hers before that, and so on. I don't know for how many generations."

"I see. You will need to show this to Dom Uss. I will have him called. Now. Please wait here."

***

61. Confidences

The Abbess rises and leaves. She shuts the door behind her. She goes downstairs, enters a small sitting room next and calls her assistant. "Please have Dom Uss found and brought to Nyx, upstairs, in my office. Please ask him to come immediately. At the same time have Lady Clara called. Please bring her to me, not to Nyx."

The Abbess sits at a small table. She again steeples her forearms and hands, closes her eyes and rests her mouth on her hands. She sits motionless listening for footsteps. A few minutes later Lady Clara enters her sitting room.

Clara closes the door behind herself and examines the Abbess shrewdly. "You look pale. Is something amiss?"

"Perhaps," says the Abbess. "Something unexpected has happened. I usually keep my own counsel. But this time I feel a need to share a confidence with someone. Would you permit me to take you into my confidence?"

"I'm honoured," says Clara. "What is it?"

"You're aware of the history of Dom Uss' disastrous marriage, and the vanished wife and daughter?"

"Yes," says Clara. "Ancient history. The wife and daughter will be long dead. Unless the daughter was an SI."

"I don't think she was. But I think one of the descendants has shown up. Nyx."

"Nyx? She travelled with Dom Us across Tarsis and made no claims to be a descendant. Why would she think so now?"

"She doesn't," says the Abbess. "I do. Nyx has just shown me an amulet that she wears. It shows a dragon's claw holding an arrow, the arrow pierces a heart, and there's an inscription that reads, 'The Hand of God'."

"Yes?"

"It's one of a matching pair. Dom Uss has one. He still wears it. It was given to him by his wife, who wore the other one. You know that back in the day he used to be a formidable archer?"

"He still is."

"He had a nickname back then, before he gave it up, before he became a physician, a nickname for his extraordinary accuracy with a bow."

"Let me guess," says Clara, "'The Hand of God'?"

"Yes. Nyx says the amulet that she wears was her mother's, and her mother's mother before that, and so on, going back several generations."

"Did you tell Nyx yet? That Uss may be her great-great I don't know how many times over 'great' grandfather?"

"No. I have had Uss called. Nyx is waiting for him upstairs. I've asked her to show the amulet to Uss when he arrives."

"I see," says Clara. "How will Uss react?"

The Abbess turns her hands palm up and shrugs her shoulders. "He may be overjoyed; he may be indifferent after all this time and all these generations - after all, the blood relationship with a great-great-granddaughter is watered down in each successive generation; he may deny any connection, who knows whether the amulet stayed in the original family or was given away; or he may be angry. He has a lot of anger stored up still about what happened all those years ago. He won't harm her, that's not in his nature, but he may accuse her of being an imposter. Or some other unpredictable reaction."

"Oh."

"Yes, 'oh'," says the Abbess. "It was a defining moment in his life when his daughter disappeared. And not a good moment. Yet, it would be unfair of me to have explained any of the history of the amulet to Nyx, with Uss not being there. And if they're both there, they don't need me."

The Abbess pauses, then resumes. "That's Uss' footsteps climbing the stairs now. I hope we don't hear the same footsteps running down the stairs alone in another moment."

Clara asks, "Do you want me to talk to him if he comes out angry?"

The Abbess shakes her head. "Perhaps after he's had time to absorb the situation. But not now. I just needed a rare opportunity to share a confidence."

Clara nods. "Thank you."

The women listen in silence. There is an indistinct murmur of conversation from upstairs.

The Abbess sinks her head onto her steepled hands again and shuts her eyes. The murmur of voices upstairs has risen in volume. Impossible to make out any words. There is a squeak of a chair being pushed back violently. Someone has jumped up. Very rapidly. Clara walks to the window and holds the curtains back a crack, looking at the scene outside while waiting. A distraction for her eyes while her ears try to interpret the rising sounds from upstairs.

They hear the upstairs door open. Footsteps descend the stairs. They sound slightly hurried. Hard to know if it's one pair of feet or two.

The Abbess raises her head. "I'll go up in a moment and talk to Nyx. If she's still sitting up there."

Clara shakes her head. "No need. Come look."

The Abbess stands next to Clara and gazes down into the monastery courtyard, through the crack between the curtains and the edge of the window. Uss and Nyx are walking through the courtyard hand in hand. Nyx pauses briefly to look back at the Abbess' quarters. Uss half turns to look at Nyx. Nyx catches sight of the window where the curtain is pulled back a crack. She waves with her free hand and then turns away again. She and Uss resume walking. Her face, briefly glimpsed by the two watching women before it turns away from them, is a mixing bowl of emotions. There is exhaustion, shock, confusion and relief - like the face of a child pulled from the waves after a near drowning. It seems to the Abbess, though, that the final emotion, before Nyx turns her face away, is overwhelming joy. Uss' face is simpler to read. It wears the look of a proud father welcoming a much-loved daughter home.

***

62. Domesticity

Uss and Nyx provide much fodder for gossip in the monastery over the coming weeks. They are now commonly referred to as grandfather and granddaughter. Tagging on 'great-great-great' an unknown number of times is too tedious.

Sal has taken to visiting Bach down at the harbour after classes most days to yarn with him. After the incident with the horses on the footbridge, Bach calls him 'Sal'. Most of the time. Today they're sitting on the afterdeck of the Ranger's ketch, sipping mugs of coffee. Sal is making himself useful, splicing the end of a frayed mainsheet.

Bach is chuckling.

"Seems that Nyx has moved into a spare bedroom in Uss' little cottage. Started by tidying up his house. Now he can't find a thing, but he's smiling like a happy fool. She's also put together a roster of regular mealtimes. And trimmed his beard.

"So, story is, Uss was supposed to take her clothes-shopping the other day. On account of she arrived here with barely nothing to wear. When they came back from the tailors, Nyx had two or three changes of clothes, and Uss had somehow acquired half a dozen for himself. In bright colours that were never his style before. Got him all confused and awkward. But happy. Almost like marriage."

Sal is taken aback. "You know about marriage, Master Bach?"

Bach eyes him in surprise. "Course I do. You didn't know? I'm married to Doma Chi, your music instructor up at the monastery. Been married for years. She's a lovely woman. Appreciates the finer sides of my nature.

Nine little savages we've got. It's because of her that
I've kept out of trouble for so many years."

Sal appears to have swallowed some coffee the
wrong way, just after the words 'finer sides of my
nature'. He splutters, clears his lungs with a last cough,
wipes his eyes, and apologizes.

Bach eyes him coldly, then continues, "It's because
of her that I don't let myself get hanged in all these
stupid places Uss takes me to. Like the jail at Gian
Major. With all them cats. Couldn't let myself be
hanged. Doma Chi would have killed me."

***

63. Assassins

It will soon be the spring equinox, the end of spring.
The Tectis Monastery holds a two-week long giant
trade fair every year at this time. Traders from Kiliman,
Tarsis, Harran and beyond congregate in Illyria with
goods to sell and for goods they wish to buy.

On the day before the equinox, the monks set up a
special tent on the beach. Traders who wish to do so
enter the tent in groups of two and three to receive an
audience and a blessing from the Abbess.

The next day, the day of the equinox itself, trade
gives way to celebration. The monks set up giant tents
on the beach, and in the Tectis town square, each tent
offering a different variety of food, drink and music.
Visitors, traders and residents alike wander from tent
to tent sampling the foods and dancing to the music.

On the subject of dancing, the Oracle at Om once said, "One man's dance is another man's funeral parade." The context is long forgotten, but the truth still holds. Take, Nyx, Clara, Uss and the Abbess Anik.

Nyx is delighted, Bach and Clara are concerned, Uss is both delighted and concerned, and the Abbess is serene.

Nyx is delighted for many reasons. Her father will be arriving in Illyria soon, perhaps with Elsin. Nyx and Uss have grown as close as any other grandfather and granddaughter. Uss is giving Nyx special lessons in physic and archery. And, Sal has invited Nyx to be his companion on the night of the equinox for the feasting and music.

Bach and Clara, by contrast, are concerned with Tarsis assassins targeting the Abbess. They are in a meeting to plan their defences. Clara has the lead in the planning and in the efforts to unmask the assassins before they can harm the Abbess.

"Their best opportunity will be to mingle with other traders seeking an audience with the Abbess, asking for her blessing. Should we cancel the blessings?"

"No," says Clara. "The Abbess insists we go ahead. And, if we cancel the event, I no longer can predict when or where they'll try to assassinate her. That would make our work much harder."

"How do you think they'll do it?" asks Bach.

Clara has thought it through. "They'll expect bodyguards between them and the Abbess. That probably rules out knives, unless they're throwing knives. So either throwing knives, or concealed miniature crossbows. Or both."

"Do you want the Rangers to provide the bodyguards? And should the Abbess wear chainmail?"

"Chainmail is good, if the Abbess is willing, Master Bach. Worn invisibly under her normal clothes. And can you give me seven Rangers as guards."

"Seven?"

I'd like two at the entrance to the audience chamber, and one on either side of the Abbess. I'd like them armed with quarterstaves and concealed cutlasses. Paint the quarterstaves so that they look like ceremonial items rather than obvious weapons. I'd like two more Rangers discretely patrolling the dock area. If an assassin escapes and makes a run for a ship, I'd like our men to know who boarded which ships when."

"Makes sense," says Bach. "I could give you more guards if you wish, Lady Clara."

"Thank you, but no, Master Bach. I want the Abbess to look lightly guarded. I want the assassins to try. In any case, your guards are my back up only. My main defences come before the assassins get to their audience with the Abbess."

"Oh, aye. What happens before they get to the Abbess?"

"They pass through an antechamber in which they go through a little ceremony. That's where I want a seventh Ranger. Someone who can play a musical instrument as part of the ceremony."

"A ceremony before seeing the Abbess? That's not our tradition, Lady Clara."

"Ah, Master Bach, this year it is."

***

64. A Really Dumb Ceremony

Istvan and Leil. Two innocent names for two hand-picked assassins. A married couple too. No one suspects a married couple. Trained by Ham, the Patriarch of the New Church of Sacrifice, himself. Dedicated to the church and willing to die on this mission for the Church.

Or at least Leil is.

She *does* believe in sacrifice. Istvan is more pragmatic. He sees the opportunities that the Church hierarchy offers to a man who proves his usefulness to the Church. He intends to prove that usefulness, without sacrificing himself.

They each endured the ordeal of having a tooth hollowed, filled with poison, and plugged with a thin coat of ceramic. Two of the very few that were strong enough to do so. To prove their dedication to the Church. They are proud of their strength, and each other.

They arrived for the Illyrian trade fair in the guise of sheep farmers looking to buy some new rams, farmers wanting to introduce new breeding strains to their herd. Istvan grew up on a sheep farm and carries the disguise convincingly.

That guise also lets them dress in thick sheepskin jackets. Jackets that thick provide excellent concealment for some unusual items.

Leil has a machete hanging from her belt. Very visible. That's mere distraction. They expect to have to give that up when entering the Abbess' audience chamber. Something obvious to satisfy any weapons search.

What's not visible are two throwing stars. These are sharpened six-point stars, concealed inside the lining of Leil's jacket. Leil prefers them to throwing knives. With throwing knives, there's always the problem of the knife spinning in its trajectory. You're never sure whether the knife will hit blade first or hilt first. With throwing stars, you can be sure that one of the points will hit. No matter how the star spins. She's coated the points with poison, a poison taken from a striped sea anemone found off the coast of Northern Sophenia. Quick acting and lethal. Throwing stars won't penetrate chain mail, but they don't have to. Leil will aim for the Abbess' face, and Leil is highly accurate.

Istvan's jacket lining conceals a tiny crossbow. It is already loaded with a single poison-tip dart. The same poison that Leil is using. Even if the Abbess wears chain mail, a small portion of the dart tip will penetrate the mail. With that poison, even a small penetration is all that's needed.

The last piece of weaponry that Istvan conceals is a bag of harmless looking white powder. It contains spores from an unusual mushroom species; a little-known cousin to the more common Agaricus Muscarius. The spores are an irritant to eyes and breathing. Once the Abbess is killed, the plan is to throw handfuls at the guards and pursuers. They will be disabled while Istvan and Leil escape in the confusion.

They've stood in line patiently outside a large two-room tent where the Abbess holds audiences. Now they're being invited into the antechamber. Two young monastery students explain to them that they will partake in a traditional ritual here. After the ritual, they will advance to the room with the Abbess.

The students are called Hanum and Alyx. Hanum is quiet but smiling. Alyx is chatty and welcoming.

"This Illyrian ceremony of thanks and purification is to prepare you spiritually to meet the Abbess. To begin, we invite you to sample the traditional salted sardines from our seas."

She holds out a small tray of delicate dried salted fish. Istvan and Leil sample the fish. They are very salty.

Alyx smiles and holds up a finger. "Whenever we Illyrians eat from the sea, we honour the sea."

A musician with an accordion steps into the room. He is a short, bald man with a huge chest and shoulders. He has a striking dragon tattoo on his face. Alyx, Hanum, Istvan and Leil stand silently while he sings a brief song of praise to the sea.

For all the silliness of this hocus-pocus, Istvan is mostly calm. Just twinges of impatience. He has done small assassinations for the Church before. This is the biggest so far. He will endure their childish rituals in order to gain access to the Abbess. This will make his name known throughout the Church.

Hanum is now speaking. "Illyria is blessed with the finest beers in the world. For which we are all grateful. Please. Try."

He holds out a tray of beer glasses for them to sample.

Istvan and Leil take a glass each. Istvan doesn't like mixing alcohol with assassinations, but they have little choice today. Besides which the salt fish has left him with a python of a thirst. He takes a large swig. The beer is much stronger than Istvan expected. Leil gives several coughs. Evidently, she took a big swig for her thirst too.

The musician is playing another short annoying song of praise to beer, malt and the hop vines of Illyria. Leil and Istvan stand still in a show of solemn deference until the tune ends.

Istvan's impatience grows. He looks at Leil. He senses she too wants to get this over quickly.

Alyx steps forward with a tray of what looks like candy-apples. "These," she says, "are sweet apples with a toffee glaze on the outside. As you will see shortly the glaze is not sweet, it's spicy. This is a traditional dessert. All those who wish to see the Abbess partake of it. It reminds us of nature's bounty, of fruit trees. The combination of spice glaze with sweet apple also reminds us of the variety of nature, for which we give thanks. Please take an apple but do not bite into it yet."

Istvan can still feel the beer burning his belly. That wasn't just beer. They must have fortified the beer with a strong distilled alcohol. It's making him even more impatient to get this over. He and Leil each hold their apple waiting.

Alyx says, "The tradition is that you two, who seek the Abbess' blessing, must join together in eating the apple. You, Istvan, hold your apple to Leil's mouth and Leil holds the apple to your mouth. When our musician begins his tune, please begin eating from each other's apples."

"What a sweet ceremony," says Leil with a smile. Istvan can see she's annoyed by this mumbo-jumbo but hiding it well. He can tell her smile is forced, but the others won't know.

They hold out the apples to each other's lips. Impatiently. The musician pulls apart the outside wings of his accordion, letting the air flow into the instrument. "On a count of three," he says to them. "One, two, three." He squeezes the accordion and the first note of his tune jumps out of the accordion. It's shockingly loud.

Istvan bites into the apple that Leil is holding for him. He hears her crunch on the apple that he is holding for her. Damn that glaze is hard as concrete! And sticky! A cracking sound reverberates throughout his skull, amplified by bone conduction from jaw to cranium. His vision shrinks, as though he's surrounded by a dark tunnel. He can dimly see that Leil has slumped to her knees. She's falling over sideways now to the ground. The light at the end of his tunnel vision shrinks. He falls.

***

65. The Night After

All who wanted an audition and the Abbess' blessing have received it. The bodies of Istvan and Leil have been disposed of so discretely that none of the other audience seekers noticed their deaths.

The Abbess and Lady Clara are in the Abbess' sitting room enjoying a late tisane. The Abbess is shaking her head in admiration.

"So they self-destructed?"

"Yes," says Clara. "Once they bit into the hard toffee glaze on the candy-apples, their hollow teeth broke and released the poison."

"How did you get them to bite into the candy-apples?"

"A dozen ways. Everyone who asked for an audience with you today had to undergo that ritual. Refusing the apples would have made the assassins stand out. They couldn't afford that. It would have broken their disguise. Also, we distracted them by overloading their senses."

"How?"

"We made them thirsty with the salt fish. Hanum deliberately oversalted it. In addition, there are tiny bones in the fish, which irritate your throat for several minutes afterwards. Because the assassins were thirsty after the fish, they welcomed some beer laced with strong alcohol. It didn't do anything for their thirst or the fish-bones. It did make them less cautious. They became increasingly impatient just to get the whole ceremony over with. The woman, Leil, was also jealous. She wanted to hurry the ceremony in order to get her husband away from Alyx. Alyx is young and beautiful. Master Bach increased their discomfort even further."

"Bach?"

"Yes, Master Bach. He's a very talented musician, but I forced him to play some dragon-awful sounding songs. Wailing and tuneless. That was just another distraction, another sensory overload for the assassins. By the time we gave them the apples to eat, they just wanted to get through the horrible ceremony. As quickly as possible."

The Abbess smiles. "Ingenious," she says. "Now the monastery and its visitors can look forward to tomorrow's equinox celebration. The start of spring. The double threats of winter and assassins behind us. Very appropriate."

The women sit in contented silence, sipping their tisanes. The Abbess puts down her cup at length. She asks Clara, "Do you have any special plans for the celebrations."

Clara's expression becomes vague. A shade too deliberately vague. "Perhaps," is all she says.

**

66. Buying a Duck Dog

"That is Svalbaard?" asks Clara.

"Yup," says Uss.

It's the evening of the spring equinox. Clara and Uss are standing in the Tectis town square. Uss is dressed, slightly uncomfortably, in a shirt three shades brighter than his normal style. Above them on the slope of the caldera, in the dark and barely visible is the monastery.

Clara and Uss have spent the day moving from giant tent to giant tent. Some are in the town square, some are on the beaches. They've sampled foods and drink. They've watched and listened to troubadours, minstrels, jugglers, harpers, sword swallowers, illusionists and the monastery choir. They've talked to friends, students, rangers, townspeople, sailors and colleagues. Now they're watching Svalbaard sell duck dogs. He has a brazier on which he cooks bread buns and the sausage-like meat. A small table stands next to his brazier, loaded with raw food for cooking, and relishes. A steady stream of customers comes and goes.

"Go on, Hugo," says Clara.

"I suppose," says Uss. They approach Svalbaard.

"Oh, it's you," says Svalbaard gloomily. "The stupid monk that caused the big ruckus and earthquake at Han-Bu." Svalbaard turns to Lady Clara. "Just about destroyed my old monastery, that one did. He's trouble, he is. He's the reason I had to leave my beloved old monastery. He's the reason poor old Svalbaard spends his last miserable days selling sausages at starvation prices in a foreign land. A word to the wise, Missus. You should find other company to hang with."

Uss ignores all this. "How much for a duck dog?"

Svalbaard sulks. "Thruppence ha'penny."

"Right," says Uss. "What do you want on yours, Clara?"

"Pickles, tomatoes and lettuce."

Svalbaard dishes up her duck dog. "I suppose you're going to want one too, Mister Monk. Destroyer of Happiness. What do you want on yours?"

Uss can't resist. "Make me one with everything."

Svalbaard makes a face. "Very Zen. I've heard that a million times already. No. You get three choices, maximum."

"All right. Pickles, mustard, ketchup."

"There. That's seven pence."

Uss hands over a shilling.

Svalbaard stares into the distance.

Uss taps him on the arm. "My change?"

Svalbaard growls at him. "You're the one making stale Zen jokes. Try this one: Change must come from within."

Uss and Svalbaard glare at each other.

There's a crash as the table next to Svalbaard's brazier tips dangerously. A dozen buns and sausages fall to the ground. Relishes, pickles and condiments teeter on the edge.

"Oops," says Lady Clara. "That was close. You almost lost everything on the table, Master Svalbaard. I'm so clumsy around tables. I hope Dom Uss gets his change soon. Before I have another accident with your table. Or knock over your brazier."

Svalbaard shakes his head. "And there I was being nice to you, Missus. Even warned you about him. Should have warned him about you. Here's your money, Mister Uss."

He hands Uss the shilling back. "Your money back. All of it. I'm an old man. Very frail. The slightest thing might put me in my grave. Like another one of your earthquakes. Don't know what else you specialize in. Volcanic eruptions? Lightning strikes? I can't be near walking disasters like you and your missus. Please don't come back anytime this century."

Clara and Uss finish their duck dogs walking down to the beach. They stand looking at the phosphorescence on the breakers.

"You're distracted, Hugo."

"I haven't seen my granddaughter since this morning. Was wondering where she'd gotten to."

Clara notices that Uss still says 'my granddaughter' with silent pride, rather than simply saying 'Nyx'.

"I saw her just after dark," says Clara. "She was walking along the beach with a boy. Heading to our right. That way. They were leaning against each other. His arm around her shoulders, hers around his waist."

"A boy?" says Uss. He's clearly horrified. "Boys around Nyx are worse than rutting goats. We should go find them and break that up."

"I don't think Nyx would appreciate that. Nor does she need your protection. She's very capable you know."

"I suppose. Who was the damn boy? I can always strangle him later. When Nyx is safely back home asleep."

"Well, it was dark, but I'm sure it was Sal."

"Sal?" says Uss. "That's not good. Nyx keeps trying to worm information out of Sal about his past on

Kiliman. That could cause great harm to several Kiliman families. We should go down there and rescue him."

Clara refuses to budge. "So, Hugo, you think each needs protecting from the other?"

Uss considers. "Well, you never know what they could get up to."

"Oh," says Clara, "I know exactly what they might get up to. Why don't we leave them to it? We could walk down the beach, the opposite direction to theirs."

He considers it again. "I suppose," he says. She turns left on the beach, takes Uss' hand and they walk together. After a dozen paces, he lets go her hand to put an arm around her shoulders. She moves in closer against him, puts an arm around his waist and they stroll into the darkness together.

*** ***

Notes on the Biology of Illyria and Tarsis

a. The Celecium prospectors' use of trees to locate mineral deposits was already considered in pre-EC times. See, e.g.

"Natural gold particles in Eucalyptus leaves and their relevance to exploration for buried gold deposit"; Nature Communications, 2013 September. Melvyn Lintern, Ravi Anand, Chris Ryan & David Paterson.
https://www.nature.com/articles/ncomms3614

b. Dom Uss' observations that the pythons on the Celecium/Sharan border kill their prey by causing cardiac arrest echoes pre-EC research papers, e.g.

"Snake constriction rapidly induces circulatory arrest in rats"; Journal of Experimental Biology, 2015 July. Boback SM, McCann KJ, Wood KA, McNeal PM, Blankenship EL, Zwemer CF.
http://jeb.biologists.org/content/218/14/2279

and

"Snake modulates constriction in response to prey's heartbeat"; Biology Letters, 2012 January.
Scott M. Boback, Allison E. Hall, Katelyn J. McCann, Amanda W. Hayes, Jeffrey S. Forrester, Charles F. Zwemer.
http://rsbl.royalsocietypublishing.org/content/early/2 012/01/11/rsbl.2011.1105

c. Master Bach's explanation of how the Illyrian lynx protects the ecology of the Illyrian shoreline echoes the pre-EC observations that the re-introduction of wolves to Yellowstone National Park was associated with a decline in elk herds, the regrowth of aspen and the reappearance of beavers. See e.g.

"Hunting Habits of Wolves Change Ecological Balance in Yellowstone"; New York Times, October 18 2005. Jim Robbins.

http://www.nytimes.com/2005/10/18/science/earth/hunting-habits-of-wolves-change-ecological-balance-in.html

d. The use of smoke to calm beehives, as used by Master Bach, is ancient. However late pre-EC research suggests the mechanism, namely that smoke interferes with alarm/attack pheromones that bees emit. See e.g.

"Alarm pheromone perception in honey bees is decreased by smoke (Hymenoptera: Apidae)"; 1994 May. P. Kirk Visscher, Richard S. Vetter, Gene E. Robinson.
https://link.springer.com/article/10.1007%2FBF01990966

e. The moth on the bridge that startled the horse, Duke, was identified by Dom Uss as belonging to the species Tegeticula. Its odd relationship with the Yucca plant was described pre-EC. For a light-hearted precis, see e.g.

"Evolution that Anyone Can Understand", 2011. Bernard Marcus. pp 59-67.
https://link.springer.com/chapter/10.1007%2F978-1-4419-6126-6_8

f. Carbon and silicon fall into the same group of periodic table elements. This suggested even pre-EC that silicon based life forms might offer an alternative to carbon-based life forms. Pre-EC scientists were able to selectively breed bacteria that naturally incorporate silicon into hydrocarbons. See e.g.

"Directed evolution of cytochrome c for carbon-silicon bond formation"; Science, Nov 2015. S. B. Jennifer Kan, Russell D. Lewis, Kai Chen, Frances H. Arnold.
http://science.sciencemag.org/content/354/6315/1048

g. Illyrian lynxes are likely related to the pre-EC caracal.

Dom Uss notes that the lynx preys on both geese and deer. The caracal, similarly, preyed on animals as varied as birds and antelope. See e.g.

"Prey selection by caracal in the Kgalagadi Transfrontier Park"; South African Journal of Wildlife Research, Volume 34, Issue 1, Apr 2004; p. 67 - 75 H.I.A.S. Melville, J. du P. Bothma and M.G.L. Mills.

The abstract notes: "... It was found that the primary prey resource was small mammals, the vast majority of which were rodents, including springhare (Pedetes capensis). Larger prey animals included steenbok (Raphicerus campestris) and smaller carnivores up to the size of a black-backed jackal (Canis mesomelas). Birds were an abundant prey resource, especially the larger ground-roosting species..."
https://journals.co.za/content/wild/34/1/EJC117182

Like Chon, the caracal was noted for its ability to swat birds out of the air. See e.g.

"Travels in Kashmir, Ladak, Iskardo, the Countries Adjoining the Mountain-Course of the Indus, and the Himalaya North of the Panjab"; G.T. Vinye, Esq, F.G.S; 1884. P42: "He often catches crows as they rise from the ground, by springing five or six feet into the air after them."
https://books.google.ca/books?id=eNzsB16GLtAC

***

A Word to The Reader

Your feedback matters. If you enjoyed this book, please leave a positive rating/review at Amazon or at whichever site you bought this book.

Thank you.

***

Acknowledgements

Thanks to my friend of many years, Daphne Cooper, who read an early draft of this book and gave me the encouragement to continue with it. Daphne is herself a superb writer, along with many other talents. Readers of one of my previous books, 'The Twelve Man Bilbo

Choir', will recognize Daphne's recurring support, for which I am recurringly grateful.

Thanks also to my friend of many years, Ron Grimes, who proofread the book with an unrelenting precision that is surprising in a man who is otherwise so relaxed and jovial. Ron also proofread one of my previous books, 'Just One More Page'. A big thank-you to Ron. Any errors that remain are mine and not his.

Special thanks to Bill Caddick, musician and songwriter, for his generous permission to quote a verse of his lovely song "John O' Dreams" in this book. Bill answered my request for his permission with speed, kindness and his best wishes. Thank you, Bill.

Lastly, thanks to my family for their support. Some of the wilder ideas and worst puns in the book were sparked by comic discussions on unrelated topics with my sons.

***

Books By Peter Staadecker

As at January 2019, books by Peter Staadecker include:

- The Twelve Man Bilbo Choir (2017, a novel of prison, justice, tragedy and love - inspired by actual events that changed legal history)

- Just One More Page (2017, for children aged six to ten-years-old)

- The Illyrian Voyages Book 1: Dropping Into Darkness (2018, an eco-Sci-Fi fantasy)

- The Illyrian Voyages Book 2: A Glimmer of Light (2019, an eco-Sci-Fi fantasy)

For updates, please see

https://publishing.staadecker.com

***

Contact The Author

Fan? Or want to be on the distribution list for news about Peter's books and book contests? Let Peter know. You can reach him through the 'contact' section at *https://publishing.staadecker.com*

and/or follow him on Facebook at

https://www.facebook.com/staadecker.books/

(Please do not send suggestions for a plot, though – Peter will delete those, unread.)

***

The Illyrian Voyages, Book 2: A Glimmer of Light

Keep reading for a preview.

***

Tamblyn: Interrupted Journey

"There is but a plank between a sailor and eternity." ~
Thomas Gibbons

"Boran One-Thumb," said the sailor opposite me.

We were sitting in a run-down waterfront bar in Port Hamelin, in Tarsis. I had completed some business in Port Hamelin; a private matter, like most of my undertakings. The bar smelled of fish, stale beer, and clogged sewers.

It was early afternoon. The only customers keeping barstools warm at that time of day were the habitual drunks and a few sailors who'd missed their tide and their ship that morning.

The latter group had celebrated heartily the night before, only to wake up late, penniless, and abandoned in some threadbare room or wet alleyway. You could tell that group by their look of bewilderment.

The sailor opposite me was one of the habitual drunks. I'd picked him because he'd forget me as soon as I walked out. His eyes were bleary. They didn't focus well, and, in the unlikely event that someone asked about me later, he was in no state to describe me accurately, or to repeat our conversation. I'd bought him two beers already in exchange for what I needed to know.

"Who's the worst skipper now docked in Port Hamelin, the one with the least seaworthy ship?" I had asked.

"Boran One-Thumb," said the drunk. "Captain Boran One-Thumb. His ship's 'The Mermaid's Folly'."

He laughed and sprayed beer. The laugh turned into a cough, then a wheeze.

When he regained his breath, he continued. "The Folly part's true, for sure. Dunno about any maidens that would hang out with Boran, though. That ship won't last another winter. The timbers are rotted, riddled with shipworm. Do yourself a favour, Merchant, whatever you're looking to ship, look elsewhere. With Boran, your cargo will only feed the fishes."

He lifted his eyes from his beer and looked at me directly – or as directly as he was able – for the first time in our conversation. He had found something to give me in exchange for my beers and, for all that he had sunk to, I saw that still mattered to him.

I nodded and put a generous coin on the table in front of him. "Fair exchange, Sailor. Buy yourself a meal, on me. I have to go.

I got up and went in search of Boran One-Thumb and his deathtrap of a ship.

I disliked Boran from the start, and my opinion didn't change during my time with him. He treated his crew like near-slaves, and barely knew a storm surge from a high tide.

I told him I'd pay him well. I told him I wanted a passage to Harran. Which was a lie – I would ensure that we never reached Harran.

I laid out my conditions. A direct route, I said, no stops until we got to Harran; no other passengers, just my servant, Dimitrios, and me.

Boran knew nothing else of me but tried to learn more.

I expected that. If his passenger was smuggling or was a wanted man on the run, there would be the possibility of blackmail and some extra profit. If his passenger was from an important family, there would be the possibility of kidnapping and a ransom to be earned. He tried casual conversation with Dimitrios but learned nothing from him.

Dimitrios was young. Hard to pinpoint his age, perhaps between sixteen and twenty years old. He looked as simple as a child's first picture book. He spoke readily, but every time the Captain questioned him about me, Dimitrios' answers danced around the question, like a butterfly evading the net. Which made Dimitrios so useful to me, and so useless to Skipper One-Thumb.

We sailed north, steering well clear of the Illyria and its myriad reefs. A sailor pointed to specs of land, just visible on our port side. The Kiliman Islands. "We'll be level with Grand Kiliman Island during the night," he said.

That was the real destination of my voyage – although it had to look like an unplanned visit, an accidental arrival.

At night, I saw the flickering lights on the Grand Kiliman shore. Boran had drunk himself into a nighttime stupor. Cheap wine half cut with rum. He had offered me some. I told him I never take alcohol.

His mate and a deckhand had the watch that night. The wind was light and steady from the southwest. No sails to be trimmed. The rest of the crew, exhausted and underfed, slept, snored and grunted, as immovable as their captain.

Which allowed me to walk undetected to the aft hold with the large wrench I had brought on board hidden in my bags.

Even for one who doesn't drink, it was sobering to stand in the hold, down deep below the surface of the water. My head was probably six feet below sea level, with only a thin shell of wood between the sea and me. The smell of dead fish and long-ago cargoes of brick, spice and coal was all around me. Overlaying all that was the strong smell of brine. I ran my hand up the wooden planks near me. They were damp. In a seam between two of the planks there were thick beads of water forming. I stood in the gloom listening to the menacing gurgle of the water on the outside of the hull.

I know this much about the sea: it hates ships.

Just as a spider skittering across naked skin repulses most people, so too, a ship sliding across the water repulses the sea.

The message in that gurgling was plain to anyone with ears.

"There is one wooden plank between you and eternity. I will test that plank with every ripple, every wave and every storm. If there is no weakness now, yet it will come. My twin, Sister Time, probes with me. You sail on her ocean too – on her smooth curving timelines. You leave ugly vortices trailing behind you on her seas and on mine. In a year, or in a month, or in a second, one of us will crush you, little, ugly wood spider with your thin planks and string and cloth."

I was facing aft in the hold. On the outside of the hull was the rudder, swinging in a set of hinges that sailors call gudgeons. These gudgeons were, in turn, bolted to the ship's hull, through the ship's hull.

In this ship, four big gudgeon bolts pierced the hull, deep below the waterline. They ran from outside where the ocean probed and pressed, to inside, where I stood; where the sea wanted to be.

I already knew what to expect. The bolts were covered in tar caulking; tightened so that the water couldn't penetrate.

Gudgeon bolts are a weak point in any ship design. Shipwrights know it. The sea knows it. I knew it.

Which was why I had the wrench. The bolts were massive, but so was my wrench. I loosened all four bolts and watched as the sea jetted into the hold. The scum of long-forgotten cargoes gave the rising water a greasy sheen.

I was wearing a tar-coated canvas cape. My normal clothes were dry underneath. No sign of what I'd been up to unless you looked closely at my shoes. On the way back to my cabin, I dropped the wrench and the cape quietly over the side. I passed the Captain's cabin quietly, then Dimitrios' cabin. His was next-door to mine and silent. No doubt, he was already asleep.

I entered my cabin, sat and breathed deep. I put my hands on my wrist and felt for my pulse. Its steady beat surprised me.

I took the tiger amulet from my neck and laid it before me on the little bunk-side table. The amulet eyes stared at me.

I lit an incense stick in a mug, concentrated on the Striped Ones and prayed for guidance.

The glowing joss reflected in the carved eyes and gave them a life of their own. Afterwards, once the amulet was again hanging from my neck, I lay back in my bunk and closed my eyes. I could still see the afterglow of shining eyes against the black of my eyelids. I pretended to sleep. The sea, my partner in sabotage, hissed and gloated in the ship's hold. The difference between us was that it wanted to kill us all. I hoped to survive.

***

Tamblyn Flashback: Hiring Dimitrios

"Nothing can be gained by extensive study and wide reading. Give them up immediately." ~ Dōgen

I first met Dimitrios in Illyria a year ago. I was being shown through the monastery school in Tectis. I told the monks I wanted to hire a monastery student as a personal assistant. I travel too much and take too many risks to attract older assistants. But for a younger person who was not academically inclined, it would be an interesting life. The duties would be light, travel would take us to all corners of the known world, and I would pay generously. The main qualifications were to be street-smart, observant and to keep my secrets. I did not mention the last part to the monks. Nor did I mention to them my main reason for being in Illyria. Which had nothing to do with hiring an assistant.

The classrooms in the monastery were sloping, amphitheatre style. Observers like me were welcome to sit at the back and peer down on classes.

Dimitrios was in a language class frustrating every attempt to teach him anything, with a vicious innocence that I quietly applauded.

His teacher, Dom Arbus, was teaching Common Language. A good man, but no match for Dimitrios' malevolent aversion to questions. Dimitrios was older than the other students. He was in the class only because Common Language was not his mother tongue. A catch-up class for him.

"Dimitrios," Dom Arbus said, "come to the front of the class. So. Good. Tell the rest of the class, how do we write the possessive case?"

Dimitrios looked embarrassed. "Dom Arbus," he said hesitantly, "in the Philosophers Isles, where I grew up, they taught that possessiveness is a sin."

Dom Arbus was good-natured at first. "Very true," he said, "but we still need to know how to write the possessive case. What if someone wanted to know how some student, let's say Paul here, was doing at the monastery school. What if they asked, 'How did Paul's exams go, last week?' How would you write 'Paul's exams'? Where would you place the possessive apostrophe-s?"

Dimitrios said, "It would be wrong of me to write about Paul's exams."

"Why?" asked Dom Arbus.

"The exams do not belong to Paul. The monastery created the exams. The exams belong to the monastery."

Dom Arbus began to fidget. "Paul is merely an example."

Dimitrios shook his head. "If you want to make an example of Paul, he should be punished for lying about who owns the exam. No offence, Dom Arbus, a monastery should choose more honest people as examples for young students."

Dom Arbus sighed. "Perhaps, Dimitrios, I should ask you about Paul's hat, then. How do you write the possessive form for the hat that belongs to Paul?"

Dimitrios looked blank. "I could not do so, Dom Arbus. Having heard how Paul has claimed ownership of an exam that is not his, I would be reluctant to take sides in any argument about whether he owned a given hat. I would need to know more about the hat's provenance."

I saw that Dom Arbus was struggling. He made a heroic effort. "There, Dimitrios, that's exactly what I want to demonstrate – the possessive case – the hat's provenance. How would you write that?"

Dimitrios looked as helpfully naïve as – I later learned – he always does. "Please tell me about the provenance. Then I can write it down for you, if that is what you wish, Dom Arbus. I would, of course, have to say 'alleged provenance', unless you have source documents for the provenance. I should want to see sworn witness statements, original invoices of sale and such. The Philosophers Isles were very strict in their quest for information accuracy."

"Were they?" said Dom Arbus helplessly; a mistake on his part, like a beginner putting slack into the line just when he hopes to reel in a mountain trout.

"Oh, yes, Dom Arbus," said Dimitrios. "I remember three Island philosophers went for a walk to the South Island, an area they had never visited before. Ahead, during a brief pullback in the mist, they glimpsed a black sheep, standing in profile on a hilltop.

"'Ah,' said the first philosopher, 'so there are black sheep on the South Island'.

"'No, no,' said the second philosopher. 'All we know is that there is at least one black sheep on the South Island'.

"'Are you both insane?' said the third. 'All we know is that on the South Island there is at least one sheep which has at least one black side'."

Dom Arbus saw that his trout had gotten away. He was a clumsy trout fisher, but he knew when to cut bait. He dismissed the class.

I offered Dimitrios the job.

Of course, I could not ask him any questions; not even a simple question like "do you want the job?" I merely told him about the job, let *him* ask questions, and put nine shekels into his palm.

"These shekels are your first month's wages. Even though the wages do not belong to the month, I would write that M-O-N-T-H-apostrophe-S. We can discuss that another time. It is unimportant. I do not care about apostrophes. If you wish to take the job, be aboard the Flying Gull tomorrow by sunrise with any belongings you wish to take. She is moored at the main dock in Freeport Harbour. If you decide against the job, return the shekels before sunrise. Think it over."

Dimitrios pocketed the shekels, looked at me, looked at the clouds scudding overhead, and then said, "Those should be gone by the morning."

It was as close as he could come to answering the question I had been careful not to ask.

The next morning, he boarded with his bags an hour before sunrise.

A dishonest person would have kept the shekels and been a no-show. The loss of nine shekels would have been a cheap price to reveal that.

Also, as I had known she would, the Flying Gull had moved dock during the night to one of the tangled back wharves. The back wharves are only accessible by water-taxi, a short rowboat voyage for a farthing fare if you can scare up the ferryman. He is unpredictable and often hungover at that hour, in which case some powerful persuasion is needed to get him to work. A less nimble person would have had difficulty finding the Gull by sunrise.

I was on deck when Dimitrios boarded. Neither one of us mentioned the change in dock or the drunken ferryman. Dimitrios guessed it was a test. We shook hands and bowed to each other.

That was a year ago. We have worked well together, with mutual respect and even a friendship of sorts. Now we are on yet another vessel. One that I am deliberately sinking. Perhaps Dimitrios and I will both survive. The Striped Ones willing.

***

END OF PREVIEW
***

Look for "A Glimmer of Light" in bookstores and online from April 2019 onwards.
Happy reading!

*** ***

CPSIA information can be obtained
at www.ICGtesting.com
Printed in the USA
LVHW080027121219
640222LV00018B/1283/P